The Charred Forest Murders

Andrew Woodward

© Andrew Woodward 2013

All rights reserved. No part of this book may be reproduced, stored in a retrieval system, or transmitted, in any form or by any means, electronic, mechanical, photocopying, recording or otherwise, without the prior permission of the author.

The book is sold subject to the condition that it shall not, by way of trade or otherwise, be lent, re-sold, hired out or otherwise circulated without the author's prior consent in any form of binding or cover other than that in which it is published and without a similar condition including this condition being imposed on the subsequent purchaser.

For Dad,

Other novels in the Elements series

The Water Dragon

The Fire Walker

The Silverbird's Sign

All books are available in print and Kindle versions from Amazon.co.uk.

Author's note

While I was researching suitable subject matter for the fourth book in my Elements series, I was hoping to find the kernel of a story ideally from the London area. That was when I stumbled across this intriguing murder case that resonated with an article I had read many years before. I had been interested at the time with the news that London's most prolific serial killer has never been caught. The more I began to research around the subject the more fascinated I became. As someone who had grown up in Chiswick, where three of the victims had been discovered, it was hard to believe that almost no one knew or had even heard of anything relating to the murders. The local library in Chiswick was an interesting source of information as they gave me access to the local papers that reported the crimes at the time (clippings can be seen on the back cover of the print version of this novel) and also they had entertained a couple of other authors researching the subject over the years. Another point that struck me as interesting was the fact that only a handful of books have been written on the subject compared to the hundreds of books, films and general media coverage that has been given over the decades to Jack the Ripper. The Stripper killed more women than the Ripper and yet surprisingly the case remains almost unknown to most Londoners and the country as a whole.

I have attempted to write about this complex case as accurately as possible from the limited and sometimes contradictory material available in both the news media and in the public arena. Interestingly, the actual police files that are now held at the National Archives (formerly the Kew Records Office) will remain sealed for another 50 years. Considering it's now half a century since most of these crimes occurred, the delay seems excessive in the extreme as it means at least a century will have passed from the time the crimes were committed to the time the files will be available to the public. This persuaded me to send a freedom of information request in an attempt to gain access to the files. The rejection letter in its entirety is attached at the end of this introduction (the names of the deceased vary slightly from the victim's names I have used as it was a common practice at the time for working girls to use alternative names). The letter raises some interesting points as to why it should be made available but also why the decision was finally made to reject my application for access to the files.

As much as possible I wanted to use the true story of the murder of these eight unfortunate women to raise awareness of the case and hopefully begin to generate enough interest for the Metropolitan Police to reopen this case and finally establish what really happened and who was responsible. Operation Yetna that features in the book is a real cold case unit that was launched in early 2012 and coincides with the timeframe of this novel.

There are many unanswered questions in these cases as well; whether or not Ms Figg and Ms Rees were part of the series of eight or whether or not they were just unfortunate victims of violence that coincided geographically with the other murders; What was the motive behind Jack the Stripper's killings? Why did they stop? How did the murderer have so much knowledge of police districts and procedures at the time? What were Inspector du Rose's motivations to frame Mungo Ireland, when he knew the Scot wasn't in London at the time of the last murder. Was it purely to close such a high profile case and to add to his reputation as London's number one murder investigator? All evidence points to the fact he must have known it wasn't possible for the perpetrator of the murders to be Ireland.

Of course I have invented a purely fictional conclusion to the Jack the Stripper case and by no means is it supposed to undermine the seriousness of these horrific crimes. The living characters that appear in this novel are all completely fictional, but all the cold case victims and those of Jack the Stripper victims are real and all remain unsolved to this day.

It is my sincere hope that by drawing attention to these cases it will, perhaps, in some small way, create an interest and then possibly the opportunity will arise for a full investigation – otherwise we will all need to wait for another half century to elapse before we can find out what really happened in the captivating case of the Jack the Stripper murders and by then, the only thing we can be certain of is that whoever committed these crimes will no longer be alive.

Andrew Woodward

Chiswick, London

July 2013

***

Dear Mr Woodward,

Thank you for your enquiry of 22 May regarding a review of:

MEPO 2/10317 - The 'Nude Murders'. Report linking the unsolved murder of Bridgette O'HARA with those of Hannah TAILFORD, Irene LOCKWOOD, Helen BARTHELEMY, Mary FLEMING, Margaret McGOWAN, and possibly that of Elizabeth FIGG, as the 'Nude Murders' (it was later considered that Tina SMART also was murdered by the same person)

We handled your request under the Freedom of Information Act 2000. All of the information in this file is covered by exemptions under the Freedom of Information Act. The exemptions we have applied are at sections 31 and 38 of the act.

Section 31 exemption: law-enforcement
Section 38 exemption: health and safety

We regret to say, after very careful consideration, that we do not think there is a public interest in releasing the information you have requested. Further information regarding the exemptions we have applied and the outcomes of the Public Interest Tests are given below:

Section 31 exemption: law-enforcement: part (1) subsections (a) the prevention or detection of crime, (b) the apprehension or prosecution of offenders, and (c) the administration of justice,

This exemption applies to all of the information because release, could put at risk certain law-enforcement matters, including preventing or detecting crime, arresting or prosecuting offenders and the proper administration of justice. This is because the murder remains unsolved and the information contained within this file may be used to reinvestigate this case at a later stage.

Section 31 Public interest test

Factors in favour of release
* *It is recognised that there is a presumption running through the Freedom of Information Act that openness is, in itself, to be regarded as something, which is in the public interest*
* *The information is 45 years old*
* *The information may shed light on police methods of investigation crimes of this nature*

Factors in favour of withholding
• This information would be used if the case was reinvestigated
• The release of this information could therefore seriously prejudice any future investigation or prosecution, thereby affecting the ability of the police to prevent or detect crime.
• It is not possible to identify information from this record that could be released into the public domain at this point without compromising future police actions
• Information that appears innocuous may have significance to an experienced investigator that is not immediately obvious to the lay reader;
• Similarly, information that appears innocuous may assume a new significance in the light of newly discovered evidence or developments in forensic or investigative techniques.

Outcome of the section 31 Public Interest Test
There remains a possibility, however remote, that this case could be opened for re-investigation at some point in the future. It is not in the public interest to jeopardise a prosecution for murder by releasing information that could be of later significance.

Section 38 exemption: health and safety: Part 1 subsection (a) endanger the physical or mental health of any individual,

This exemption applies to some of the information.

Factors in favour of release
• It is recognised that there is a presumption running through the Freedom of Information Act that openness is, in itself, to be regarded as something, which is in the public interest.
• A number of the issues regarding this murder are already known to the public

Factors in favour of withholding
• This file relates to a tragic crime of a disturbing nature.

- *All of the information contained within this file, including statements, medical examinations and reports detailing the injuries sustained by the victim and especially information on the circumstances leading to the event, are of such a nature that mental endangerment of living relatives is rendered highly likely.*

Outcome of the section 38 Public Interest Test

The National Archives and the Metropolitan Police have a duty to openness, and to the public's 'right to know'. But such a duty cannot be allowed to override their parallel duty to protect vulnerable parties from shock, harm and distress. Victims, families of victims and mentally disturbed defendants and their families need the reassurance of knowing that FoI Act access rights are not going to be allowed to be exercised to their detriment. The National Archives and the Metropolitan Police must also continue to protect public confidence that victims, victims' families and mentally disturbed defendants are allowed to be given privacy.

In addition some of the information in the file is also covered by Section 40: Personal information: subsection (2). This section exempts personal information relating to a third party (that is, someone other than the applicant), if its disclosure would contravene the Data Protection Act 1998. The 1998 Act prohibits the disclosure of personal information where, for example, it would be unfair, or incompatible with the purpose for which it was obtained.

Why this exemption applies

Section 40 (2) applies as the file contains unsubstantiated allegations of a criminal nature against living identifiable individuals, as well as expressions of intention towards them as individuals. Disclosure of this would be deemed to be unfair as there is no expectation that the information would be released during the lifetime of these individuals. This is an absolute exemption and as such we do not conduct a public interest test in relation to releasing this information.

If you are dissatisfied with any aspect of our response to your request for information and/or wish to appeal against information being withheld from you please send full details within two calendar months of the date of this letter to:

The Quality Manager
Public Services Development Unit
The National Archives
Kew
Richmond
Surrey
TW9 4DU
<u>COMPLAINTS@NATIONALARCHIVES.GOV.UK</u>

You have the right to ask the Information Commissioner (ICO) to investigate any aspect of your complaint. Please note that the ICO is likely to expect internal complaints procedures to have been exhausted before beginning his investigation.

If I can be of further assistance, please do not hesitate to contact me.
Yours sincerely,

FOI and Data Protection Officer
The National Archives

***

Prologue

Deathly Forges

Sunday 22nd April 2012 – 1:03am

'Baszd meg!' The man swore, remembering too late to lower his voice. After a quick look over his shoulder he relaxed. It was unlikely he would be seen or heard at this time of night.

It had been an unexpected struggle to hold the heavy sack at shoulder height. Eventually he allowed the deadweight to slide down the cold, black metal railings. He stood upright sucking in several deep lungfuls of the chilly night air as he stretched his arms trying to release the lactic acid that had been building up in his forearms. Taking off his dark green woollen hat, he ran his fingers briefly through his closely cropped blond hair. The latex gloves he was wearing were thin enough that he could feel the warm, wet sensation from the pinpricks of perspiration generated by his recent exertion. He cursed again, quieter this time, at his latest failure that had compounded his earlier error. Initially, he had been unable to find the exact location, and now at his impromptu new site, he had been incapable of shifting the heavy sack over the high, wrought iron fence.

It was shameful, a young man in his condition, he admonished himself. Pulling the hat back down onto his head, he bent his knees and took a more measured approach. In one swift movement, like a weightlifter, he jerked the sack up to shoulder height, spread his legs and shifted his hands into a better position. Taking several more deep breaths, his face reddening quickly, the veins throbbing on his temples he thrust the heavy weight clean over the fence. A quick look around to make sure no one had seen him, then he vaulted fluently up and over, landing quietly on the short grass on the other side that ran by the footpath.

Dragging the dark tarpaulin sack towards some bushes near a low wall, he rolled the contents out. Stopping briefly he pulled a folded sheet of paper from his back pocket and opened it, squinting in the poor light emanating from a the streetlamp on the far side of the road. He looked briefly at the diagram then back at the naked body lying in front of him. Copying the image on the paper he carefully aligned the position of the body to correspond to the piece of paper. He had at least got lucky on one point; near the bushes was a pile of leaves. Checking the neck again to make sure the scratch marks were visible he stood and admired his handiwork. Then leaning in he dealt a powerful right jab to the left side of the bridge of the nose and across the left cheekbone.

Moving back towards where he had entered the park, he continued a few metres on until he came to a small stand of trees at the edge of a forest. Bending down he gathered a few twigs together at the base of one of the trees. Using the piece of paper that he had consulted earlier, he screwed it into a ball and pushed it in among the small pieces of wood. Fishing a lighter from his pocket he bent in close and lit a corner of the balled up paper. He stood back and watched the flame take hold and briefly flare as the paper burned itself quickly into ashes while the damp kindling refused to catch.

He smiled briefly. This last step wasn't on his list of orders. This was his own little touch. His own mark. His own ritual.

After he climbed back over the fence he carefully removed his gloves and placed them in his bomber jacket pocket making sure he zipped it up before he climbed into the white Ford Transit van. He drove a little way up Boston Gardens before completing a 360-degree turn as the road swung away to his right and as quietly as possible rolled the van back towards the junction with Boston Manor Road. He took his time, waited for a red double decker to pass along the main road before he checked again to make sure there was no traffic coming from either direction. The last thing he needed was to execute a hasty manoeuvre and become involved in some sort of traffic incident by being in too much of a rush. This wasn't the first time he had done a job like this and he knew how imperative it was to keep calm in these situations.

There were no headlights to indicate oncoming traffic so he eased the vehicle left onto the main road and at a mini roundabout 50 metres on he indicated and swung a sharp right. The street was also clear of traffic but the man swore as he read the road sign - Swyncombe Avenue. What fool had put the sign there? It was half hidden behind a tree growing in the garden of the corner house. So difficult for anyone driving past to see. He looked to his left as he drove down the street. There was a narrow alley running away to the north. This is where he should have placed the body. But it was too late now. He hoped the man who had given him the instructions for how the job should be done would be happy enough. He would have to be. There was no going back now. And anyway it wasn't his fault he couldn't find the right place. What did the man expect? Hiring a foreigner to do his dirty work. His rates were cheap and the buyer knew that. In this day and age you get what you pay for. *Caveat emptor.*

***

Chapter 1.
Large borrow

Monday, 2nd April 2012 – 9:15am

'Detective Inspector Chambers?' The voice came from further along the corridor from where Chambers was standing gawping through the small window in the wooden door. The man's voice snapped him from his trance just before a door slammed violently shut from somewhere behind the voice.

Chambers slowly shifted his gaze from the varnished wooden door and looked to his right, towards the jovial figure. A short, stocky, uniformed man with a reddish complexion and neatly parted brown hair was walking briskly towards him. As the man neared, he slowly held his hand out in front of him.

'You are DI Chambers, aren't you?' Chambers initial lack of response had caused the man's broad smile to loosen into something less certain.

Finally, nodding slowly, Chambers accepted the firm, if somewhat warm and moist, handshake. The three pips on the uniform's shoulder badge identified the man's rank as that of Chief Inspector.

The jolly smile returned. 'Good, that's good. Very good. Please, if you don't mind, come with me.' He turned, 'it's best I give you a briefing before you meet your new team.' He gestured with his thumb over his shoulder towards the room into which Chambers had been staring.

THE CHARRED FOREST MURDERS

He had noticed the office contained six desks in two columns of three. At the back there was a window that stretched across the full width of the room. The plastic horizontal blinds slightly open, allowing the watery light of the weak, morning London sun to compete in vain with the electric strip lighting that was casting its own incandescent sickly yellow glow over the office. The wall on the right was taken up mainly by a large white board with an empty desk adjacent to it. On the left wall, an assortment of filing cabinets stood erect next to an outdated printer. Chambers had stopped short of opening the door and introducing himself. As he'd looked through the glass he realised all of the six desks were occupied. Maybe he had arrived at the wrong room. The sign on the wooden door read 201. He appeared to be where he was supposed to be.

It was a simple matter of asking one of the people in the room for clarification, but just before he reached for the handle he'd felt overcome by weariness. Not just in a physical sense, but more an accumulation of mental and emotional fatigue. The last few months were catching up with him and he knew it wouldn't be long before he paid the price. But for now, looking blankly through the narrow window into what was to be his new office, he felt like the new kid at school. Normally he didn't give a second thought to situations such as these. It was common for him to join bespoke teams or lead a special unit full of officers unknown to him but today everything just felt different. In reality a lot of things were different now. He'd been through hell since the last time he had set foot in a London police station. And now he was due to return to something resembling normality, he wasn't sure this was the career he wanted or needed anymore.

'Come along, come along.' The uniformed officer was marching back in the direction from which Chambers had heard the door slam moments before. As he turned to follow, Chambers thought he had detected a slight Welsh accent.

***

'Take a seat while I introduce myself, bring you up to speed with what you'll be tasked with. I'm Chief Inspector Roger Barlow, I'm heading the West London section of a new national crime initiative. We, and now you, are part of Operation Yetna.' Barlow paused to gauge Chambers' reaction. All he got in return was a blank look. 'Ring any bells?'

Chambers shook his head slightly.

'Hmmm, I'm guessing you're not familiar with Operation Yetna?'

Chambers glanced around the office. It had a strange smell of old biscuits and dampness. The small office was compact but not cramped. The wooden desk was covered in paperwork, an odd assortment of files and reports. There was only just room for the flat screen monitor while the keyboard and mouse that had to be somewhere were hidden from view under the usual office detritus. Apart from the modern monitor there was nothing else visible that placed the office in the 21st century. It looked like every police station Chambers had visited during his London career – drab, soulless, barely functional. He felt suddenly claustrophobic. The large window behind Barlow had its vertical plastic blinds drawn. A solitary overhead strip light illuminated the room. On the desk was a photograph in a slightly tarnished silver frame. Chambers could just see the image from the angle he was at. It was of Barlow with his arm around an Asian woman, they were both smiling. Wherever they were it looked warm, the smiling Barlow looked tanned and content. The couple looked genuinely happy Chambers decided.

'No? OK, well that's interesting,' Barlow opened a file on his desk and skimmed a few pages, silently mouthing phrases. 'I see, right, well of course, you have been …' he paused, drumming his fingers lightly on the desk and looking towards the photograph briefly before returning his gaze to Chambers, '… away, so to speak. Let me bring you up to speed. Operation Yetna has been running for a few months now, but as the BBC ran a story on their website in March, it's now common knowledge to every man and his dog. Not that we have anything to hide, and it's hardly classified information anyway – it just means we're fair game for the journos in terms of producing results. Yetna involves systematically working through files of unsolved murders to see which of them would benefit from further investigation. Initially we'll focus on about 200 cases from the 1980s and 1990s. Advances in DNA testing will hopefully bring about some new leads. But we are also tasked with looking at cases dating all the way back to the 1960s.' He paused again looking for a reaction from Chambers.

'It's an interesting assignment don't you think?' Barlow cajoled, trying to get a reaction out of the unemotional Chambers. 'Since we've technically split from the MIT guys it's given me a chance to embrace a more holistic approach to solving these really fascinating cases.'

Chambers was becoming aware that Barlow not only liked the sound of his own voice but had somewhere got lost in the mumbo jumbo of meaningless office babble, but the man seemed harmless enough.

'Basically' Barlow continued, 'it reminds of those US cold case shows on TV that are so popular these days. Teams have been set up all over the country and your old boss, Inspector Asbury, who as you know has been kind enough to send you here on secondment for a year.'

The name Asbury jarred with Chambers. The old bastard couldn't wait to get him reassigned. It was Asbury who was responsible for Chambers suspension from the force after the Hong Kong incident, and it was Asbury who, Chambers had subsequently found out, had pushed for the issuance of an arrest warrant for Chambers during the murder hunt up in Fife earlier in the year. How it must have hurt Asbury's pride to have his superiors not only reinstate Chambers when all the facts came to light, but also for Chambers to receive a commendation for bravery for his part in flushing out the killer in Scotland.

Now that Chambers was back from his short excursion in Africa, Asbury had shifted him out of his team as quickly and quietly as time would permit. Even Chambers who was used to Asbury's underhanded manner was amazed that it had all happened so rapidly. Before he'd even had a chance to return to his old desk at the Westminster Chinese Unit situated at the West End Central Station, he'd received a curt telephone call at home from Asbury congratulating him on promotion to a newly formed team in West London and that although the WCU was disappointed to see him go, they wished him well. And as a parting by the way, there was no need to come by his old station, as Asbury would thoughtfully forward his belongings to his new office. Further instructions of where and who to report to would be emailed to him in due course. Asbury had rung off leaving Chambers standing in his living room in Shepherd's Bush staring blankly at his mobile phone.

It had been less than two weeks since Chambers had been reinstated into the Met police and little over a week after receiving his commendation in front of a room full of press – it was hard to believe he was now persona non grata in the office where he'd worked for the past decade.

'We've been together as a team for two months.' Barlow continued in lieu of Chambers expected response, 'you're the final piece in the jigsaw so to speak. Granted it's a bit of a mixed bag you've got there, but when all is said and done you've got a lot of good, solid experience and if I may say, a lot of it gained across a wide arena of different police departments. The five of them all have their strengths and weaknesses, but …'

'Five?' Chambers interrupted, finally breaking his silence.

'Yes, five, why?'

'It's just that when I was about to enter the room, I saw six desks and each of them occupied.'

Barlow nodded. 'Aha, well no doubt that means our illustrious retired consultant is with us today. My guess is he's sitting at your desk. He's a good man is old Charlie. But he's had some bad news recently. That's one of the reasons I turn a blind eye to his comings and goings. Really he shouldn't be here. However, he was on the force for decades and, to be honest, we could do with all the additional help we can get and he brings a wealth of knowledge to the team. At the end of the day he works for us for free and he's been crucial in a couple of breakthroughs we've made already. Plus, I really do feel a bit sorry for him. I can't imagine how I would cope with what he has. It's a death sentence really. And he's all alone to boot.'

Chambers waited for Barlow to fill in the crucial missing elements to the story but the Chief Inspector was looking thoughtfully at the silver frame on his desk.

'Is that your wife?' Chambers asked.

Barlow snapped out of his abstraction, turning his ruddy-cheeked smile towards Chambers. 'Yes, yes it is. Maggie. We've been happily married since 1977. Don't know what I'd do without her. We met in Singapore you know? I was over there briefly, working with the Republic of Singapore Police Force as it was known back in the day, its heyday if you ask me but that's another story,' he paused flicking back through the file, 'I see you were out East.' He looked up, tapping the page with his index finger.

Chambers nodded briefly.

'It's a different world isn't it? Gets under your skin. Can't quite put my finger on it.' He looked briefly back at the photograph, 'I miss it though. We go back from time to time to visit a few of her relatives, but it's not the same is it?' He was drumming his fingers on the desk again.

Chambers nodded. For the time being he didn't want to think about the Far East. If he thought about Hong Kong it meant thinking about Lucy and that was simply too painful at present.

Barlow continued, 'last time we were there was October 2010 on our way to Australia for the Ashes. Do you like cricket?' He looked up and smiled broadly at Chambers, 'I'm a devotee, don't you know. Teaches you a lot about life if you ask me.'

Chambers gave a shrug of his shoulders. Cricket? He could take it or leave it.

'So are you up for the challenge?' Barlow chuckled as if he had just told an amusing anecdote. 'Yetna I mean, not a cricket challenge! Hardly going to torment you with my famous Barlow bosey right here on the first floor corridor.'

Chambers raised his eyebrows slightly but didn't reply.

'Can I call you John?' Barlow asked leaning forward, the smile had disappeared.

Chambers nodded again.

'John look here. I'm no fool. I know you're probably looking on this as a sideways move, perhaps even a demotion. It's clear from your file that you've been around the block more than once and I'm damn sure you know what's what, but it seems you've ruffled a few feathers in the past few months. But let me tell you, I was brought up to see the good in people. Yes I know some people bear grudges, but I just want you to look at this as a fresh start, a new opportunity as it were. We'll have no trouble here. I genuinely don't care what happened before. What's done is done. I'm talking about a clean slate.' He sat back, the hint of a smile played on his lips.

Chambers nodded, he appreciated the show of support.

Barlow went on. 'It's about integrity. We're police officers after all, and we've been given the chance to solve some murders that in some cases date back nearly 50 years. It's a challenge and I believe it's our duty. Plus we've got this state of the art software in the database. The bigwigs say it's a major step forward. We've got the latest in forensics technology at our beck and call from Dr Parvati Bhanji at the Forensic Services Command Unit in Fulham. It's probably worth reaching out to her and getting the team in for a presentation of what those boffins are up to.'

Again Chambers nodded.

'I'm up for the challenge and I hope that you are too. I'm willing to give you complete freedom in how you operate and how you run the team if you can promise me that you will be committed to the cause, act with integrity, demand the most out of yourself and the team and basically give it your best shot. No one can ask for any more than that. Can they? Now do we have a deal?' He extended his hand again and looked expectantly over at the DI.

Chambers shook his hand and smiled. 'Yes. You got yourself a deal Chief Inspector.'

'That's absolutely smashing! And please, call me Roger. We'll have no standing on ceremony here. Now let me introduce you to your new team.' As he stood up a phone rang. Barlow leaned in and lifted a folder revealing a cream plastic telephone. He read the caller ID and rolled his eyes heavenward. 'It's the blasted Super; I really had better take this. You head on in and introduce yourself I'll be along as soon as I deal with our omnipotent leader.' He smiled again and picked up the receiver.

'Ronnie, hello and what can I do you for today?'

Whatever was said in response quickly wiped the smile from Barlow's face. His other hand smoothing down his already neatly parted hair. Chambers took the opportunity to take his leave, quietly closing the door behind him and making his way back to where the Chief Inspector had found him earlier.

***

"A mixed bag?" Chambers mused to himself. What exactly had Barlow meant when he'd described the new team as a mixed bag? It didn't exactly fill him with confidence. He tried to shake the feeling of lethargy that he felt was threatening to envelop him. If he could just get through today, he thought, then just take it one day at a time. Hopefully he'd be back to his usual self before too long. His words of encouragement to himself felt hollow. Whatever was the source that caused him to feel this flat, there was little respite and for now he would just have to grin and bear it. What else could he realistically do?

He eventually turned the door handle and entered the room. Four sets of eyes looked over in his direction, but no one spoke, or smiled for that matter.

Chambers was aware that the front two desks that had been occupied earlier were now empty.

'Operation Yetna?' He asked as a way of introduction, looking around the room for some camaraderie. 'I'm Detective inspector John Chambers. Would someone mind showing me which desk is mine?'

Chambers again looked around the room's four members. Two younger men, who were now smirking and looking at each other, occupied the middle two desks. The man on the left as Chambers looked, was thin with short reddish hair and pasty skin, he was wearing a black cardigan over a grey shirt with a short, button-down collar. The man to his right had a neatly trimmed goatee, slicked back dark brown, slightly wavy hair and he was wearing a red Ralph Lauren polo shirt. Behind the pair sat two much older men. On the left a heavyset, bald man in a plain white T-shirt, scowled back at him, while on the right an equally bald, but bearded and much smaller, thinner man in a pale blue shirt looked casually in his direction. The man on the right was wearing a large pair of enormous headphones that reminded Chambers of Doctor Who's cybermen. Slowly the man reached up and removed the headphones, placing them carefully on the desk in front of him.

Rubbing his short, neat silver beard he said, 'Morning squire. Anything I can help you with?' Chambers could hear the man's strong London accent.

'I'm DI Chambers,' he reiterated, 'I've been assigned to Operation Yetna. This is the office for the Operation Yetna team?'

The man in the black cardigan sniggered but didn't speak.

'Yep, this is the place.' The man with the headphones said, ' you'd better come in. Roger said you'd be starting today.' He turned to the man next to him, 'come on mate, you better get up and give the DI his desk.'

Without taking his eyes from Chambers the heavyset man struggled to his feet with what appeared to be a great deal of difficulty. Chambers was surprised at the man's size, well over six feet and weighing beyond 100kg, the T-shirt taught against his large beer gut. He had to be in his seventies, although bald on top he had a shock of white hair wrapping around the back of his head falling almost to the collar of his T-shirt. The scowl combined with his heavy brow gave him a bizarre yet somewhat intimidating look.

As he shuffled past Chambers without acknowledgement, Chambers noted the man was also wearing a pair of carpet slippers and faded maroon, cotton jogging pants.

As he reached the door, the man in the red polo shirt shouted out, 'Take it easy uncle. I'll buzz you later or bell me if you got any problems.'

The old man continued shuffling towards the door, simply raising his hand in acknowledgement but neither turning nor speaking. He just gave a grunt and slammed the door as he left.

Chambers remained motionless, staring at the door in sheer astonishment at the man's complete lack of social refinement.

'Hounslow's finest.' The man with the headphones said. 'What can I say? Come and take a seat and I'll do the introductions.' The man was now standing and gesturing at the recently vacated chair. 'Sorry for the mess by the way.'

Chambers moved past the empty row of desks closest to the door, past the two younger men before coming parallel to his new workspace. The desk was bare except for a monitor, keyboard and mouse, penholder and some pads of yellow Post-It notes. A dog-eared puzzle magazine was the solitary item of paperwork on the desk. The only other article of note was the detritus of what Chambers guessed was, the remains of a sausage roll and tomato sauce smeared across part of the desk. The chair had crumbs and odd stains on it that made him reluctant to sit down.

'Welcome to Yetna. Take a seat,' he nodded at the chair, 'it won't bite you – I hope.' The blue shirted man said with a crafty smile, 'I'm Terrence Buchanan, Detective Sergeant and I'm guessing I'll be your number two from here on in. I'd prefer it if you call me Terry rather than your number two.' He smiled and the other two men chuckled in their seats.

Chambers eased himself into the chair, the fact it felt warm made it feel even more uncomfortable. 'Nice to meet you Terry.' Chambers nodded, he immediately warmed to the older policeman. There was something about him that Chambers found reassuring maybe it was the contrast between the warmth of Buchanan and the initial hostility he felt emanating from the others.

Buchanan continued, 'this is Detective Constable Russell Polk,' he indicated the man in the cardigan, 'and DC Paul Pierce.' He concluded the brief introductions by pointing to the man in the red polo shirt.

'Hello.' Chambers nodded in turn to the two men who had turned to look at him.

'Alright,' Pierce said turning back to his monitor. Polk just nodded and continued to watch him, a sarcastic grin on his face.

'Obviously I'm new to the team, so I'll try and arrange to get some time with you both later for a quick overview on what your working on. But for now just carry on with what you're doing.'

Chambers turned to Buchanan, who had sat back down, 'when I passed the office earlier, I noticed there were two other people here.'

'Yes, they've gone off to Heathrow, should be back by lunchtime. The bird is Sandra Hayes and the coloured lad is Eddie Adams. Both DCs as well.'

Chambers nodded. He was a bit surprised at Buchanan's antiquated descriptive terms of the two other members, it could hardly be described as something for a tribunal but also it had been a while since he'd heard those terms in use in a modern Met police station. Well not inside the confines of the office with the strict codes on equal opportunities that were now strongly enforced. At least that was the protocol at his old station – these days the PCs were assuredly PC.

'I had a quick chat with the Chief Inspector, he'll be along shortly, but in the meantime can you bring me up to speed on where we're at with Yetna?' Chambers had rotated his chair to address Buchanan rather than the group.

'Yetna was formed in January of this year. Paul, Russell and myself were already working here in the Brentford Murder Investigation Team. Barlow was senior in that so it was a straightforward enough change for him and the three of us to move office to here. Literally we just shifted our stuff over from the main building. Sandra and Eddie joined us a couple of weeks ago, he's come over from Taskforce Trident she's back from extended sick leave as far as I know. And my guess is you complete the team.'

'What about …' Chambers looked towards the door then towards the mess on the desk.

'Old Charlie you mean? I wouldn't mind him if I was you.'

Chambers nodded.

'Charles, or Chad as pretty much everyone calls him, he's been back with us since,' he paused, 'must be November last year, before we shifted into here anyway.'

'So what's the full scope of Yetna?'

'Not sure what Roge has already told you, but it's all cold case stuff. Our area is covering out to Heathrow, round there and all way into town basically. So when I say cold case, we got loads to work with. I mean your talking cases like Dando, Lamplugh, you know real big hitting media stuff, but anything that hasn't be solved. Going all the way back to the war. I mean I said to Roge why not make the bleeding scope a bit bigger, go back another 60 years and we can have a pop at solving the bloody Ripper case as well!' Buchanan laughed.

'What did the Chief Inspector say?'

'What old Roge the Dodge? He just gave one of his hearty chuckles. He doesn't want to rock the boat that one. He's a couple of months away from his big golden handshake. He'll be made up he's got you to smooth his path out of this place. He's got that Northern bint giving him both barrels all day. He's just sucking up all the shit she can serve him till he can do one and get his arse out of here.'

'Northern? His wife? I thought …' Chambers trailed off. He was thinking Buchanan had to be at least 10 years older than the Chief Inspector.

'No, not his wife Maggie. She's a lovely bird. I'm talking about the Super. You'll know what I mean when you get to meet her. Luckily for you she sits over in the main building, so you might get to steer clear of her for a while. She's not one for visiting the poor relations over here in the cheap seats.'

'Eh? I thought when I just left him, he was talking to the Super, someone by the name of Ronnie.'

'Yeah that's her. Ronnie is a she. Detective Superintendent Ronnie McKinley. One of Manchester's finest.' He said sarcastically. 'Fast tracked through that bloody ridiculous scheme to give the bird's in the force a leg up.

'Yeah, she needs a leg over not a leg up.' Pierce chimed in without turning. Polk snorted loudly at the joke.'

Buchanan ignored them. 'What's its name? The course?'

'The accelerated promotion course at Bramshill College?' Chambers knew a few colleagues in Westminster who'd benefitted from the course that was designed to get more women into senior roles at the Met.

'Yeah, that's the one. PC one minute, next she's a bleeding Super, and I tell you she don't like anyone mentioning it. She's got a chip on her shoulder that one. Anyway fair's fair, she's rarely in here bothering the shitkickers. She gives Roge a hard time; he's the buffer see? We just got to piece him back together afterwards. The good news is she's the senior investigating officer for the Specialist Crime Directorate's Homicide Command, the posh name for our MIT so, in reality she's just the token head of this new team. If we're lucky she'll have her hands full with the MIT mob here and we can stay under the radar.'

Chambers nodded. He didn't know the woman personally, but it appeared that once Roger retired, and judging from what he's just heard it sounded imminent, then he'd be next to step into her firing line.

'Oh, I nearly forgot. This is for you.' Buchanan passed him a couple of printed sheets of A4. 'It's from the HR and IT guys.

Your log in codes and passwords for your email and access to the mainframe and database, all that sort of stuff. Also there's a log in there for HOLMES 2, the database we are to use for Yetna. Speak to Paul here; he's our resident expert. Now if you'll excuse me I've got to crack on.'

Chambers thanked him and watched the neat, wiry man carefully place the oversize headphones back over his ears and return to tapping away on his keyboard.

***

Chapter 2.

Rating ban

Monday, 2nd April 2012 – 11:12am

Less than an hour later the office was empty save Chambers. Barlow still hadn't appeared, Pierce and Polk had slipped off somewhere without informing him where, and Buchanan had been about as apocryphal by stating he had "to go to see a man about a dog".

Chambers opened the web browser and logged on to his personal email account. Finally there was a mail from Hong Kong. It was from his ex-colleague Detective Inspector Brian Tang.

'John, Apologies for the delay I am only today back from leave. I received your messages. Please call me when you have the opportunity.'

Brian'

Chambers immediately picked up the phone on his desk and dialled Tang's number that he located at the bottom of the email. It was just before 11am in London making it about 7pm in Hong Kong. Chambers hoped Tang would still be in the office.

'Wai,' On the fifth ring a man answered in Cantonese.

'Brian Tang?'

'Yes, this is Brian.' There was a short pause. 'Is that you John?'

'Yes it is, I just got your email. How's things over there?'

'Fine, fine. I just had a couple of weeks away in Sanya with my family. I had to get away. The office here,' he trailed off, 'you can imagine after such a tragedy.'

'I'm so sorry Brian. I've heard some things but in your absence I got put through to a DI C.F. Mak, I don't remember him and, whether or not that was the issue, he was reluctant to give me any more info than I already got from the SCMP website.'

'Ah, C.F., he joined the team after you left. He's been around for years. C.F. was the first senior officer at the murder site. From what I can gather he made a, what was your lovely English saying? "A balls up", of how he handled it. He waited too long to go in. They estimate it was nearly an hour between the witnesses hearing the shot and when he finally allowed the Flying Tigers in for a look.'

'Who the hell are the Flying Tigers?'

'Sorry, that's the nickname of the Special Duties Unit, the hostage negotiation team. What they found? Inspector James Pang's body. Shot once in the chest. That's why C.F. is getting so much criticism. They think if he'd authorised going in earlier Pang would still be alive. The Coroner's report says he didn't die immediately. I don't know if they could have saved him and now we'll never know. But in C.F.'s defence, he couldn't be sure the shooter wasn't still inside.'

'But the report in the newspaper said there was another body in there.'

'Yes, there was the mutilated remains of Horace Wu. From what I can gather he was one of Lucy's leading informants.'

The mention of her name made Chambers' stomach turn a somersault.

'And Lucy?' Chambers was scared to ask, 'any word about her?' He was terrified Tang was going to tell him something he wasn't ready to hear.

There was a long pause, 'I'm sorry John.'

Chambers heart sank. He could feel his chest tighten and tears pricked his eyes. Blinking quickly he struggled to keep calm. He simply couldn't accept the fact that the woman he loved was dead.

'What, how … do you know what happened?'

'Nothing. I mean she's still missing. By the time the Tigers got in, there was no sign of her or the killer. I know this is going to sound ridiculous, but after it was ascertained Lucy had also been inside there were questions raised as to whether one or two people had escaped.'

'What do you mean …' Chambers hesitated while he tried to get a handle on what Tang was telling him, 'shit, are you seriously trying to tell me that people, and people who worked closely with Lucy, could even for a moment think she had killed Pang? He was like a father to her.'

'I know John. I feel the same way. But see it from their perspective. There was little in the way of evidence. Lucy was closely linked to the two dead people. She's not been herself since the assault. She's hardly spoken to anyone since she came back to the office. Not many officers in here even know about this murder suspect from London, so at first no one could put an name on the suspect.'

'Tomar Shen, AKA Hak Loong. You know who it is.'

'Yes, you're right I do. And so did James and Lucy. One dead, one missing. Jenny Greening knows as well and she's still on extended sick leave since the whole Water Dragon thing. All the people that worked closely with you on that investigation accounted for, except me. By the time the rumours had started I was unfortunately already on leave. I put people straight as soon as I could. I'm sorry John.'

'Come on Brian, it's not your fault. But how come nothing has been seen or heard from her? I don't understand. It's been how long now? The last mail I received from her was dated 1st of March, over a month ago.'

'I know. We've scoured Peng Chau. It appears he must have taken her from the house and the best guess now is he must have spirited her away into one of the sampan's moored up close to the building and from there out to one of the hundreds of islands dotted about here or onto a larger boat and into the South China Sea and then where? The Pearl River Delta and into China? Across to Vietnam? Up to Korea or Japan. She could be anywhere by now. That's assuming he didn't just put a bullet in her, weigh her down and dump her overboard.'

Chambers breathed deeply trying to maintain his composure. 'What did they find at the scene? Anything we can use?'

'One shell casing. It's been tested and it was definitely fired from Li's weapon and matched the bullet that killed Pang. That didn't help her much either at the beginning. The place has been fingerprinted but there's plenty of prints and not just from Pang and Li but also from about twenty other people. Some we've matched, some we haven't. It was a derelict house. All sorts of people could have been in there. We also found some cigarette butts which we've sent for DNA testing but no match as yet.'

'OK,' Chambers was thinking about other possible leads, but there was little to go on. 'Anything else?'

'Oh yes, when DI Mak made an earlier aborted attempt to enter the building, he found a cover of a Japanese passport by the front door. We don't know if somehow it happened when Shen and Li left the building or it might just be something that was dropped there on another occasion. Again there's nothing on the cover to identify the owner and no fingerprints.'

'Japan? What do we know about Shen?'

'As for the scant info I have on him, all I know is he's a Canadian-born Korean.'

Chambers heard a short rat-a-tat at the door, before it opened and Roger's head popped into the gap. A wide grin on his face.

Holding up one finger in the Chief Inspector's direction, Chambers said 'Brian, I've got to go. I'm really sorry for you and the team's loss. Pang was a good man. And please, can you call me if you hear anything?'

'Of course. Just one thing before you go. We've received some mail. Looks like it might be expenses and a few other things letters, some internal and some external mail. Do you want me to forward it on to you?'

'Sure. Probably easier to send it to my home address. I'll email you the details now. Thanks and let's speak soon.'

'OK. Stay positive John. I'm sure she'll turn up. You know she's tough,' he cleared his throat. 'She will be OK John.'

'Cheers. Take care,' Chambers hung up.

'No one about, John?' Barlow asked, stating the obvious.

Chambers opened his palms to the sky. 'No idea. Out and about.'

'No problem. The blasted super's got me chasing my tail. Basically formal introductions are off for this afternoon. Might be best if we line up a quick drink after work. Do the introductions in a less formal setting. Better for team morale I always think. Let's say The Beehive at 6pm. It's a Fuller's pub so it does a lovely pint of London Pride, if you appreciate a fine ale.'

'Sounds good to me.' Chambers offered him a brief smile.

'Righto, I'll fire off an email to the rest of the team and I'll leave you settling in. See you at the pub at six.'

Pressing reply on Tang's email, Chambers thanked him for the information and added his home address for the Hong Kong DI to forward his mail on to, before clicking on send.

The phone call had made Chambers' miserable mood even worse. It just didn't make any sense to him. The last thing the Hong Kong police needed to do was waste any of their time focusing on Lucy as the killer. That was completely and utterly ridiculous. But as the inspector had been killed with her weapon, and her leading informer also dead at the scene he begrudgingly understood their initial confusion and waste of critical time. Hardly anyone knew anything about the identity of Tomar Shen. Lucy had only recently discovered his real name and it sounded like she hadn't shared that information with many others except Inspector Pang and himself. Brian worked closely with them all when Chambers had been in Hong Kong and was probably privy to some of the information or at least knew Lucy was still searching for the killer who had fled from London the previous year.

But why hadn't he just killed Lucy and left her there? It didn't make sense, but crucially it gave Chambers a slight glimmer of hope that she was still alive and some belief to desperately cling on to. At least until a body turned up he would keep believing. If Tang was right though, and she'd been dumped at sea, then there always the chance her body would never be recovered. He just had to hope that whatever psychotic reason Shen had to spirit Lucy away, it meant she might still be alive. Where though? That was anyone's guess. And what of the Japanese passport cover? It had no obvious links to Shen, but then what else did he have to go on?

***

When Chambers pushed his way through the narrow spring-loaded doors into The Beehive pub at about a quarter to six, he was still feeling distracted by the scant information DI Tang had relayed to him earlier in the day. He'd spent a lot of the afternoon looking at Google maps and trying to figure out where Lucy might have been taken. His memory of Hong Kong's vast Victoria Harbour was that it was teeming with craft from enormous super freighters and navy ships right down to tiny sampans that bobbed so precariously on the undulating surface that it was a miracle that they remained afloat. He would email Brian later from home and see if he could get some harbour police reports of activity around Peng Chau on the day in question. But he was sure this would already have been done and that the thousands of small, unlicensed craft would render the task nigh on impossible.

There had been little in the way of action in the office. When he left the office to go for a walk about 5pm, the two DCs, whom he still hadn't met had been delayed investigating a lead at the airport. He had spoken briefly to DS Buchanan, but the older man clearly was keen to be left to get on with whatever he was working on and Chambers was in no mood for small talk.

Looking around the bar, Chambers couldn't locate any of the team so he ordered a pint of London Pride. When he paid the barman he claimed a corner table on the other side of the bar down a couple of steps near the pool table, big enough to seat a party of eight. The jukebox on the far wall was pumping out Electric Avenue by Eddie Grant. Although there were only a handful of patrons they were making quite a racket, a few middle-aged blokes cursing at the bar with a couple of old men sitting at another table.

He didn't have to wait long to be joined by the Chief Inspector. Barlow gave him a mock salute on entering and seeing Chambers still had a full pint, ordered himself one and came over.

'How was the first day? No trouble from the natives I hope.' Barlow beamed as he sat down.

'Actually very quiet. Most of the team have been out all day. I'll make a point of sitting down with each member individually to see what they're working on and where they're up to.'

'Jolly good.'

The saloon bar door opened and DC Buchanan came in and glanced around. Seeing his colleagues he came over and nodded to them each in turn.

'How do Terrence. Not getting yourself a drink?'

'No Roge, just popped in to say a quick hello then I'll be getting off. I see no one else is here. Not sure where Russell and Paul are. Haven't seen them all afternoon. But Eddie and Sandra just got back from the airport so they'll be here any minute.'

'Take a seat for a minute can you? I'm sure you can't be in that much of a rush. While it's just the three of us, do you want to assist me and give DI Chambers a little of the colourful background on what's going on with the team.'

Chambers interceded, 'Terry's already given me an overview on Yetna. What would be good is some background info on the team, if you don't mind. Experience, strengths, that kind of thing.'

As Buchanan sat down he looked towards Barlow who nodded encouragement.

'Well, let's start with Charlie. He's been retired for about 10 years. He came back in one day completely out of the blue like. When was that Roge? November?'

'Late October, early November yes.' Barlow agreed.

'First of all I thought it was a bit odd. After a decade or so with no contact. And there's this big lumbering oaf all of a sudden. He would show up and hang about with the guys in MIT. His nephew is DC Paul Pierce. Chad and I worked Vice up the West End in the late seventies and eighties, so I guess it was a couple of friendly faces for the old fella. He'd had some bad news see? Once I winkled that out of him it all made perfect sense.'

Barlow picked up the baton. Glancing towards the pub's door. 'Basically what Terrence here is alluding to is, that Chad was diagnosed with bladder cancer last year. He lives alone at home and so I think the poor bloke was in dire need of some company. I can't imagine what it would be like sitting at home with a death sentence like that hanging over you. So that's why I've been turning a blind eye. Also, as I mentioned before, he's got an encyclopedic knowledge of many of the Met's murder cases for the past few decades. In my opinion it's worth having him about even if it appears he's just sitting doing puzzles all day. In actual fact he's normally in at the crack of dawn and does a lot of stuff then. Basically I think he likes to give the impression that he's just lazing about doing puzzles but I can assure you it's not the case. He's more like a duck on the water, looks like he's cruising along but I can assure you, those little feet will be going ten to dozen out of sight.' Barlow gave a perplexed look at his own analogy.

'Anyway, he's got a very methodical brain and understands systems very well. For an old guy he's very good with computers and software. At the end of the day he just has a knack for it, I guess.'

Chambers felt they were desperate to justify the old man's presence in the office and he was happy not to rock the boat for the time being.

'I'm fine with him coming in. But let's just try and limit it so it's not every day so he becomes a distraction to the team. Maybe we can tailor a few cases to his strengths to make him feel more involved.' Chambers suggested helpfully, although from the man's initial rudeness to him he didn't feel like he owed him anything.

'That's great John, really great. That means a lot. I'm glad you're on board with making this a harmonious team. It basically makes everyone's life that much easier.'

'What about the others?' Chambers pushed. Hoping to take advantage of the cordial atmosphere to gain an insight into his new team.

Buchanan looked past Chambers towards the bar. 'Sounds as though we might be here for a while, I'd better get myself an half. Anyone want anything while I'm up?'

Barlow and Chambers shook their heads and Buchanan moved towards the bar.

Barlow's gaze followed Buchanan until he saw the man speak to the barman. 'Now you see Terrence is one of life's good guy. He's a bit like Charlie in some ways.' He looked back towards Chambers. 'What I mean by that is, he could have retired years ago on a full pension. But he lives on his own.' Barlow looked puzzled for a moment, 'or maybe he has a cat. Whatever it is there's no wife or kids, I'm sure of that. He told me once that this job is all he has, which always makes me count my blessings for meeting Maggie. Don't get me wrong. I'm dedicated to this job, but one needs an escape, a valve to let off the pressure. Don't you agree?

Chambers nodded again, it was easy enough to humour Barlow, who clearly loved the sound of his own voice.

'Despite the Super's repeated suggestion that it's high time Terrence moved on – he's a bloody good detective and the most dedicated officer you're likely to come across. I'd have to check my records but I don't think he's had a sick day in nearly a decade.'

'Really? That is impressive.' Chambers glanced out of the pub's frosted glass window. The texture of the glass making it impossible to make out exactly the faces of people passing close to the window, causing their features to morph bizarrely as they streamed by, rushing home from work.

Barlow was nodding. 'Yes indeed. In fact, if it hadn't been for the allegations when he was in Vice, who knows where he'd be. My superior, I can say that for sure. Now he's content just working as a DS and keeping himself to himself. You might have noticed he's not the most forthcoming conversationalist. I'm guessing that's what those ridiculously large headphones are for. Making sure everyone keeps their distance. Let me reiterate, he's a bloody smart fellow and a real ace up your sleeve on this team.'

Chambers hadn't particularly noticed Buchanan's perceived reticence. He returned his gaze to Barlow 'Trouble in Vice? When? What was …'

'Peanuts? Thanks Terrence. Very thoughtful.' Barlow announced loudly.

Chambers turned to see Buchanan was almost back from the bar with his half pint and a bag of salted peanuts.

'So where were we?' Barlow continued. 'Aha, yes, DC Paul Pierce, nephew of Charlie. Local lad, comes from Isleworth, just down the road. Good with computers, software. Smart one, a bit like his uncle.'

'Too smart for his own good, if you ask me.' Buchanan added as he retook his seat by the window.

'Yes, well, you might have a point.' Barlow paused, 'what I'd say, if I was writing his school report, I'd give him a "C. Could do better". He's a good copper but he's easily distracted and I just think he's got so much more to offer the job. He's cruising. If he could get someone to show him his true potential.' The Chief Inspector looked at Chambers. 'Someone with experience. A robust chap. Someone with integrity.'

'And he bleeding well leads Russell astray. Sometimes I think that the Brummie kid is a bit soft in the head. But he passed his detective exam so there must be a brain in there somewhere. But I tell you, put the two of them together and you have a right pair of blockheads.'

'Do you think it's worth splitting them up? How long have they been paired up?' Chambers suggested helpfully.

'Paul's been on board since 2007, ever since he got kicked to touch by CID and Russell's been with us from 2009. He joined us from a stint at the British Transport Police, London North Division, based over in Paddington. We're looking at the best part of three years those two have been together.'

'Is it worth putting one with Sandra and the other with Eddie?' Chambers continued.

'It's a good idea in theory. But I'm not convinced we would strengthen the team as a collective or weaken it. Sandra and Eddie seem to have hit it off and appear to be working well together. I'd be reluctant to split them up. I'm not sure that it would help so much as just drag them down. You know Eddie came to us from SCD8 a few weeks back.'

'SCD8?' Chambers had heard of it but couldn't recall its actual scope.

'Operation Trident – focusing on major crime, shootings and drug sales in the Afro-Caribbean communities. He's been earmarked as one with great potential. I think he felt he had more to offer than the scope Trident was allowing him to achieve. Seems to have had a bit of friction with the Detective Chief Superintendent over there.'

'Interesting.' Chambers said by way of encouragement.

'That brings us on to our last but not least member of the group – Sandra.' Barlow continued. 'Bloody good copper by all accounts. Basically she's been off on sick leave. Actually she'd been recovering from a very nasty injury. She used to be in the Mounted Branch. Had a fall from her horse policing a night game up at Loftus Road. There'd been a bit of bother before kick off. Liverpool were the visitors if I'm not mistaken. She'd been told to get around to the exit where the trouble was. As she was galloping off down Ellerslie Road this young fan runs out in front of the horse – completely oblivious to what was going on, looking completely the other way and then the blasted fool stops dead. She had no time to react. The horse catches the kid, loses its footing on the slippery tarmac and they all go down in a heap. The fan's got the mother of all bruises on his thigh but he's basically OK, the horse is shaken but fine, but poor old Sandra caught the full weight of the horse as it fell on top of her. Shattered her pelvis, I believe.'

Buchanan helped himself to the open packet of peanuts and looked out towards the street, clearly, thought Chambers, it wasn't the first time he'd heard the story. Chambers shook his head. 'Sounds nasty.'

'Off for the best part of a year and declared unfit to ride again. She was redirected to a deskbound job with us. She was doing long distance study for her detective badge. At the end of the day she might be green and new to plainclothes, she comes highly recommended.' Barlow gave one of his trademark smiles before taking a large quaff of his beer.

'A mixed bag.' Chambers smiled.

'Eh, oh yes. Very much so.' Barlow nodded, squirming in his chair and looking awkwardly at Buchanan, who was sitting with his fingers intertwined contemplating something or someone over at the bar.

Mixed bag indeed, thought Chambers. Two retirees, a couple of blockheads, an angry young man, someone whose been out of the game for a while with no practical detecting experience and a boss who can't wait to retire. Great when do we start? He smiled at his lot, unsure how with 20 years of experience he had ended up here – at Brentford police station with a cold case team of misfits. It sounded like a big enough task for someone who was committed to the cause. Right at this moment that person certainly wasn't Chambers. He had an overwhelming urge to get up, shake the two men by the hand and resign on the spot.

'Speak of the devil.' Barlow was already getting to his feet as two people came into the bar.

They looked briefly around before acknowledging the seated group as Barlow waved them over. The man was tall, Chambers guessed over six feet. He looked lean and in good shape. The woman was shorter, maybe 5'5" with a mousy bob. As she turned and walked towards them, it was clear she had very pronounced limp. Here were the remaining members of the group.

***

Chapter 3.

Ads made

Thursday, 5th April 2012 – 3:17pm

By the Thursday of his first week at the new station, Chambers was beginning to acclimatise to work back at the Met. Of course the disappearance and possible death of Lucy cast a long shadow over his general mood, but other than that he felt things were starting to come together. Although Polk and Pierce hadn't joined the welcome drinks, and probably because of that, they'd all had a good time. North Londoner Eddie had only stayed for a couple of soft drinks before making his excuses and heading off to his Muay Thai class at a gym near his flat in Harlesden. The Thai boxing explained his toned physique and although he'd only stayed with the group for less than an hour, Chambers had already formed a positive opinion of him. He was switched on, clever, confident and for his age, which he guessed to be mid-twenties, he was wise or at least streetwise. Out of all of the team he was the one who Chambers thought could be his 'go to' man to get things done.

The next to leave had been Buchanan. He'd nursed several halves of bitter over a couple of hours and, Chambers noted, had become much quieter when the others had joined the group. Or maybe he'd just supposed that after Barlow's comments about Buchanan's perceived silence. It was as though he was aloof or at least distant from the others. It was a little odd, as he'd seemed friendly enough to Chambers on his arrival. But with the new members he appeared guarded, while both Adams and

Hayes had been engaging conversationalists. Maybe it was because he was from a different era of policing. Times were changing rapidly and maybe he no longer felt a part of modern policing methods.

After Buchanan made his departure, there was only Barlow, Hayes and Chambers left. They had another couple of pints, Hayes managed to slip in a couple of inbetweeners and by the time Chambers took his leave, DC Sandra Hayes and Chief Inspector appeared to be quite merry and were ordering pints and chasers and discussing some cricket related matters.

Yet the biggest surprise of the night was still in store for Chambers. He walked the short distance to the bus stop outside Morrisons supermarket and caught the 237 back to Shepherd's Bush. His demotion to Yetna and subsequent change of office at least meant he now had a door-to-door bus service. It was a very minor consolation.

As was his wont he sat upstairs. It was just coming up for 10pm and he hadn't been paying much attention when he took his seat. But it hadn't taken long for him to become aware that there was group of teenage girls cursing and shouting out threats to people on the street every time the bus pulled up at a stop or at a set of traffic lights. It was odd and unsettling behaviour and Chambers felt ill at ease. Not wanting to provoke the situation by pulling out his warrant card, Chambers endured the noise and offensive activities until the group of unruly girls got off on Chiswick High Road abusing most of the passengers on their way out.

For the rest of the journey back to Shepherds Bush he berated himself for his lack of action. Something told him not to get involved. What did he expect he could provoke? If truth be told he was suddenly aware of his vulnerability. He'd never felt it before. Maybe it had been Adams's passing comment in the pub earlier about the rise in random knife crime and associated unsolved murders. And although they didn't fall under the remit of Yetna, as they were still active cases, it was shocking to think of how many knife-related murders had taken place in London over the past few years. Was that it? Had he not stepped in for fear of getting stabbed? Or was it more than that? Had he really lost his desire to be a policeman? The thought depressed him and took him back to his black mood from earlier in the day.

When Chambers had woken slightly fuzzyheaded from the night out, he had made a decision. The past few months had been physically, mentally and emotionally draining. If he could start building up his physical strength then following the mantra – healthy body, healthy mind – surely it would help his recovery. Still troubled by headaches since the accident in Africa, he was pleased to have recovered his memory save for the day of the crash until he had woken in the nurses' room in central Uganda.

He'd caught the bus to work and after establishing there were showers and changing rooms he made the decision to start jogging to work in the morning and home again in the evenings as much as possible. There was a route from his place that travelled almost alongside the Thames for the most part. He would just need to make his way up through Ravenscourt Park towards Hammersmith Bridge, run the footpath along to Chiswick Mall, onto Duke's Meadows and along the gravel path that was hemmed in by blooming wildflowers and weeping willows, until at Chiswick Bridge he could head down Hartington Road until he hit the towpath at Strand-on-the-Green, past the riverside pubs to Kew Bridge. From there he could go under the arches and back along the towpath until he came back up to the road at O'Riordan's Tavern before cutting through Waterman's Park and along past the old, weather-beaten houseboats before finally the last stretch down the hill to Brentford police station.

Chambers began his campaign on Wednesday morning. A beautiful, sunny, spring day and the perfect conditions for his new health regime. Digging out an old pair of Adidas tennis shoes, he'd packed a small rucksack with a bottle of water. A change of clothes he'd already left at the office the day before, and off he set at 8am into the chilly morning air. It hadn't taken him long to warm up though and to say the run had been much harder than he imagined was a massive understatement. He'd eventually made it to his desk just past 10am. Over an hour late. Mainly due to his collapsing red faced and sweating on a number of park benches along the scenic route. At least most of the time he'd been afforded lovely views of the river Thames with its dark swirling waters that slid by and the early morning activity that consisted mainly of rowing boats effortlessly gliding across the moody water's surface.

The atmosphere in the office had also improved after Chambers hostile reception. He'd been surprised at how bright eyed Hayes had been on the Tuesday morning despite having put away at least twice what he'd had. Chambers was also reserving judgment on Pierce and Polk. The former had been helpful and patient in teaching Chambers how to use the updated HOLMES 2 software. They'd spent most of Tuesday afternoon together at Chambers desk.

While Pierce had been explaining the shortcut keys and essential fields that required entry to get the best results from the database, Chambers had been carefully studying his tutor. He was perfectly groomed, what was the expression he'd heard? Metrosexual? There was not a waxed hair out of place; his slightly wavy hair was immaculately coiffured. His goatee was trimmed to within an inch of its life. The cologne he used liberally was definitely bordering on feminine to Chambers unrefined appreciation of modern masculine perfumery. Chambers could even see his nails had been manicured. The only thing that seemed out of place was that despite all his grooming, was that Pierce was quite overweight. It jarred with his immaculate appearance, the length of time it took Pierce to get ready for work intrigued Chambers and it was a question he nearly asked on several occasions.

THE CHARRED FOREST MURDERS

It began to dawn on Chambers, as he watched Pierce explain fields in the database and explain the complexities of the back end system that powered HOLMES 2, that despite the younger man's surly manner, Pierce was quite effeminate in many of his gestures. There was no wedding ring, but then Chambers didn't have cause to wear one either so that didn't reveal much. He'd tried to casually elicit information about his new colleague, but Pierce was evasive and revealed little about his personal life or the reason that he'd been unceremoniously shifted out of the CID team at Hammersmith station that Barlow had alluded to the previous evening. The only time Pierce varied from his methodical explanation of the technical workings and in some cases shortcoming of the new software was to make a disparaging remark about one of the other team members, just loud enough for Polk, occupying the seat directly in front, to hear. Polk would snort or guffaw, often to the chagrin of others in the room. Except Buchanan, of course, his headphones cutting him off from the juvenile and banal office banter.

Chambers was struggling to stifle yawns as Pierce continued in his monotone explanation of the capabilities of the database. Although it was often referred to as the new system it was already several years old and currently Chambers only had experience using the original system at his previous office. Pierce was extolling the virtues of the system's two-tier approach for local database access and three-tier approach for remote database access, whereby – and Pierce's eyes lit up at this point – remote database access was user-configurable from the front end. It confirmed what Chambers had been beginning to suspect, Pierce was a closet IT nerd and that he tried to cover his perceived social shortcomings by being the office bully in the form of a 'try hard' office comedian. But here he was in his element, showing off his superior knowledge to someone of a higher rank and trying to baffle him with IT jargon.

'Furthermore,' Pierce continued as Chambers stifled yet another yawn, his eyes watering with the effort. 'HOLMES 2 is a freetext database that allows users to ask unstructured questions and to present the results in order of relevance. Apart from that, a dual operation has been adopted to increase the speed of the system. While searches themselves are tuned at the SQL,' he turned and sneered at Chambers. 'Surely you know what that is right?'

Chambers shook his head, inexplicably reminded of long, boring chemistry lessons from his youth. 'Structured Query Language.' It was Pierce's turn to shake his head, as if in shock that anyone with half a brain couldn't know that. 'At the SQL level, additional indexes on the RDBMS,' again a long pause and a pained sigh before he slowly explained the initials as the 'Relational DataBase Management System,' then he repeated himself in a bored tone, 'at the SQL level, additional indexes on the RDBMS' tables are deployed.'

The lesson had descended into gobbledegook as far as Chambers was concerned, he wasn't sure what he'd learned at the end but he had a grasp of the system's improved functionality as an easier way to use the database for coordinating case notes and material across the network. What he had found useful was that it had allowed him to gain an insight into how the petulant Detective Constable operated. Pierce's patronising approach and the juvenile antics of him and Polk did little to raise the pair's value in Chambers' eyes. There was something going on with them and he was determined to get to the bottom of it, or at least he would be looking to push one of them towards the exit over the coming months or weeks to create a more harmonious office atmosphere. His afternoon working with Pierce had shown Chambers that the man was technologically smart, but there was something not right about him. Polk, like Buchanan had suggested, was definitely being led astray, but was it better to shift the cause of the trouble or the effect? If he got rid of Polk, there was a chance the replacement might fall under the same negative influence. For the time being Chambers was looking at preparing a sharp exit for Pierce, that way he might take his troublesome old uncle with him. At least that is till Chambers had the chance to see what made Polk tick and to see whether he had something to offer the team.

Charles 'Chad' Forster hadn't returned to the office since he slouched out on Monday morning and Chambers took the opportunity to find out what he could from his nephew. But Pierce was reticent about passing on too much information. He would only say his uncle had grown up in Hounslow, had been on the force 'for a bloody long time' and that he was struggling with his battle against cancer. When Chambers pressed Pierce about how often his uncle came in. Pierce became unnaturally defensive.

'I can tell you don't like him or want him here.' Pierce said sullenly not taking his eyes from the screen.

'That's not true Paul. I think his experience and knowledge can be an essential tool for the team. It's just we don't have much room,' Chambers gestured around the office. What little floor space that wasn't taken up by desks or filing cabinets was limited. 'Of course he can come in and use the desk in the corner but he's not going to have access to a PC.'

'He won't like that. He knows more about computer systems than everyone in here, except me.' Pierce shot Chambers a nasty look. 'You're missing an opportunity. Anyway he only comes in on a Monday and Friday usually; sometimes a Wednesday. Depends how he's feeling. I'm not the boss of him, so I can't tell him what and where to go. He does what he wants, when he wants. But he'll be bloody pissed off he won't have access to a computer. He's on loads of forums and he's buying and selling all sorts of stuff on eBay, Amazon and Craigslist.'

Chambers was a regular user of the first two but not the latter. 'Craigslist?' He asked.

'Yeah, it's a classified ad website, you can buy and sell loads of crap, he loves all that kind of thing. It's been around for nearly 20 years, I'm surprised you've never heard of it.'

Chambers considered himself relatively au fait with technology, but he was clearly not in the same league as Pierce nor evidently the cocky young man's elderly uncle either. Maybe he wasn't as switched on as he thought when it came to being tech savvy, he'd only recently got himself a smartphone and he was still getting used to the number and variety of apps on offer. Slowly he shook his head, before moving the conversation on. 'That's fine then. Let's get him in here on Mondays and Fridays. He can use the spare desk and we'll get him helping you and Russell out on your case.' Chambers said in his most conciliatory tone while making a mental note to stay off site as much as possible on the days Forster would be in. He couldn't put his finger on it, but there was something in the old man's mannerisms and attitude that antagonised Chambers, and he was pretty sure the old guy had picked up on how he felt. It would probably be a good idea that he try and make a concerted effort to get to know Forster and find out how to bring out the best in the old man.

By the time the team had left on Thursday night, Chambers had a much better idea of what his mixed bag were capable off, and also what they were working on. Buchanan was currently involved in assessing which cases warranted further investigation in the West London area. Eventually this task would be handed on to Chambers but for now Buchanan was the man in charge. It was imperative that the scant resources available to him could handle the cases he took on. They would have access to forensics, old case files, most of which was still sitting in storage in a variety of police stations across West London, Chambers guessed the majority of it would still be undigitised or off the database. There was the national police computer network and the bespoke HOLMES 2 database but that was their lot. Manpower would be limited to what the team could provide. They didn't have much so they would have to be selective about just what cases they could take on with a chance of getting a result.

Buchanan explained his logic for not taking on the two most famous unsolved murders in West London from the 1980s and 1990s. Namely the disappearance of Suzy Lamplugh in Fulham in 1986 and the murder of Jill Dando less than a mile and just a few streets away in 1999. Both of these cases had received enormous exposure in the press and equally large attention from the Met Police in terms of resources. Buchanan was at a loss to how a small team could offer any new insights into these cases without bringing unnecessary press attention and conducting their enquiries in such a public arena. For this reason Buchanan had explained, he had decided to investigate three other cases from the local area: The 1993 murder of Jean Bradley in Acton; the 1991 murder of Penny Bell in Perivale; and the 1971 murder of Gloria Booth in South Ruislip.

Adams and Hayes had been assigned to the Bell case, Polk and Pierce were working on the Bradley case and for now Buchanan was looking at the much older case of Booth.

Once Chambers had established the running order he was happy enough for now to let the detectives handle their own investigations in their own way. Over the next few weeks he'd go through the case files and get familiar with where the previous investigations had got to, and then to explore any items that would be worth getting forensically analysed. Although there had been drastic leaps forward in terms of DNA testing, it would all depend on what condition the original items had been stored in and even if they were still being kept. Chambers knew it was a definite possibility that some of the critical material might have been thrown out over the decades.

Late on Friday afternoon he was sitting reading through the notes on the original Penny Bell case. It appeared there had been an exhaustive investigation involving 8,000 interviews and

2,500 written statements but no firm DNA links had been established to any suspects. In 2000, a review of the case re-examined bloodstains from the scene but found no new leads. Chambers closed the file and looked over to where Adams and Hayes were deep in discussion. To say they had a tough task ahead was an understatement. He sent an email to the pair of them requesting a meeting on Monday morning to discuss their progress on the case.

Chambers logged out and shut down his PC. There was plenty of work ahead, but for now he was relieved just to make it through his first week. He would get changed into his running gear and walk/jog his way back. His calves here still letting him know that his newfound enthusiasm for running was going to come at a price. He would gradually build up and hopefully sooner, rather than later, he'd be able to make the journey without stopping. He said his goodbyes to the team and took off at 5pm. He would be going to see his sister Ruth and her husband Gareth in Southgate the following day. It would be his first chance to see them since he'd come back from Africa and he was looking forward to seeing her and getting pampered for the weekend before hopefully returning to work on Monday morning with a rekindled desire to once again be a policeman.

***

Chapter 4.

Small hart

Monday, 9th April 2012 – 6:40am

It was 6:40 when the alarm clock violently buzzed Chambers awake. Wiping the sleep from his eyes he could see through the open curtains that the faint rays of early morning sunshine were already trying to barge their way through the thick bank of grey cloud. As part of his new regime, he wanted to be on the road by 7am. He was aware now that he needed to allow himself the best part of two hours to make the journey and allow time to shower and cool down at his destination. He hadn't done any running over the weekend, something the muscles in his legs and particularly his calves were very appreciative of. Although he was aware that his overindulgence in his sister's hearty home cooking might have an effect on his return to early morning exercise. He'd also borrowed a yoga DVD from his sister. She had insisted when he'd told her about wanting to improve his fitness but his 44-year-old body wasn't exactly coming to the party. He watched the first 15 minutes of the DVD while he had his breakfast of oats, chopped banana and manuka honey. Assuring himself that he would begin a few of the exercises when he returned from work that night, or possibly the following morning.

The weather looked grim as he left his block of flats in Lime Grove. It was overcast and the skies were threatening to open any moment, the early sunshine had disappeared behind the blanket of cloud, but Chambers had made the decision to run no matter come rain or shine. He had managed to find time to get to the Nike store at the nearby Westfields at Shepherds Bush and invested in a pair of proper running shoes, although he wasn't too impressed that they were luminous yellow. The young shop assistant, who professed to be an avid runner, had talked him into a pair of Free Run 3.0.

Twenty minutes later, having crossed Ravenscourt Park and moved easily along St Peter's Square, Chambers made his way through the underpass below the A4-Great West Road and up onto the towpath and swung right along the footpath that occasionally hugged the riverbank and sometimes ran parallel one street away. He jogged past huge houses with the occasional blue plaque denoting a former house of a famous inhabitant. This was now Chiswick Mall, the stretch of road that carried on past the large river island, Chiswick Eyot, until at the back of the Fuller's Griffin Brewery, the mall eventually veered to the right away from the river at St Nicholas Church. Chambers swung a sharp left along a very narrow paved footpath that then came out back at the riverbank It was here he stopped suddenly, surprised to see the flashing blue light of several police cars and an ambulance in one of the short dead end streets that ran perpendicular away from the waterfront back towards the A4.

In need of a breather, Chambers stopped against the shiny, black metal fence that ran along the water's edge of the path and watched the proceedings while doing some stretching – his calves were definitely in need of some relief. The tide was far out and there were several people standing on the dismal, brown, muddy bank. Near where the group was standing was a worn, white metal walkway leading at a shallow angle down to a pontoon with a variety of modern and older river craft moored to it. Several canoes were tied to the back of the nearest houseboat.

A uniformed policeman was in the process of unraveling blue and white tape to seal off a raised stepped area on the towpath that led to the entrance to the walkway down to the pontoon.

THE CHARRED FOREST MURDERS

Moving along the metal fence to try and get a better look at proceedings, he could see a small group comprised of several uniformed officers, what he guessed were plain clothed police and a couple of paramedics. Moving rapidly down the walkway to the pontoon in front of Chambers were a couple of other uniformed policemen carrying large rolls of white material. Chambers guessed they were trying to set up a tent to preserve some kind of crime scene and also to prevent the prying eyes off passing rubberneckers and the media. It was hard to see what was the item of such great interest until one of the officers stepped back to help with the assembly of the tent allowing him to catch a glimpse of the naked body of what looked to be a young man on the sloping muddy riverbank. Instinctively Chambers checked his watch. It was 7:20am. The towpath was quiet save the emergency services. Looking back towards the body, Chambers just had a chance to see what looked like a long red gash across the chest and that the hair of the corpse was strawberry blond. The first of the makeshift tent walls was erected blocking his view so he moved over towards the policeman who had finished putting police tape over the entrance to the stairs.

Chambers reached for his pocket to show his warrant card, while at the same time realising it was sitting in his desk drawer back at the Brentford police station. The policeman watched him as Chambers approached.

'What's going on?' Chambers asked, while at the same time pulling his right leg up behind him and stretching his quad.

'Sorry sir, this is a crime scene, so I'll have to ask you to move along.'

Despite Chambers curiosity, he knew that without ID and not knowing anyone who worked this patch, his enquiry wouldn't be acknowledged, and after all the bodies he'd had the misfortune to see over the past few months, he was almost glad that this one had nothing to do with him and that he really had no need to get involved. It dawned on him that he no longer had the passion. Here was a crime scene, possibly a murder scene and he was happy to be fended off by a junior PC at the scene without so much as pulling rank or forcing the issue. It just reinforced his feeling that his time as a police officer had run its course.

As he had got his breath back, he simply smiled at the officer and said 'Sure, no worries.'

Probably out of habit as he left, Chambers took note of the police vehicles numbers so he could trace their origins when he got to the office if he decided to take an interest in the case. Judging from the location of the body it was either going to fall under the jurisdiction of either the Chiswick or Hammersmith police. Less than a hundred metres further on the concrete towpath abruptly stopped at the entrance to Dukes Meadows and Chambers was able to join the gravel track that for the next mile was no longer hemmed in by expensive riverside properties but only by a continuous wall of mauve and white flowers in full bloom, high stands of nettles in among which Chambers spotted dock leaves, that as a child he'd been taught to crush and mix with saliva as the perfect antidote to the painful rash caused by the nearby nettles. It always intrigued him how even in nature a solution to a problem almost always could be found close by.

It was just before 9am when Chambers finally arrived at his desk. He had the chance to shower and change before getting to the office. When he entered the room he was disappointed to see the old man Forster lounging in Chambers' chair, grumbling to himself, a pair of glasses pushed up on his forehead as he intently studied a puzzle magazine. Chambers closed the door loudly but Forster didn't look up. Moving closer he cleared his throat loudly but it was only when he moved into Forster's eye line that the old man looked up. The initial blank expression changed to a scowl.

'Good morning.' Chambers tried to sound upbeat.

'Is it?' Forster answered gruffly. 'What's so fucking good about it?'

It was the first time Chambers had heard Forster speak, the voice was deep and coarse, like he needed to clear his throat, with a strong London accent.

Chambers was surprised by the man's clear lack of social etiquette. 'If you don't mind, I've got a lot to do today. So I'd like my desk back.'

'What if I do mind?' Forster had put down the magazine and was staring at Chambers.

The two men had a standoff for nearly thirty seconds before Forster broke into a wide smile and began a cackling laugh. 'I'm just pulling your pisser. 'Aving a wind up like. You need to lighten up mate.'

Unfortunately Chambers didn't see the funny side, and he didn't like the emphasis Forster put on the 'mate'. In fact he had to take a few seconds to keep himself from saying something he might regret.

'We've assigned you a seat over there.' Chambers said pointing to the spare desk. 'I'll work out what hours and days you can come to the office and what case you'll be working on. OK?'

'Whatever you say, boss.' Forster replied with more than a hint of sarcasm.

'I'm going to get a coffee, can you have your stuff moved over to the other desk when I get back. Please.' Chambers turned and walked back to the door, not waiting for a reply.

***

Fifteen minutes later, when Chambers had returned to the office, he felt he was more in control of his emotions. Trying to factor in that the cantankerous old man was in effect dealing with a death sentence, had convinced Chambers that he really ought to give the old man some leeway. It had to be the best way to deal with the bizarre and confrontational actions of Forster. But Chambers was worried, more about himself. He'd noticed that since the accident in Africa, he was having a harder time keeping his emotions in check. Whether it was the head injury, or the level of stress he'd been under recently, or maybe a combination of the two, he definitely thought he was getting more likely to lose his temper over seemingly irrelevant issues like Forster's obstinate attitude.

The office was still empty save for Forster who had shifted to the new desk. He watched Chambers as he entered.

'Do you like puzzles?' He held up the magazine. Chambers wanted to ask the old man to clear his throat, his voice sounded laden with phlegm.

Chambers was not really in the mood to talk to the old man, just because he now deigned to begin a conversation.

'Sometimes.' Chambers said abruptly, making his way towards his desk at the back of the office.

'I'm intrigued by them. I've always loved a good puzzle. Even when I were a kid. I'm a member of MENSA. I found being good at puzzles helped my detective work.' Forster had returned to studying a page in the magazine, but carried on talking. 'Gave me another perspective to look at crime scenes and the objectives. I'm not opposed to all this modern policing, profiling and what not. I see it as an extension of what I was already doing decades ago.'

As he was logging on, Chambers was distracted by the sound of a chair scraping across the floor. He looked up to see the huge figure of Forster lumbering towards him with his hand outstretched.

'See this?'

Chambers couldn't work out what it was until Forster flipped it open. It was a sky blue plastic case about the size of a credit card. Inside was a mirror.

'I've used this over four decades of police work. I don't know many other coppers that use one. I've found it gives me a different sense of perspective. Reveals things, hidden things. You know what I mean?'

Chambers didn't know or care for that matter. He just wanted the old man to bugger off back to his desk while he got on with some work.

'You get to things from a different point of view. That's critical.' Forster continued, turning back towards his desk, seemingly unaware of Chambers complete lack of interest into his unique and groundbreaking form of police work. He continued to regale his captive audience with how his inspirational insights had been critical to the capture of a number of otherwise elusive criminals, but Chambers had zoned him out. He was having problems accessing the HOLMES 2 database and it was a while before he noticed the login name that automatically appeared above the password field was not his own but was in that of Paul Pierce. It struck Chambers as odd that Pierce would want to log in to his computer to search the database when he could do it from his own PC. Even if he did log in from Chambers' terminal could Pierce gain any greater access to information. He wasn't sure if there were different levels of security clearance but what other reason would Pierce have to use his machine? It struck him as odd. As he was pondering why this might have happened the door opened and in came Buchanan. The arrival of the Detective Sergeant meant it was 9:30am. Chambers had noticed that Buchanan always arrived on the dot of 9:30am. Same time every day. He glanced at his watch; already knowing what time it would read.

The new arrival distracted Chambers and he took a moment to watch Buchanan on his way to his seat. As usual without acknowledging either of the men already in the room. He was in his early- to mid-sixties, Chambers guessed. He was thin, quite short with a baldhead and neatly trimmed white beard. The hair that remained on his head had been shaved close. He had a well-lined face that could be described as weather beaten, a flat nose that gave Chambers the impression he'd either been a barroom brawler or a boxer in his earlier days. He was wearing a pressed white shirt tucked in to a pair of plain grey flannel trousers with a single turn up over a pair of highly polished black slip on shoes. The contrast between Buchanan's neat attire and Forster's slovenly appearance couldn't have been greater. Buchanan was wiry and compact – all his movements took place quickly in short bursts giving Chambers an even greater impression that the man used to box.

When Buchanan sat down his mannerisms changed. He seemed to relax. Taking off his oversized headphones he looked at the two men in turn. 'Morning Chad. Morning John.'

Chad responded in his usual caustic manner. 'Buck, why on earth do you persist in wearing those god-awful farking headphones. They make you look like a nutter. Like you've just escaped from Acton Lodge. They'll have you back up the looney bin before you know what's happened if they catch you wearing them outside.' He cackled.

Buchanan was still looking at Chambers and simply rolled his eyes and gave Chambers the slightest hint of a smile before replacing his headphones and logging in to his computer. Buchanan's headphones were beginning to make sense. It was the perfect buffer between the irritating old man and relative peace and quiet. Chambers had spent a fair bit of the previous week watching how the team interacted, but Forster had been absent making it hard to see the impact he had on the group. It would be interesting to see how he dealt with the other members, particularly the newer ones like Hayes and Adams.

THE CHARRED FOREST MURDERS

Buchanan and Forster had worked together in the past, but there didn't seem to be any great affinity or repartee between the two men. It would be fascinating to see the office dynamic with and without Forster in the room.

The rest of the Monday Chambers spent with Adams and Hayes going over the files for the Bell case and what new leads they had managed to uncover.

Instead of the detectives continuing on from where the case was left off, Chambers wanted them to start again, not take anything for granted and to try and reassess the whole case. There were definitely some factors about the murder that jumped out at him. Ruth Penelope Bell was a businesswoman from Bakers Wood in Buckinghamshire. She was found dead at noon on the 6 June 1991 in her car in the car park of the Gunnell Leisure Centre in Perivale, Greenford. She had been stabbed over 50 times.

Greenford was only a few miles away and all three of them were familiar with the area. But Chambers didn't think it was necessarily as important to know as much about the crime location as to understand how that late on a Thursday morning in an average London suburb near a busy street no one had seen the crime committed or anyone fleeing the scene. Surely the person responsible would have been covered in blood. That seemed odd to him. There were a couple of eyewitnesses who had reported seeing Bell's Jaguar XJS driving very slowly along Greenford High Street with its hazard lights on and the female driver apparently in distress. The witness at the time ignored her. What other leads did the initial investigation have? Bell was in the middle of major renovation work at home and when she left her house at 9:40am she allegedly told one of the builders she was late for a 10:50am appointment but she never said who she was meeting and there were no appointments listed in her diary for that time. Her business address was in Kilburn and she would normally travel along the A40 to into central London. The Greenford turn off was just off her normal route. A variety of carpet display samples were discovered in the back of her car.

When she was discovered at noon, the hazard lights were still flashing, an indication perhaps that the eyewitness was accurate in what he had seen. Chambers read on. One of the builders was initially charged after his fingerprints were discovered in the vehicle but was later released. There was also the intriguing fact that Bell had withdrawn £8,500 from her and her husband's joint bank account that morning without his prior knowledge.

The initial case had been closed in 1999 and reopened in 2002 by a murder review team but this investigation had also led nowhere and the case was soon dropped. The last possibly significant fact that the investigation team looked into was the sexual orientation of Bell's husband Alistair. The press had had a field day when it discovered that prior to marrying Bell he had been in a relationship with another man for 11 years before meeting Penny, implying that Bell had been murdered by a jealous gay lover. Chambers couldn't believe that such an enormous amount of time had been wasted exploring this dead end.

'What else have you discovered?' Chambers opened the floor to the two detectives.

'Not much to be honest.' Hayes said, her accent was Home Counties, but Chambers hadn't discovered exactly where. 'The first investigation was very, very thorough. They conducted house-to-house enquiries around the area, followed up on all carpet manufacturers, and checked all the builders' alibis. Went through her phone records, fingerprints and blood analysis. Nothing.'

'OK well I don't think that we should necessarily get sidetracked. What I mean to say is we're not looking for fault with the way the first investigation was conducted. What we need to focus on is what we can reinvestigate in terms of forensics; advances in technology and also that people's situations have changed. If someone was married or in a relationship with the killer their situation might have changed and they may be more willing to speak to us now. It's worth a try.'

Hayes nodded. 'What about the people that were previously brought in? Shall we take another look at them?'

Chambers nodded and flipped a page in the file and pointed to a photo. 'What? You mean this guy? The family friend that was arrested?'

'Richmond? He came forward saying he'd seen Bell earlier in the day.' It was Adams this time, his accent was London but not as strong as Buchanan or Forster. 'But eventually he was released. There was simply no evidence against him. I don't get it.'

'Get what?' Chambers asked.

'That there appears to be no obvious motive for the killing. No signs of sexual assault, her handbag was found in the car.'

'You think it was just a random attack? But what about her withdrawing the money without letting her husband know? Or not making a diary entry? Something doesn't add up.' Chambers was puzzled. 'What about the murder weapon, was it ever discovered?'

'No. It never showed up. The post mortem report indicated that judging by the injuries sustained the blade was at least six inches in length.' Adams responded. 'Could have been chucked anywhere or even taken back to the killer's home.'

'Don't you think it's strange though that uniformed officers made house to house inquiries and questioned any other potential witnesses, including almost 800 car park users, but failed to produce any significant leads?' Hayes pressed. 'Surely someone had to have seen something. It was the middle of the day for God's sake.'

'Have you read the crime scene investigation report?' Chamber asked.

Adams pulled the file towards him and sifted through the pages, eventually handing back a stapled report to Chambers. 'Seems standard to me. The crime scene was sealed off to allow forensic scientists to examine the car and search for anything that might lead to the identity of the killer. The detective superintendent assigned to the case set up an incident room and gathered a team of detectives who put all the info in the old HOLMES database.'

'OK well let's set up interviews with the Flying Squad Commander and the detective superintendent from the original investigation. What about the physical evidence?'

'It's mostly held in storage at Ealing police station. The car though is long gone.' Hayes said.

'OK Sandra can you request and see what can be sent over here? If not, one of you will have to work in tandem with the Ealing team. I want to see if there's anything that might be worth retesting for DNA, saliva or blood. There has to be something that was missed or that we can use. Eddie I want you to take a look at the original HOLMES database entries and see if you can get them transferred to the new system if they are not already there. Then I think we've got no choice but to begin the ball-breaking job of going over every interview and alibi.'

'Off the record. How are you two, as relative newcomers I mean, getting along with the rest of the team?'

Hayes looked at Adams before answering. 'I can't speak for Ed here, but personally speaking Buck's a bit distant but if you ask for his help he'll give it. Chad is a bit of a pain in the arse but he's not here that often, thankfully.'

'I agree. Yeah the old bloke is forever challenging us with his ridiculous quiz questions. It was OK at the beginning.

Humouring him. Letting him get his kicks from thinking he knows more than everyone else. But now it's getting boring.'

'He tends to spend a lot of time with Paul and Russell. Whether it's because Paul's his nephew or he just knows them but he's not that helpful to us particularly.'

'Chad and Chav. A right bloody double act, Piercy and his uncle are. Russell's just along for the ride. He's harmless but I wouldn't trust the other pair as far as I could throw them.' Adams added.

Chambers thanked them for their honesty and called an end to the meeting and the two detectives filed out of the incident room they had used as a makeshift meeting room. It certainly wasn't going to be easy. Chambers removed a photograph of a smiling Penny Bell from the file and took it back to their office to stick on the whiteboard. He wanted the team to see a constant reminder of the difficult task ahead.

He'd been impressed by the two detectives, and he was confident to let them take control of the investigation with him only acting in a supervisory capacity. He was not so confident he could have such a hands off role with Pierce and Polk in the Bradley case. He'd scheduled a meeting with the pair of them for the following day.

***

Chapter 5.

Shady arenas

Monday, 22nd April 2012 – 9:25am

Slowing down from a jog to a walk, Chambers eventually came to a complete stop outside the Heidelberg Graphic Equipment building on Brentford High Street. He put his foot up on the low red brick wall that hemmed in an area of low hedge that ran around the showroom. His calves ached and he needed to give them a long stretch, they were the only part of his body that steadfastly refused to come onboard with his new fitness regime. On the other side of the low hedge was a long window into which Chambers peered inquisitively into the gargantuan printing presses on display.

Chambers had started to time his Monday morning run to appear at the office just after nine. By the time he'd showered, changed and grabbed a coffee it meant Buchanan and at least one other were there and he wasn't left alone with Forster. Over the past fortnight he'd watched Forster's interaction with the team, which so far was only on Mondays and Fridays. He was always in the office before anyone else and tended to take off early in the afternoon. As he was an unpaid free agent there was little Chambers could say or do about the man's casual attendance.

That morning, before leaving for work Chambers had checked his home mailbox. There were a couple of bills and a postcard from the post office informing him they had tried to deliver a parcel the previous Friday that was available for collection from the Shepherd's Bush Post Office and would be held for the next seven days. He couldn't think what it could be as he hadn't ordered anything online. It was a pain, as he would have to collect it during work hours.

As he continued stretching his troublesome calf, he noticed a familiar figure on the other side of the street in the window's reflection. Turning around he saw Adams quickly cross the narrow side lane of Alexandra Road and make his way past the Brentford County Court and the stone marker indicating where Julius Caesar had crossed the Thames in 54BC, and continued towards Morrsions and The Beehive pub on the corner where the team had previously met for a drink. Chambers walked parallel to Adams and gingerly crossed at the lights that marked the beginning of Brentford High Street proper and the perpendicular road, the Half Acre, that morphed into Boston Manor Road as it headed north towards the A4/M4.

Chambers was able to catch Adams as he turned the corner at the pub head down engrossed in something on his smartphone.

'Eddie.' Chambers called out.

Adams looked up from his phone. 'Alright John. How's it going? Good weekend?'

'Yes, not bad, quiet you know. How was yours?'

'OK Hey I'm just reading this article about the murder in Brentford over the weekend. Did you hear about it?'

Chambers shook his head. He hadn't seen the TV news over the weekend. He'd picked up a Sunday Times newspaper but hadn't seen anything in there relating to the murder. The two men had passed the green tile-fronted Fuller's pub and were now level with the entrance to the police station. A single decker 235 Sunbury bound bus screeched up to the lights adjacent to the pair drowning out what Adams was saying.

'Body was discovered yesterday morning it seems.'

'What, here in Brentford?'

They had stopped at the short set of steps that led up to the navy blue front doors of the police station. 'It says here a man's naked body was found up by the junction of Boston Manor Road and Boston Gardens,' Adams was pointing further up the way they were facing.

Chambers let his gaze drift further along the street, past the long off white, two storey police station with its royal blue fence and grey upper panelling that ran along it's flat roof. The station reminded him of an oversized portakabin. It was an ugly building in an ugly part of Brentford. Back at the junction were a couple of grimy derelict buildings and opposite the station was a funeral parlour and a public toilet. Attached, as if as an afterthought, to the police station was a 12-storey appendage. Both buildings looked as though an architect who had clearly flunked all his exams in aesthetics had built them.

Chambers' office was on the second floor along with Barlow's. There were a couple of admin offices located there as well. The ground floor was taken up with the front enquiry desk, the office for the beat coppers and more admin staff. There was a basement with several holding cells and a storage area. The car park held a pool of marked and unmarked police cars, the latter were at the disposal of Chambers team should the need arise. The 12 storey building, Chambers had yet to set foot in but he was of the understanding it housed the elusive Chief Super McKinley, the local MIT team, who would have their hands full with the local murder, plus several levels of storage and the IT department with several more floor of admin staff.

'Boston Gardens? Where's that?'

'Not sure, I'll have to look it up on Google maps.' Adams moved up the stairs and into the reception area, nodding to the uniformed officer on the desk who recognised the pair of them and buzzed them in.

THE CHARRED FOREST MURDERS

'Cheers Des.' Adams said to the officer on the desk, 'hey do you know Boston Gardens?'

'You talking about the murder? It's up the other side of the M4. About halfway between the motorway and Boston Manor tube station. There's a park there on the left. Boston Manor Park about a mile up the road from here. The body was found in there yesterday morning.'

'Thanks Des. I bet the MIT boys are having a field day.'

'Yeah, they're buzzing. It's been a while since we've had a murder on our patch.'

Chambers nodded to the policeman as they passed through the security door and headed up to their office.

***

Two weeks on and Chambers and the rest of the team had settled into a fairly harmonious routine. Adams and Hayes were spending most of their time out of the office whether working at the Ealing police station with the physical evidence of pounding the pavements to go and re-interview people in the area surrounding the attack. Chambers didn't envy them their mundane tasks, but it was the real and essential crime detection work that needed to be done and he felt confident they would conduct a thorough investigation. If there was something, anything to be found, he trusted them to find it.

As for the other pair, he was less confident. The meetings he'd had with them the previous week had been less than inspiring. When Chambers opened the file on Jean Bradley and began discussing the case, neither of the detectives appeared to have any opinions or even to be particularly well versed on the case.

The first thing that struck Chambers was the similarity to the Bell case that Adams and Hayes were investigating. Bradley had been stabbed to death as she got into her car near Acton Town tube station on Thursday evening 25 March 1993. Less than three miles from where Bell had been murdered. Both women were in their forties, had short, coiffured hair, drove expensive cars, commuted to work along the A40 and were both stabbed to death with a long bladed knife. The coroner's report stated the injuries were the result of an 8" blade. As Chambers read on he could see there were other noticeable similarities, neither woman was robbed or sexually abused.

'What do you think the motive was?' Chamber asked the pair.

Polk looked at Pierce. Neither replied.

'It's clearly not a sexual attack. Do you find anything in her records indicating she was having an affair? Or owed someone money? What was her job?'

Pierce eventually spoke up. 'The report says she worked for a New Bond Street company for about 10 years, specialising in helping employees of United States businesses to move to Britain. Her colleagues described her as "a dedicated professional woman". That's all I got.'

'Well that's a start I suppose. Do you know anything about the Penny Bell case that Eddie and Sandra are looking at?'

The pair shook their heads.

'I suggest you two pull your collective fingers out and go and discuss your case with them. I can see too many similarities between the cases and I think you need to be working in tandem with them.' Chambers flicked through another couple of pages in the file.

'Have you spoken to this eyewitness?'

'Which one?' Polk finally spoke.

'Jesus! Russell. Who do you think I'm talking about? This bloody carpenter bloke?' Chambers read from the notes: 'A passing carpenter in his van saw the incident and drove after the attacker. After a short distance, he stopped his vehicle and confronted the man, who ignored him and walked away. After pleading, unsuccessfully, with passersby to call police, he continued to follow the attacker into a housing estate, where the man disappeared in an underground car park. Detectives said this suggested the murderer had local knowledge. He gave a description to police: white, aged about 40, 6 feet tall, with gaunt features and a large nose. He was wearing a black shiny hat that looked like a sou'wester and a three-quarter length grey coat.'

'We'll look into it guv,' Pierce said eventually.

'Too bloody right you will. I want a full report from the witness by the end of the week. I want you Russell, to assess the similarities between this and the Bell case. Paul, I want you to go to Acton Town tube station taking interviews with any staff that might have seen something.'

'What? It was 20 years ago!'

'Well then you'd better hope some of them still work there, or that the London Underground HR department have kept accurate records of past employees. Now I suggest you get off your arses, stop fannying about and get some bloody work done.'

Chambers closed the file, stood up and as he left, he made sure he slammed the door behind him. He'd give them till the end of the week and if nothing was forthcoming he'd get on to Barlow and get rid of the pair of layabouts. A mixed bloody bag indeed.

***

Friday 27 April 2012

Standing at the bar of the Brewery Tap with a pint of London Pride, Chambers was talking to Adams about his plans for the weekend. Chambers had made a point of emailing the team every Thursday to arrange a quick drink after work on Fridays. The collective had decided to move from the more hostile environs of The Beehive to the slightly more welcoming pub across Brentford High Street and closer to the Thames. It was a good opportunity for the team to relax and, Chambers hoped, to bond over one or two pints. He was desperate to get Polk and Pierce integrating better with the rest of the team. It was just coming up for 6pm when Pierce and Polk arrived together, followed by Hayes and Buchanan. Barlow was a no show due to a prior arrangement and Forster never socialised on principle.

Watching the two blockheads at the bar ordering Red Bull and vodka, Chambers made his way over. Polk spotted his approach and nudged Pierce, the pair stopped talking and watched his arrival.

The barman put the two clear drinks down with a can of Red Bull for them to share.

'Thanks Nev.' Pierce said holding out a tenner but not taking his eyes of Chambers.

Chambers indicated the drinks. 'Big night planned lads?'

The pair nodded.

'Going anywhere special?'

'Club uptown.' Pierce said hardly acknowledging Chambers as he poured the amber-coloured energy drink into his glass.

'Are you going to come and join us for a quick drink?' Chambers indicated the corner table where Adams was just sitting down with Buchanan and Hayes.

'What with old peg leg and the toucan? No thanks.' Polk said smiling. 'Not good for our image, is it Paul?'

Pierce laughed. 'Yes, who wants to be seen with a raspberry and that old fart?'

Chambers had an overwhelming desire to crack their heads together. In fact he imagined doing just that. He counted to 10. 'Suit yourselves.' Chambers said and just as he turned to leave he glanced back. 'Do me one favour though.'

'What's that guv?'

'Drop the name calling.' He stepped in closer. 'If I ever hear you make a derogatory comment about another team member again I'll personally smack some sense into the pair of you. Got that?' Chambers stared hard at Pierce, ignoring his sidekick.

Pierce didn't say anything. He just took a sip of his drink, before finally dropping his gaze and looking away.

Chambers turned and walked back towards the rest of the team.

'Oooooh, who's the tough guy,' he heard a Midlands accent whisper behind him and the pair began to laugh. Chambers didn't react even when he heard Pierce call him a wanker. Their time would come. Of that he was certain.

Later in the evening, when Adams had departed to go training it just left the three of them. Hayes drinking pints with the occasional chaser that she put down to medicinal purposes on account of her hip problems, Buchanan nursing his familiar half pint and Chambers limiting himself to three pints of Pride. He'd had two and it was his shout. Moving to the bar he saw that Pierce was no longer there and Polk was deep in discussion with a tall, attractive brunette. Chambers first thought was that it was someone who was definitely out of the lanky ginger Brummie's league.

Giving his order to the barman, Chambers was aware that Polk and the woman were looking in his direction and Polk was saying something in the woman's ear while she didn't take her eyes off Chambers. The general hubbub in the bar made it impossible for him to hear what was being said. Chambers collected his round nodded in the general direction of Polk and the woman and returned to his seat by the window. It was getting dark outside and the streetlights were beginning to come on.

'Who's Russell talking to?'

Hayes turned to look. 'No idea. Never seen her before.'

'It's not his wife is it?'

Buchanan came to life. 'No. I've met the wife. She's blonde and much shorter.'

The woman turned and glanced at the table.

'Oh, that's Jess Tucker. She's the fit bird from the MIT. Sandra you might not have met her yet. She's based over in the main building. Rarely ventures up to see us. None of them do. We're the poor cousins they keep hidden away in the portakabin.'

Hayes didn't react to Buchanan's colourful description of Tucker. 'She's attractive, I'll give you that much Buck.'

Over the three weeks since he'd first set foot in the Brentford police station, Chambers was getting used to the team's nicknames, some official, others, more often than not, instigated by the caustic tongues of Polk and Pierce, were less flattering. Terry Buchanan was known as Buck to his face or Two Can Dan, sometimes the Toucan for short, behind his back. Chambers could only figure out that he was alleged to be a lightweight drinker; he couldn't make any other logical connection. Charles Forster was Chad to everyone; maybe as he was Pierce's uncle he escaped any other nicknames although Chambers could think of a few less than flattering suggestions. Sandra Hayes was known as Purple to her face, but more often referred to as the bird (Buchanan), Peg Leg and the Sloany Pony (Pierce, Polk) or Clump (Forster). Eddie Adams was just Ed, but Chambers had heard Forster refer to him as Chalky, the other two seemed to have enough common sense not to be caught making racist comments about the six foot tall Thai boxing specialist. That only left Chambers. In the office he was simply John or Guv, what he was called behind his back, he had no idea but plenty of reason to believe the blockheads had a nickname or two for him. It didn't bother him. What bothered him was the pair of them causing unrest and ill feeling among the rest of the team.

THE CHARRED FOREST MURDERS

Chambers watched the woman at the bar. She seemed familiar to him but he was almost certain he hadn't met her before. Although there was something compelling about her, but what could she possibly find of interest in a Neanderthal like Polk? He was intrigued and continued to watch as he took a sip from his beer, she was certainly attractive. He was only distracted by the loud scraping of a chair next to him as Hayes struggled to her feet and made off across the lounge bar towards the ladies toilet.

'John.'

Chambers looked over at Buchanan. 'What?'

'If you can drag your beady eyes off DS Tucker for a second, I got a proposal you might be interested in.'

Swivelling in his chair he gave Buchanan his full attention. 'Go on. What have you got for me?'

'Two things. First, my mate Stan can't make the game tomorrow so I was wondering if you fancied joining me up at the game tomorrow.'

'What game?'

'Bees against Sheff Wednesday. 3pm kick off. We can meet in here for a quick half about 2. I'm a season ticket holder like Stan so it will be gratis. What do you say?'

It had been over a decade, closer to two, since Chambers had last been to a football match. Since returning to London, work was all Chambers had done. He'd spent the weekends catching up with family but hadn't done anything in the way of entertainment for a while.

'OK why not.' Chambers held out his pint and clinked glasses with Buchanan. See you here at two tomorrow.'

The two men sipped their drinks.

'Hang on. You said there were two things. What's the second?'

'I think that bird over there has got the hots for you.' Buchanan raised his eyebrows and looked over Chambers' shoulder.

Quickly Chambers swivelled in his seat and looked in the direction of the bar expecting to see Tucker looking back in his direction. But instead of seeing Tucker, he saw the solid outline of Hayes limping awkwardly back towards them from the bar.

Buchanan let out a hearty chuckle.

'What's so funny?' Hayes said as she sat back in her chair.

'Nothing love, nothing.' Buchanan smiled into his pint. Chambers stared blankly out of the window at the passing traffic.

***

Chapter 6.

Cyan heartburn

Saturday, 28th April 2012 – 2:03pm

It was just past 2pm when Chambers hopped off the 237 bus outside the Heidelberg building. He thought he would be late to meet Buchanan and if he had gone back home to drop off the mail he collected from the Shepherd's Bush Post Office, then he certainly would have been.

It could have been that he'd been working hard since he'd got back, and combined with running to and from the office most days, but his body needed the rest, clearly indicated by Chambers waking up at 10:45am. By the time he'd got himself together on Saturday morning and joined the long queue at the post office it was nearly midday. Caught behind a series of difficult customers Chamber had watched as the minute hand on the clock wound slowly by. The delay just meant he'd have to go straight to the pub rather than return home.

On the bus he'd opened the envelope and taken a cursory look at its contents. He had guessed from the Hong Kong postmark that it was the mail Brian Tang had promised to send from the Wanchai Police Station several weeks before. In the meantime he'd sent Tang a few emails to find out if there were any updates of Lucy's disappearance but as yet there was nothing, no new leads, no sightings, nothing from the Harbour Police, no new forensic evidence. It was as if she had disappeared in a puff of smoke. But Chambers knew if he could find Shen he would at least find out Li's fate. He couldn't stop thinking about her.

Everyday, from the moment his alarm went off and he was woken, he had a sinking feeling, the loss of Li had hit him hard. At times during the day he would find himself staring morosely out of the window or looking deep into his screen unaware of how long he had been lost in thoughts about Li. But all this thinking had produced no new ideas as to her fate. Part of him wanted to accept that she was gone. But until a body was found he had to continue to believe no matter how hard it was proving to be.

The worry was affecting his work and his sleep. Since his accident he was aware that he was forgetting simple things, but he couldn't be sure that it was the lack of sleep, Li's predicament or the effects of the accident. But what he did know was he had developed a very short fuse and was finding himself at times overcome with anger. At the moment most of it was reserved for Polk and Pierce, but he found more and more he was becoming impatient with strangers. Small things that had never bothered him before were now looming large and at times he would notice that he was standing fists clenched, teeth grinding at some minor inconvenience.

The parcel appeared to hold a bundle of smaller recyclable, brown office envelopes, their contents secured by a string fastening on the flap for reuse. Chambers didn't bother to get any of them out. They would be office memos, expenses forms or invoices that required his signature. He pushed them back into the envelope and when he alighted from the bus he took a quick detour to his office to drop the letter in his inbox before joining Buchanan at the pub.

After a quick drink, the pair walked up the Half Acre, took the right fork onto Windmill Road and turned at the Brentford Library into Clifden Road, walked past the old, now derelict swimming baths and came to a T-junction at Brook Road South. Buchanan led the way, briskly taking a left then a right at The Royal Oak pub that was packed with Brentford fans spilling out

THE CHARRED FOREST MURDERS

on to the street, enjoying a pre-match pint and a bit of banter on a glorious spring day.

Brentford football club was unique in the professional footballing landscape of England in so much as its home, Griffin Park, was the only ground to have a pub on each corner. A short distance along New Road brought them to the entrance of the Bill Axbey Stand where they had their seats in Block E. It was just past 2:40pm when they sat down 20 minutes before kick off and the ground was slowly beginning to fill. Buchanan had bought a programme and began flicking through it as soon as they were seated.

Chambers was intrigued as to why Buchanan had invited him, but he was sure he would find out sooner rather than later. The previous week they had been through the case the older DS was now looking into, namely the murder of Gloria Booth, whose body was dumped in a South Ruislip park in June 1971. It was assumed at the time that the murderer had abducted her outside a pub near the Polish War Memorial and took her off to a garage somewhere near Ruislip. There he had tortured, mutilated, and murdered her that same night. The killer was thought to be impotent, as no sexual intercourse took place. At the time, Queen's Park Rangers Football Club used the park where she was found as their training ground.

Gloria's partially clothed body was found the following day, Friday, 13th June, 1971, dumped in a park by the Polish war memorial near the A40. One of her shoes had been carefully hidden under a hedge, in contrast to the rest of her clothes, which were strewn around her body.

At the time the police set up a murder room in Ruislip Police Station and the Detective Chief Superintendent from Scotland Yard had a team of 30 officers investigating the murder. But no leads had materialised and the case soon went cold.

Chambers had looked through the rest of the report. Gloria Booth was a barmaid at The White Hart pub in Northolt when she died. A 15-year-old boy on his paper round found her body on the morning of 13th June, 1971. Here was another murder then that had taken place near a tube station by the A40 and on a Thursday. Chambers knew the link to the others murders his team were investigating were tenuous, there was over two decades between this one and the others while this was death by strangulation with a sexual element unlike the others.

When Chambers had mentioned these vague links to the Bradley and Bell cases, Buchanan looked at him. 'No I don't think those ones are linked. I had a look at that at the time I initially assigned them. I think we're looking at the micro when we need to examine the macro. Of course if we study all the murders for West London we are going to see clear geographical links but the MO is too different. But I do have another one I think we should consider.'

Buchanan had another file with him. Clearly he had already planned to show it to Chambers.

'Have you heard about the Jean Townsend case?'

Chambers shook his head. Before he'd joined the cold case team his knowledge or exposure to unsolved murder cases in London was limited to what he'd read about Jack the Ripper. He hadn't got into policing to solve murders per se. His career up until the last few months had been relatively murder free, the past five years was involved with policing the growing Triad-related drug crime in Central London. It was only through his trips to Hong Kong, Scotland and Africa that he'd had become immersed in several grisly murders to the point that he almost felt immune to any emotional distress that it probably should have been causing him, but somewhere deep down he knew it was taking its toll.

As Chambers took a look at the file Buchanan began filling him in on the details.

'Jean Mary Townsend worked as a theatrical costumier in London's West End. On the evening of Tuesday, 14 September 1954 after she'd attended a function up the West End, returning to South Ruislip later that night on the last Central Line train. At around 11.45pm she was seen leaving South Ruislip station and walking alone along Victoria Road. Her body was discovered the following morning on waste ground to the north side of Victoria Road, near to the junction with Angus Drive in the area now occupied by St Gregory the Great Catholic Church.' Buchanan watched as Chambers flicked through the file before continuing. 'The autopsy report stated that she had been strangled with her own scarf and it was reported that – despite various items of her clothing being removed – there was no sign of sexual assault. Now what makes this case interesting and one of the main reason's I flagged it for us to investigate it, is another young woman, Joan Gala, reported being attacked by a man late at night on Victoria Road on the Saturday before the murder. Interestingly, another young woman – Ellen Carlin – had been murdered in London earlier that very same month. Three years later, in 1957, a young mother called Muriel Maitland was murdered in Cranford Woods near Heathrow Airport. She had been beaten and strangled. Clearly there's a link there.'

Chambers nodded. 'No arrests or leads at the time?'

The area was close to a US airbase and some witnesses mentioned a man in a US soldier's uniform acting strangely but extensive investigations in collaboration with the US military produced nothing significant.'

'So what's your plan of attack?'

'I've been working through the names of the detectives on the original investigation. I've worked with a few over the years, I'm going to contact as many as possible to see if there's anything else they can remember that didn't make it into the files. My initial request for tangible evidence has hit a brick wall. Apparently her clothes hadn't been stored properly at Ruislip police station and it appears some if not all of it has been disposed of. Oh and sorry John.'

'Sorry for what?'

'Passing you all the unsolved murder files.'

'Oh yeah.' Chambers thought back to the enormous pile of grey manila folders that had magically appeared in his intray when he had arrived at work that morning. Now he was in charge, it was his job to find other cases for the team to follow up on if and when they had any success with their current investigations. 'Thanks, I'll start working my way through them later, see if there's anything I can give to Chad. By the way is that all of it?'

'Not at all. Most of them are just the overviews to the case. Some witness statements and transcriptions. A few have the crime scene photos. But on the whole most of the paperwork is still in storage. There's about 20 possible cases we can look at, but for now we need to break it down into cases we might actually have a chance of solving.'

'Do you need my help on anything to do with your case?'

'Nah guv.' And after that short outburst Buchanan returned to his monosyllabic ways and Chambers guessed the meeting must be over.

They hadn't spoken much since then except for the usual morning formalities until Buchanan had invited him to the match in the pub the night before.

Chambers checked his watch. It was 2:55pm the ground was now just over half full and both sets of fans were in good voice as the players came out on to the pitch. Brentford in red and white striped shirts, black shirts and black socks. The visitors, Sheffield Wednesday were in blue and white striped shirts, white shorts and white socks.

THE CHARRED FOREST MURDERS

The fans in the away end were making more noise and Buchanan registered Chambers interest. 'We blew our chances for the playoffs last week. Lost 2-1 at Stevenage. We can't make it now. That lot are still in with a shout for automatic promotion. It's either them or their city rivals Sheffield United.' Buchanan said in way of explanation.

It might explain why Buchanan's mate didn't want to come. It was the penultimate game of the season and the team's hopes had been extinguished. So near and yet so far.

'Two bloody nil nils with Hartlepool and Notts County in the games before that. That's where we blew it.' Buchanan said almost to himself as he continued to look to his right towards the vociferous away support. Chambers could see something in Buchanan he'd not registered before. There seemed to be a latent aggression in him, the older man's teeth were gritted and his normal affable demeanour had been replaced with something less friendly. He wasn't watching the other fans out of interest, almost with a look of malice.

The ref blew his whistle and the game got underway. The pitch looked in great condition, the sun was shining, the fans were in full voice it was a perfect day for football. Putting his hand up to shield his eyes from the sun, Chambers sat back in the narrow plastic, red seat and watched the proceedings. He wasn't averse to football and on the rare occasion he was in a pub on a Sunday afternoon he'd quite happily watch a live premier league game, or from time to time Match of the Day on BBC1 late on a Saturday night, but he followed no team with any passion and hadn't been to watch a match since he used to go with a mate to Loftus Road to watch QPR in the nineties. His random viewings of games and the fact that the TV and print media were full of the latest dramas taking place on and off the pitch meant he was relatively up to speed with the premier league. But this was something else. Brentford were in the third tier and this was a different world far removed from dating models, driving Ferraris and earning salaries in the millions.

This was the arena of broken dreams. Players on the fringes of the elite, journeymen, has-beens, never-will-bes and those young enough to think they might have a chance at cracking the big time. But for all that, and maybe because of that, it felt more real. This wasn't the glossy and glamourous premier league TV football. It was hard, gritty and ugly and all the more compelling.

Chambers knew enough to know a good team when he saw one and during the first half, he was aware that neither of these teams, despite being near the top of League One, would be winning any awards for their stylish play. For all Brentford's huff and puff, they were predominantly a long ball team, repeatedly pumping balls into the opposition penalty box hoping to get some lucky ricochet and almost being rewarded on several occasions. Although they had created the better chances they went into the break trailing by one goal to nil. Wednesday scoring a few minutes before the halftime whistle with their first shot on target.

Chambers was surprised by Buchanan's reaction as the older man let out a string of expletives blaming the ref, the linesman, the Brentford defenders and finally the team's German coach with such an aggressive force Chambers began to believe Buchanan might be suffering from some rare form of football related Tourette's Syndrome. As the game had worn on Buchanan had looked more and more like a coiled spring and the goal was enough to unleash all that the pent up aggression. By the whistle though Buchanan appeared to have regained his composure and as the players trooped off, he turned to Chambers.

'You see that body that turned up near Boston Manor Park?' He said it in little over a whisper as the crowd around them thinned out. Most of the spectators off in search of a pie, a drink or a quick visit to the toilet.

THE CHARRED FOREST MURDERS

Chambers was caught off guard. He had assumed Buchanan would want to analyse the team's first half performance.

'What about it?' The discovery of the naked body in Brentford had, naturally, created a buzz of excitement, but it was one for the MIT team. In reality it had nothing to do with Chambers' unit.

'I see Ed's taken an interest in it.' Buchanan said rubbing his beard. 'I think he'd like to have a crack at working with MIT.'

'He's a good copper. I don't begrudge him wanting to get himself over there. Much easier to get yourself noticed there, than working in cold case.'

Buchanan nodded and returned his gaze to the pitch that was now vacant except for a couple of groundsmen moving around the playing surface repairing divots or putting sand down in the fresh holes. The condition of the pitch surprised Chambers. From his experience the lower league pitches turned into mudbaths in the winters and remained brown bogs for the rest of the season. Everything was changing, evolving, developing – no doubt some new form of durable grass had been artificially engineered and was now cheap enough to be used in the lower divisions.

'So what about the body?' Chambers prompted eventually.

'Did you go through all those cases I left on your desk?'

'Not yet. A couple. But there's a load of them.'

'See the one on the London nude murders?'

'London nudes?'

'AKA the Hammersmith nudes? I left it in the pile.'

'No. Why? Are you saying there's a connection to this body in Brentford?'

'All I'm saying is have a look at the file I left and then check the details on the murder last weekend. See what you think.

That's all.' Buchanan said cryptically, rubbing his hands. It was late April and despite the sunshine a cold breeze was blowing across the stand.

Chambers searched his memory. He'd taken a quick look at the murder report in the paper on Monday after Adams had mentioned it. The body of a 25 year old man, Daniel Tompkins, had been found naked in Boston Manor Park early on the previous Sunday morning by a man out walking his dog. The body was found under some bushes near the metal railings at the entrance to the park. The man had ligature marks around his neck and had been strangled. Some teeth were missing. He couldn't recall anything else.

'Why do you think there's a link? You said the Hammersmith nudes, this one was found in Brentford.'

Buchanan looked up from the programme he was reading again. 'I grew up not far from here, in Isleworth. When I was a teenager we used to run wild around the borough as kids, you know? Looking for a bit of adventure. We used to bomb about to Hounslow, Brentford, Chiswick, over to Richmond. I remember there was this murder in Brentford. Me and my mates, we went up there the next day to take a look. All the police were still around. Of course the body was gone, but there were lots of uniform coppers and the like. I got a buzz from it. The excitement of it all. That's when I decided I wanted to join the police when I got a bit older.'

'When was this?'

'A couple of days over 48 years ago.'

'How can you be so precise?' Chambers was intrigued.

'I was 16 years old and it was the 25th of April 1964. I'll never forget it. Never.' Buchanan said without taking his eyes off of the centre circle.

THE CHARRED FOREST MURDERS

Chambers glanced at his watch. Today was the 28th of April. Meaning the previous Sunday, when the body was found, was the 22nd. Close but no cigar.

Chambers shook his head, but before he said anything, Buchanan turned to face him. 'Do you know where they found the body back in 64?' He didn't wait for Chambers to answer, 'Swyncombe Avenue. Near the junction with Boston Manor Road.' Now he paused. 'That's about 50 metres from where they found Tomkins last week. Her name was Helen Barthelemy. She was found naked. Strangled to death. Dumped. She was only in her early twenties.' Buchanan had turned his head and was now looking straight ahead again. Slowly the older copper massaged his intertwined fingers, his face set almost in a scowl, as he stared off into space.

The pair sat in silence for a couple of minutes, before Buchanan snapped out of his melancholia and stood up swiftly. 'Queues should have died down. Fancy a brew?'

Chambers shook his head and Buchanan squeezed past him in the narrow aisle and made his way down the concrete steps leaving Chambers bemused by what he had just heard.

Why hadn't Buchanan mentioned this before? It had been a week since Tompkins' naked body had been discovered.

Just as the second half got under way Buchanan returned with a plastic cup of steaming hot tea. He nodded to a few people in the row, possibly other season ticket holders that he knew.

'I fancy we'll get something out of this. We had the better chances in the first half. Come on you Bees!' He shouted the last four words then sat down in his seat leaning forward engrossed in the action. 'You know until this day no one's been charged with her murder, or the others.' He said eventually.

Chambers didn't want to interrupt the man's intense concentration on the game. He just sat pondering the coincidences in the cases. Both found naked and strangled in relatively close proximity. But 48 years and a couple of days apart? The inaccuracy of the dates puzzled him. Maybe if it was 50 it would be significant. But 48 and why not the same day? It had to be a coincidence. He had made his mind up when Buchanan went for his tea that he'd have to go to the police station straight from the ground. This couldn't wait until Monday morning. It struck Chambers as odd that Buchanan wanted to tell him this at a football match and not back at the station.

Near the hour mark Buchanan and most of the fans around Chambers leapt to their feet. 'Penalty!' They cried almost in unison. There was a long pause, where the ref got some rather unfair criticism and some choice name calling from some members of the crowd before he eventually pointed to the spot amid raucous cheering from the home support. The Brentford striker Clayton Donaldson duly stepped up and dispatched the penalty into the back of the net.

'Get in there!' Buchanan screamed and turned and hugged Chambers much to the surprise of both of them. 'Game on!' Buchanan said clapping his hands, before launching into some chanting of 'we're by far the greatest team the world has ever seen', with his fellow supporters while Chambers looked on amused by the older man's unexpected and forceful show of passion. Normally so quiet and unobtrusive here was another side to the old policeman. Chambers couldn't help getting caught up in the emotion of the game and soon joined in the singing.

The joy didn't last long however. Within a couple of minutes Wednesday were ahead again. A goal scored in front of the away support was an odd experience. Most of the ground suddenly went quiet, and there was a second between the ball hitting the net and the away support celebrating until it could be heard where Chambers and Buchanan were sitting. And unless he was much mistaken it was only Wednesday's second attempt on goal compared to numerous chances for Brentford including hitting the woodwork only moments before.

'Bloody typical!' Was all Buchanan volunteered on the subject. The rest of the game continued in the same vein. Brentford streaming forward but Wednesday always looking more dangerous on the counter attack. The ref played a couple of minutes of injury time before blowing his whistle to indicate the end of the match. The end of the game was met by a mixture of cheering and booing as the Brentford players made a slow lap of honour to applaud their fans on their last home game of the season.

Chambers looked over at the despondent Buchanan. 'I've been a bloody Brentford fan since the 1950s. You think I'd be used to this rubbish by now. Wouldn't you?' he said leaning forward in his seat and rubbing the palms of his hands together before joining in the muted applauses from the rest of the fans. Eventually he turned and gave Chambers a wry smile. 'Come on let's get a pint at the New Inn round the corner.'

***

Chapter 7.

Hey there, bellman

Saturday, 28th April 2012 – 6:37pm

After a pint in the packed New Inn pub almost opposite to where they had entered the ground, Chambers left Buchanan who walked away down South Ealing Road to catch the 237 bus back to his home in Isleworth, while Chambers retraced his steps from earlier back to the Brentford police station.

Flicking quickly through the grey files piled up in his inbox and several more in untidy stacks next to his desk he soon came across eight files tied together with cord. Scrawled on a note taped to the top file in the bundle was written Hammersmith / London Nude Murders. Written on the file itself was the name Elizabeth Figg. The name meant nothing to him. He untied the cord and spread out the eight old dog-eared files on his desk. The fifth one down in the pile had Helen Barthelemy's name typed on a white label stuck to the cover.

Chambers stacked the other seven files neatly back into his inbox to give himself space to work and carefully opened the file on Barthelemy, undoing the green tag that held all the pages together so that he could separate the contents of the folder into their relative sections. There were a collection of crime scene photos, witness statements and police and forensic reports.

Helen Catherine Barthelemy – born 9 June 1941, East Lothian, Scotland, was found murdered 24th April 1964 in Swyncombe Avenue, Brentford. She had an arrest sheet that included charges of aggravated robbery and unlawful wounding, running a brothel and soliciting. At the time of her murder she was known to police as a prostitute who mainly worked in and around the Notting Hill area.

Chambers had a look at the post-mortem report. It stated that when the post mortem occurred later on the day the body was found, that she had been dead somewhere between 20 hours and three days as rigor mortis had completely disappeared. The body was dirty; the report noted that this had occurred after death. Indications were that from the hypostatis, or livor mortis, present – the body must have lain on its back for several hours after death. She had also been stripped several hours after death. Her death had been caused by asphyxiation. Although the coroner had refused to state whether this was by manual means or by ligature. She had abrasions around her throat that could have been self-inflicted in trying to stave off the strangulation. Also visible was swelling to the nose and cheekbone on the left side of the face.

Putting the report down Chambers swivelled in his chair and looked out of the station window. It was still light at half past six and would be for another hour. Again the question came into his mind. What did Buchanan see as the connection between the murder of this prostitute 48 years ago and that of the young man a few days before? And why had he not wanted to talk about it previously? Why wait until they were in the anonymity of a crowded football match?

Chambers next turned his attention to the thick pile of witness interviews. Quickly flicking past the pages of handwritten statements to the much easier to read transcribed versions. Looking at the wedge of interviews he settled in for a long evening.

Over three hours later and Chambers had finally finished reading the confusing, contradictory reports of Barthelemy's last few days. It seemed she had a great interest in the West

Indian scene found around Notting Hill in the late fifties and early sixties, and was often seen in bars and clubs like the Roaring Twenties in Carnaby Street, The Flamingo and the Jazz Club on Westbourne Park Road. All well known Ska clubs catering to a West Indian and liberal white crowd. Illegal drugs and prostitution were commonplace as was the regular presence of Barthelemy. It appeared no one was precisely sure when she was last seen in any of these bars that often didn't get going until after midnight and finished when the sun came up. And as the police couldn't be precisely sure when she was murdered it was difficult to pinpoint who had last seen her. They had pinned 8:30pm on Tuesday 21st April as the last definitive sighting of her near her flat at 34 Talbot Road in Harlesden until her body was discovered at 7:15am on Friday 24th April in an alleyway of Swyncombe Avenue in Brentford. There was a witness from the street who has passed the alleyway at 10:55pm the previous evening and hadn't seen a body, while a passing motorist who had been driving along Boston Manor Road had nearly crashed into a speeding vehicle that exited Swyncombe Avenue at 6am just an hour before the body was discovered. The witness thought the car was a grey Hillman type.

Chambers stopped and looked at the dates again. Barthelemy went missing on the 21st April and the coroner suggested the time of death could be up to a couple of days before the body was found on the 24th. So it was possible that she had been murdered the night she was last seen – the 21st, stored somewhere for what ever reason and dumped on the 24th. But Chambers was sure Buchanan had said the 25th. It didn't make sense at first, and then it suddenly dawned on him. Buchanan had said as a kid he'd been up there the day after the body was found, the 25th. And when had the young man been found? The morning of the 22nd? Which probably meant he had been murdered the night before. He would need to check the details with the Brentford MIT team when they came back in on Monday. No wonder it had resonated so clearly with Buchanan. The appearance of the body was exactly 48 years to the day that

THE CHARRED FOREST MURDERS

Helen Barthelemy had been murdered. So what did it mean? What was the significance of the 48 years? Chambers was beginning to think this might not be a coincidence after all.

***

Chapter 8.

Clowned rookie

Monday, 30th April 2012 – 9:30am

Monday morning and Chambers rolled into work bang on 9:30am, later than normal as per his new plan that was principally to limit alone time with the difficult Forster character. Instead he entered to a cacophony of noise and a rare full house. Buchanan was the only person present who appeared to be aloof from the noise, sitting as usual bolt upright in his chair tapping away at his keyboard with his oversize headphones shutting out the world. There appeared to be a debate between all the other team members as to who'd had the most memorable weekend. Hayes and Polk were discussing which one of them had had the most units of alcohol at The Brewery Tap on the Friday night and wherever they had carried on the party. Hayes as usual looked completely normal, but one glance at Polk and he appeared considerably the worse for wear. As Chambers said a quick hello and made his way to his desk he heard Polk telling them about what had happened after his Sunday league match the day before which quickly explained why he looked rough and clarified to Chambers why it was Polk had 'been out of the office on investigation' on other Monday mornings. Now Chambers realised that the Polk was pulling the wool over his eyes, he would make sure to line up some 9am meetings with the young DC to keep him on his toes.

Chambers sat down and after switching on his PC, turned to observe how Forster was engaging the others. It didn't take long to see. Forster was quick to harangue the others that 'back in his day, they did everything twice as hard and for twice as long'. He went into one long rant about how him and the other coppers would use their sway to get lock ins at many local pubs and would still be at work at 9am sharp therefore proving that he and his generation where harder than the soft modern copper. Chambers thought about how he'd seen Hayes drink on at least two occasions and was pretty sure she could hold her own against anybody past or present.

Now it was Pierce's turn to get involved. 'As I was saying, who cares what you lot drink in that shithole. I was up the West End. At a top club. I don't hang out anywhere as dry as The Tap. Give me some credit. That's for old farts. No offence Unc.'

'Ooh, you are so cool aren't you?' Hayes cooed at him. 'What tips have you got for us common folk?'

'Shut it you...' Pierce tailed off, flicking a look over at Chambers.

The look gave Chambers the impression Pierce would have said something much more cutting if he hadn't just arrived. 'All I'm saying is you're drinking in an old man's pub when you could be out larging it. The only thing that was good about it was I got that bang tidy bird from MIT to come clubbing with me.'

'What bird? Not Tucker?' Polk seemed incredulous.

Pierce sat back and put his hands behind his head. 'Yes Tucker the one with the top bangers. What a night!' He gave Polk a wink. 'Up all night we were. If you know what I mean.'

The smile disappeared from Polk's face. His gaze shifted over to Chambers, whose own face was registering confusion. Pierce had left long before him and when he'd gone Polk had been talking to Tucker at the bar for quite a while. Something didn't add up.

But for now he'd seen and heard enough. He picked up the Barthelemy file and made his way back out of the office and down to the staff canteen for a coffee and bacon sandwich and the chance to look over the file in something more akin to peace and quiet.

Finding a table in the corner of the canteen Chambers sat down to review what he had learned about the case on the Saturday night. The canteen was sparsely furnished and had seating for 30 although there were only a few uniformed officers currently occupying one of the tables. But he couldn't get his mind off what Pierce had claimed he had been up to Friday night. His first impression of Tucker was that she was in a different league to Polk and Pierce, plus he wasn't even 100% sure of the latter's sexual persuasion. He took a sip of his coffee and winced at the sudden sharp pain in his tooth. He was long overdue a trip to the dentist but as it was one of his least favourite things in life he had relegated it way down his list of priorities. But the pain meant a trip would need to be arranged sooner rather than later.

The canteen door opened and three plainclothes officers came in. Chambers was surprised to see that one of them was DS Tucker. As they made their way to the counter she looked over in his direction and smiled before saying something to the to men she was with and peeled off to come over to Chambers table. As he pushed himself to his feet she said.

'You must be the new DI working in team Yetna?' She said smiling at him and holding out her hand.

Chambers was surprised to hear that she had a very thick Northern Irish accent.

'That's right. DI Chambers' He replied shaking her hand.

'I've heard a lot about you.' She smiled again. 'Don't look so worried, most of it's good. I'm Jess, Jess Tucker, nice to meet you. I'm a DS over with MIT.' She was tall, with jet-black, wavy collar length hair. When she smiled her dark brown eyes twinkled. Chambers got the impression she smiled a lot. She had broad shoulders that made him think she was a swimmer, and had a tan that looked out of place during a wet and cold Brentford springtime.

Chambers couldn't think what to say. 'Were you in The Tap on Friday?' He blurted out.

'Aye, I was there for a wee while. I was talking to,' she paused, 'Russell is it? Russell Polk. He was pointing you out to me as his new guv'nor.'

'So you know my team then?'

'Aye, well I know him and a couple of others. Paul Pierce and Terry Buchanan. They were working with us in MIT until we split a few months back and managed to foist off the deadwood.' She laughed at this. 'Don't you go telling them I just said that. But you look smart enough to me to know what you've got on your hands.'

Chambers nodded. He didn't know what this woman's motives were and didn't know what her relationship was with Pierce and Polk, so he decided silence was his best option. He changed tack. 'So you had a good time on Friday in the pub.' He paused for a moment, 'and afterwards?'

She gave him an odd look. 'I don't know what you are implying cheeky chops. But if you consider an orange juice while talking to the idiot Russell Polk followed by a 3km swim a good night out, then I think you might need to reconsider how you define enjoyment.'

One of the other officers called out to her asking what she wanted to drink.

'So its been grand speaking with you DI Chambers I'm sure we'll be seeing a wee bit more of each other since we're based in the same station.' Her eyes flashed as she said it causing Chambers to go red, or at least to feel as if he was blushing.

What was it with this woman? She was so forward that he didn't know how to react.

'Yes lovely to meet you.' Chambers said awkwardly as he sat back down and watched her return to her colleagues; she said something and the three of them laughed together.

Flipping open the file, Chambers couldn't concentrate. He was aware that the three officers were moving back towards the exit. He looked over just as they reached the door. Tucker turned her head towards him and flashed another of her smiles and then she was gone leaving Chambers sitting bewildered at what had just happened.

His first thought was of Pierce. Why had he said he had been clubbing with her and implying they had spent the night together? Polk's reaction seemed to suggest otherwise and although Tucker said she had been for a long distance swim after a visit to the pub it didn't completely rule out that she had gone clubbing much later.

And why did he find that it bothered him that Pierce might have spent the night with her? He didn't know her at all. He was still in love with Li, despite his inner demons convincing him she was dead. It had been over eight weeks now since she had disappeared. There had been no sightings, no word, nothing. At what point did he face reality and accept she was gone forever? Two months, two years, two decades? His rational side was trying to convince him to move on. Move on from what? They had been partners, and only in the police sense, for six months. There had never been anything physical between them and if truth be told they hadn't exactly been on the best of terms when he had left Hong Kong. In fact, he was almost certain she held no feelings towards him at all. In the back of his mind he thought it was possible she just considered him an awkward work partner during the time he'd been in Hong Kong. But what could he do really? He couldn't put his life on hold forever. Chambers picked up the transcribed witness statements from the

THE CHARRED FOREST MURDERS

Barthelemy case folder and began reading them once again. At the same time he decided to stop waiting around and get on with his life.

***

Chapter 9.

Crinkly nominee

Monday, 14th May 2012 – 9:02am

Chambers was feeling particularly apprehensive as he walked into Brentford police station on that Monday morning. It was two weeks since DS Tucker had introduced herself in the staff canteen and things had moved quickly since then, too quickly for Chambers' liking. The day after she had introduced herself, he had received an email from her. It was casual in tone and served on first glance simply to reiterate her introduction. There was mention of some of the MIT group going for a drink in The Brewery Tap after work on the Friday, and as a slightly improved version of The Beehive it had become part of his team's weekly routine. The offer seemed innocent enough.

When he had entered the pub with Hayes and Chief Inspector Barlow that Friday night, Chambers already had an agenda. The week had passed quickly; the rest of the Monday was spent cajoling the reluctant Forster to take a more active role in helping out Buchanan with his Booth case. The downside was it meant losing Buchanan for the week as it was easier for the pair to work together from Forster's residence in Hounslow as it wasn't far from where Buchanan lived in Isleworth and Forster had made it clear he worked from his own schedule and didn't like coming into Brentford every day. Chambers was more of the impression that Forster was the kind of bloke who would deliberately do the opposite of what he was asked out of sheer bloody mindedness. What had possessed him to come into the office in the first place seemed to be based on making everyone else as miserable as he was.

The other cases continued on in the same vein. Despite the dogged approach of Adams and Hayes, and the numerous re-interviews they had carried out in the area and working with the Ealing police there was yet to be a tangible break through. As for Pierce and Polk, their feeble attempts at any police work merely continued to infuriate Chambers who had sought out Barlow to ask to transfer one or both of them.

Barlow had been succinct on the matter. There were to be no new additions, changes or upheaval in the team for the next few months. Apparently that had come down from the Super. McKinley had her hands full with the murder in Brentford and was under pressure for her all-star MIT team to quickly get a result. Chambers also had the feeling that it was partly due to Barlow wanting to maintain an even keel until he could slip his resignation letter under the Super's door and make a clean getaway.

What was on Chambers' mind was the link that Buchanan had mentioned, the time between the appearances of two naked bodies in the same vicinity being 48 years apart. He wanted access to the ongoing investigation, the one in which DS Tucker was the lead investigator on.

As Chambers had entered the bar he immediately saw Tucker at the bar with the two men he had seen her with in the canteen earlier in the week. She beckoned him over and quickly made the introductions. There was a tall, blond man she introduced as DI Lew Hutchinson, who looked to be in his late forties, and was heading up the investigation. Chambers had heard talk of him in his unit as a capable detective who was known to prefer the older police methods to the new touchy feely ones. He gave Chambers a firm handshake and looked him hard in the eyes with his piercing blue eyes before uttering a quick hello. Chambers thought he heard a Glaswegian accent and recalled the Polk had disparagingly referred to him as a 'Sweaty' when Hutchinson's name had cropped up in conversation.

The other man was introduced as DC Rob Black. He was shorter, in his late twenties and had scruffy brown hair and a few days of stubble that Chambers couldn't work out whether it was supposed to be designer or the man just hadn't bothered to shave. Pleasantries over with, Chambers peeled off to the side of the group to a spare place at the bar where he had called out his order of two pints of London Pride for Barlow and himself and a pint of Stella for Hayes when he was aware of someone standing close behind him. He turned and saw that Tucker had bridged the gap between the group and him.

'I hope that the Stella is for you.' She flashed a smile at him. 'I don't want you drinking the old man's rubbish.'

Chambers smiled back. 'Can I get you anything?'

'No, I'm away back to the pool tonight.'

'You seem to spend a lot of time in the pool, are you in training for something?'

'Well done detective,' she smiled sarcastically, 'I'm gearing up for a triathlon. I've been competing for a few years. It means I have to sacrifice the booze for a few months a year, but I still like to socialise and I love to dance, so I do.' She took a step back and assessed him. 'You look like you take care of yourself as well. Do you still go clubbing?'

Chambers shook his head and laughed. 'The last time I was in a club was probably 20 years ago!'

She leaned in closer to him, 'you have an awfully sexy laugh. Do you know that? I think it's high time you got yourself back in to a club. What do you say to that?'

'I bet you say that to all the boys.' Chambers said, thinking of what Pierce had claimed earlier in the week.

She smiled and looked suggestively at him. 'No, I tend to be very selective about who I invite to dance with me.'

Chambers could feel himself going red again and suddenly his mind went blank. He felt under pressure to say something witty or clever and the only thing that sprung into his mind was the naff joke Barlow had told him on the way to work, before he could control his tongue he blurted it out.

'What do you call the world champion boxer who is half Irish and half Native American?'

'What?' Tucker looked surprised at the change in conversation. 'I don't know?'

Chambers knew he was digging a hole for himself. 'Barry McWigwam.' He said meekly.

'What?' She looked genuinely puzzled.

'You know. Barry McGuigan. Barry McWigwam.' Chambers offered in way of explanation, aware it was a terrible joke and wondering why his brain had been cruel enough to only suggest that as a conversation piece.

'I get it alright. It's just that it's not funny.' She leaned back as if she was reappraising him.

Chambers was struggling to think of something when his eyes alighted on her North Face rucksack. 'What have you got in your bag?' He offered in way of moving the conversation on.

'Your personality.' She said without showing any indication she was joking.

Fair enough thought Chambers. He was not doing a very smart job of holding a mature conversation. 'Good point. He took a deep breath. 'How's your investigation going into the murder up at Boston Manor?'

Tucker looked mildly relieved that he had finally been able to say something coherent. 'It's been three weeks and we don't have an arrest. We have a couple of suspects, but the usual avenues of love, lust, revenge and money haven't got us anywhere yet.' She hesitated, while she sized him up. 'Why detective, are you going to tell me you know who did it? Or better still maybe you are looking for a transfer into our team. There's still a bit of deadwood that needs replacing.' She cast a meaningful glance along the bar at DC Black, who was oblivious to the aspersion as he was deep in conversation with Barlow.

'Not at all. It's just I found something that might be of interest in one of cold cases that we're looking into.'

'I see, so are you going to invite me up to your office to take a look at it? Is it a case of you show me yours and I'll show you mine?' She laughed.

Before Chambers could stammer out an answer Tucker's phone rang and she stepped away to answer it. A minute later she was back.

'Saved by the bell eh, Detective? I've got to run. Literally. Training calls. I'll be done by 9.30 tonight.' She dug about in her tailored leather jacket and fished out a business card. 'If you're not already at home with your pipe and slippers. Call me and we can go out.' She smiled again then said a quick goodbye to the others and left. Chambers watched her go, expecting a look back that never came. He could see her cross the road towards the bus stop. She was talking on her mobile phone again.

'Everything OK John?' It was Sandra Hayes, who had come to join him. 'You look a million miles away. People dying of thirst here.' She winked at him.

'Do I? Did I?' He stuttered. 'Hey, here's your drink.' He passed her the pint of Stella. She had followed his gaze out of the window and seen Tucker jogging the last few metres to the bus.

THE CHARRED FOREST MURDERS

'I'd watch her if I were you.'

'Who? Oh yes, her.' Chambers paused and took a deep breath before turning to face Hayes. 'Thanks for the advice. I was just talking to her about the case I'm looking at.'

Hayes gave him a knowing nod that told him all he needed to know and made her way back to the group.

Chambers hadn't called Tucker that night. And when he checked his email on the Monday morning there was an email from her. She didn't make reference to his lack of communication over the weekend. Simply suggesting they meet up to discuss in more detail what he had alluded to in the pub about the recent murder case.

The pair met several times over the next week in different interview rooms within the Brentford police station to discuss the similarities in his Barthelemy cold case and her current investigation into the death of Daniel Tomkins. Chambers felt slightly uneasy when Tucker admitted to knowing nothing of the case he was now looking into. Over the previous week he had taken the opportunity to read through the case notes of the other seven victims that had been associated with a murderer known to the press as Jack the Stripper.

The first case was that of Elizabeth Figg, who was found dead, leaning against a tree at Dukes Meadows, on the banks of the Thames at Chiswick, on 17th June 1959. There was some discussion in the case notes as to whether this was one of the serial killer's victims. As she was murdered over four years before the next victim, Gwynneth Rees who was found almost opposite Figg on the other side of the river. Rees had been found half-buried on a council rubbish dump at Kew on the 8th November 1963. Again the file indicated the investigating officers at the time were loath to include this in the killer's repertoire as Rees' colourful past linked her with the Profumo affair. The 1963 political scandal involving John Profumo, the then Secretary of State for War and his relationship with

Christine Keeler who was the alleged mistress of a soviet spy at the height of the Cold War. The pair had met at a private party where Dr Stephen Ward, a well-known party arranger was also present. The upshot of the affair was that Harold MacMillan resigned on grounds of ill health and Ward was prosecuted for living off immoral earnings. Ward committed suicide before sentencing. It was Dr Ward that the police had linked to Rees, and her involvement in some of the private parties that he had organised for the aristocracy. Police at the time appeared to be under the impression that as a possible witness for the prosecution she might have been silenced. She was also a known associate of Ronnie and Reggie the infamous Kray Twins, who ruled the East End of London through their organised crime network in the 1950s and 1960s. This murder was the one that the investigators back at the time appeared uncertain whether or not it was linked to the other killings associated with Jack the Stripper.

After he had brought Tucker up to speed on the unsolved cases he sat back and waited to see her reaction.

'I don't understand how I've never heard of this.' She looked genuinely surprised.

'Well me neither, and at least you have the excuse of not growing up in West London. If Terry hadn't turned me on to this, I don't think I would have known about it either. It's crazy, the bodies at Hammersmith Bridge and along the …' Chambers stopped abruptly.

'What is it? You look like you've seen a ghost.'

'Worse. Shit, how could I have forgotten that?'

'What? Forgotten what?' Tucker pressed him for clarification.

'With everything that's been going on recently, I've been walking round with my head up my arse.'

'What are you talking about?'

'I jogged passed the police pulling a body out of the river last month. It wasn't my patch and as I said I was not really thinking clearly at the time, so I chose to ignore it. I've had a lot on my mind and at the time I didn't know anything about these old London nude murders.'

'And?'

'And I need to check but I think the body was pulled out about the same place as where they found Irene Lockwood. Jack the Stripper's possible fourth victim or second depending if we count Figg and Rees. I need to see the date Lockwood was discovered.'

'The body at Chiswick Mall a few weeks back? That victim was a man by the name of Tom Marshall if I remember correctly. That case is being handled by the MIT at Hammersmith police station. At this stage we certainly haven't linked it to that of our Tomkins one and we've not heard anything from them, indicating they haven't seen a possible connection. Don't you think you're grasping ...' she tailed off.

'What do you mean?' Chambers challenged unable to keep the annoyance out of his voice.

'Nothing. It's just ... well I took the liberty of asking a few people about you. You're a bit of an enigma Mr Chambers. All this stuff in Hong Kong. Your suspension. The trip to Scotland and then you disappearing off to Africa. All very exciting and mysterious if I may say so. Maybe you're finding life in Brentford isn't as exciting as you would like it to be. So you try and work a couple of deaths together to create something out of nothing.' She looked at him, her trademark smile nowhere to be seen.

'Far from it Jess. If anything I'm looking for a quiet life right now. I've seen enough dead bodies in the past few months to last me a lifetime. It's just Buck pointed out something that seemed too coincidental to overlook.' He explained.

Tucker grinned again. 'Good. I'm happy to bend a few rules, so as we can help each other out, I just wanted to be sure you're not off your head and seeing conspiracies everywhere or trying to play the big shot.'

Chambers nodded briefly, 'thanks for the vote of confidence. If that's what it was.'

Over the next few days the pair met intermittently to discuss the similarities in the Boston Manor killings that were 48 years apart. Chambers had followed up on the murder of Lockwood and discovered that her body was found naked on the riverbank at Chiswick Mall on the 8th April 1964. Chambers had seen the police removing the body of who he now knew to be Thomas Marshall on 9th April 2012. Again there was something slightly off with the dates, but Marshall, like Lockwood 48 years ago almost to the day had been found naked in almost exactly the same location. It simply couldn't be a coincidence. Chambers was keen to take an active role in the investigation but technically he wasn't involved in the current murder case and as soon as Tucker elevated the connection to her superior Detective Superintendent Ronnie McKinley, Chambers guessed he would have little involvement in what developed from there. He wasn't vain or particularly egotistical, but he wanted to be a part of this. His gut feeling was that solving the recent two murders might shed some light on the largest unsolved serial killing in the history of London. That was too good an opportunity to pass up on. But for now, he needed Tucker to keep these developments to herself until they could establish more facts.

The week had culminated in the usual Friday night drinks in The Brewery Tap. The only change was that Tucker wasn't going training after and had joined in the drinking. What happened next was a blur. She had got things going with a round of Jägerbombs. Jägermeister shots dropped into a glass of Red Bull that Chambers had reluctantly, and under great pressure from his peers, agreed to take part in. The evening soon descended into a huge drinking session, in which Chambers somehow, despite his many attempts to slip away, had become deeply embroiled.

On Saturday morning Chambers had woken up alone in a strange bed with a cracking headache and no recollection of how he got there. Laying back on the soft pillows he'd massaged his throbbing temples for a minute before getting up and locating his clothes scattered about the unfamiliar room. Making his way cautiously down the stairs, he popped his head in the kitchen. The clock above the cooker informed him it was just shy of 8am. There was a note on the counter top.

'Sleeping beauty, I've gone for a run. Help yourself to breakfast. Jess x'

Chambers rubbed his face for a minute. All he could think of was Lucy. How could he have done this to her? He felt a gnawing sickness in the pit of his stomach. Without waiting for Tucker to return, Chambers slipped out of the front door and walked until he saw a street sign at the end of the road by a betting shop on the corner. Niagara Avenue W5. He wasn't familiar with the street but he knew the postcode W5 meant he was in Ealing. He asked a passing man for directions to the nearest bus or train and was informed that Northfields tube station was just up the rise to the left. Chambers was familiar enough to know it was on the Piccadilly line which would get him to Hammersmith where he could change to the Hammersmith and City for the one stop journey to Goldhawk Road and home. He thanked the man and made the morning walk of shame the few hundred metres to the train station. Hoping he wouldn't bump into Tucker. All the while feeling grubby, shallow, embarrassed and ashamed of what he had done the night before and also for not having the integrity to wait and face Tucker in the morning.

The rest of the weekend Chambers had been nursing his hangover and feeling particularly anxious at his inability to recall exactly what had happened on the Friday night. So it was with great trepidation that he entered the office on Monday morning. He'd forgotten his usual ploy of arriving slightly late so to avoid alone time with Forster, only realising his mistake as he opened the door to the office.

Forster was the only one there. Sitting off to the side of the room at his makeshift new home. The desk without a computer. Chambers tried to slide in unnoticed and got half way to his desk before the big man swivelled round in his chair.

'Morning squire.' Forster said in a surprisingly friendly tone a wide grin on his old creased face.

'Morning Chad. Everything OK?'

'I'm OK. You know. In my condition any day that I'm not pissing blood has to be taken as a good day.'

Thanks for that insight; thought Chambers, 'glad to hear it,' he said sitting in his chair and pressing the power button on his PC.

'I hear you got your end away with the Irish bird on Friday night? Good for you. I was beginning to think you were a wrong 'un.' Forster said in a matter of fact manner.

Chambers froze. How did the old bloke know about what he'd done? He wasn't even sure of what had taken place. It could only be the office grapevine that started with Forster's nephew Pierce who had been in The Brewery Tap on the Friday night.

Chambers let out a sigh. 'All I can say is I had a few drinks,' he gestured with his palms upwards, hoping this would end the conversation.

'Don't be such a ponce. Was she a good ride? She does all that fitness so she must have a bit of stamina. She's not my cup of tea mind. A bit masculine, you know what I mean?' Forster said screwing his already ugly visage into something more akin to a gargoyle.

THE CHARRED FOREST MURDERS

'Come on Chad, You're going to be disappointed if you think I'm going to sit here and let you get your kicks from me describing what happened. So you'll have to get your rocks off by some other means.' Chambers grabbed a couple of files and an envelope from his in tray and headed towards the door.

'Fair enough. But you're a bit touchy ain't you? You want to calm down mate, just having a bit of banter. You should think yourself lucky you get still get your leg over.' Forster harrumphed and turned back to his puzzle book as Chambers slammed the door behind him and made for the canteen.

Grabbing a coffee and a bacon roll he sat in the corner and looked at the files he'd hurriedly brought with him. They were two folders completely unrelated to those of Jack the Stripper. He cursed himself for not taking a closer look, but he was reluctant to return to the office while it was only Forster that was in there. He turned his attention to the envelope that he'd also swept up, realising after a moment's confusion that it was the one that Brian Tang had sent to him. It had arrived from Hong Kong almost a month before and had been sitting in his intray for nearly a fortnight. With nothing else to do for the next half hour until the rest of the team turned up, he decided to use his time to take care of the admin duties from his time in Hong Kong. There might be a few quid in expenses owing to him. This Forster shaped, depressing cloud might have a silver lining after all.

Emptying the contents of the envelope onto the table he sorted the mail into three piles. There was a pile of internal DL envelopes from the accounts department that Chambers knew would be from his expenses, some other larger envelopes that contained office circulars and finally one external letter with a stamp and a handwritten address that simply read: Det. J. Chambers, Wanchai Police Station. Hong Kong.

Opening the letter, Chambers removed a single photograph from the envelope. Written on the back in the same handwriting as the address on the envelope were the words.

Wish you were here

?

Chambers looked puzzled and flipped the photograph over. At first it was hard to discern what the photo showed, as it was so dark. It appeared to be a photograph of three women kneeling down in a badly lit room. The photograph was taken from above and behind them. Their clothes were dirty and dishevelled. There was a mirror on the floor that reflected part of the face of one of the women. Chambers took a closer look.

It was Lucy.

He was positive it was her.

At once he felt a massive surge of fear and adrenalin. It felt like he couldn't breathe. His heart was pounding to the point he thought it might burst. He flicked the photograph over looking desperately for a date stamp or anything to indicate a location or something that might help. Grabbing the envelope he looked at the stamp. It was postmarked in Hong Kong on the 16th March 2012. It was now 14th May. Chambers gasped. At the very least it had to prove that Li was still alive two weeks after she went missing after the shootout at the derelict house on the island of Peng Chau on 1st March. But this meant the picture was at least two months old. The letter must have sat at the police station in Hong Kong for a fortnight before Tang knew where to send it. Why hadn't he opened it? Then Chambers had inadvertently sat on it for nearly three weeks. He cursed himself and wanted to scream out loud. She was alive then. But what about now? If something had happened to her in the past two months he had only himself to blame. He turned the photograph over again and looked closely at the sliver of mirror that revealed Li's delicate features.

THE CHARRED FOREST MURDERS

Momentarily he was distracted as the canteen door swung open and Jess Tucker walked in.

***

Chapter 10.

Cute idyll

It was picture postcard perfect. The bright sunshine was dancing on the surface of the crystal clear ocean that stretched invitingly to the horizon where it met with the bright blue sky. As she walked lightly along the water's edge she could feel the soft, fine sand making small squeaking noises under her feet. Somewhere out to sea she could hear the sound of a boat engine sluggishly making its way to some unknown but no doubt equally exotic destination. Taking a moment she looked along the shoreline. It was a dream location. A deserted, palm-fringed beach that ran to what looked like the tip of the island, an empty hammock stretched between two trees in front of a solitary bungalow. There was no one else anywhere to be seen on the beach. She could feel the warm water gently lapping against her toes. Returning her gaze to the azure blue horizon, she looked out to see if she could locate the elusive craft. Its gentle put-putting was the only noise apart from the chattering noise of parakeets feeding in the nearby palms. But there was nothing. The noise gently fading away until all she could hear was that of the voluminous ocean.

Slowly the soporific sounds of the sea surfaced. She surveyed the sand, as small shimmering suds of spume settled sporadically on the shore among the shells. She felt like a somnambulist, unsure if she was seeing or sleeping. She drifted gently along the beach as if in a dream. But it was so bright. Where were her sunglasses? Maybe they were still on top of her head where she often left them. She wanted to lift her hand up to feel for them, but she couldn't. Her arm felt too heavy; suddenly she was too tired to perform even the simplest of tasks. She had an overwhelming desire to lie down, to rest for just a short while.

Open your eyes.

She looked over her shoulder for the voice but she couldn't see anyone. Just the long crescent-shaped, deserted beach. Something touched her foot. She looked down and saw a small gelatinous, opaque sphere no bigger than a golf ball. It was some kind of jellyfish She guessed. As she took a closer look, a small ripple caused it to brush along her foot. But instead of feeling the sensation where it touched her skin, oddly she felt it tickle against her cheek. The sound of the boat engine grew louder. But still she couldn't see the source of the noise. As she looked back at the water near her feet she could see the clear water had a film on the surface. It perfectly reflected the colours of the rainbow. It had to be some kind of oil but where was it coming from? Maybe it was her sun lotion or was it from an engine? She could see no boat, but now she could also smell petrol. The overpowering yet strangely addictive aroma was mixed with something else, something with a sweet smell, familiar but equally just out of her grasp. The sun was so bright now she wanted to turn away. She felt confused as she was already looking down at the shallow water, yet the sun seemed to be getting brighter and brighter, it made her head hurt. She tried and failed once more to lift her arms to shield her eyes from the glare. Something was tapping gently against her cheek

. The petrol smell was so strong it was almost as though she could taste it.

Wake up!

She coughed violently, Her eyes suddenly open. What was happening? She felt immediately disorientated. She was lying supine on something hard and extremely uncomfortable. She was immersed in some sort of fluid, the smell of petrol stronger now, almost overwhelming, making her gag. There was the other aroma again. But what was it? A bare bulb was hanging down swinging with a rocking motion of whatever she was encased in. The light was so bright she couldn't see much beyond it. The light bulb was now swaying violently, causing her to feel even more nauseous. Something touched her face again. She twisted round lifting her head slightly out of the oily liquid; the effort took most of her strength. Her arms felt pinned behind her back making the movement both painful and awkward. At first she couldn't focus on the object, it was too close and she was too confused to comprehend what was going on. Then as the light above swung over her shoulder and illuminating the iridescent liquid, she realised what the item was that had been brushing against her cheek. She let out an ear-piercing scream. Bobbing innocuously on the surface was a human eyeball.

When she had screamed and gagged herself hoarse she could hear the sound of a man laughing. The sweet smell that was mixed with salt water, petrol and rotting fish, was clear now. It was the unmistakable aroma of clove cigarettes. It took her a moment to come to a realisation of what was going on. The clove smell had to be that of Tomar Shen. It was his laugh she could hear and the sickly sweet smell was from the disgusting clove cigarettes that he smoked.

***

Chapter 11.

Kind postman

Monday, 14th May 2012 – 9:32am

Chambers looked away in embarrassment as Tucker made her way to the counter. At this point she hadn't looked over in his direction and he was hopeful she might not notice his presence as he slid down in the chair lifting one of the files from the table to hold up in front of him.

The door swung noisily open again and in came Buchanan, who looked around the room until his gaze settled on Chambers.

'Oh there you are John. I got something I think you'll be interested in.' He called across the canteen causing a few people to look up towards the voice. Chambers automatically looked over to where Tucker was and he inevitably locked eyes with the Northern Irish detective. She gave a brief nod of her head and returned to her conversation with the woman behind the till, leaving Chambers flushed and even more embarrassed about his recent behaviour.

Buchanan moved towards Chambers' table with his compact, economical, measured step.

'Mind if I join you?' He said placing a folder on the table.

'Please do,' Chambers indicated the empty chair opposite.

'I've been over with Chad all week at his place.'

'How was that?' Chambers interrupted. He could think of nothing worse than a week in a confined space with that nasty old man.

'It's OK, you know? His place is pretty grotty, a real pigsty if I'm honest. Hard to believe I've never been round there before. I've known him for decades and he only lives a mile up the road.' When Chambers didn't respond, Buchanan continued. 'It needs a bit of work, the wallpapers all tatty and the carpet is damp in places. Smells like …' he tailed off as if he didn't need to fully explain. 'Plus he's prone to these wild mood swings. You just gotta let the old fella burn himself out I guess. He's angry at the world for his cancer see?'

Chambers nodded again, trying to imagine himself living alone in his seventies with a cancer growing inside him that he knew would inevitably kill him. He would try and be more understanding of what the old bloke was going through.

'I brought him up to date with the new investigation,' Buchanan continued, 'he's promised to get on to a few of the coppers he knew from out west around Hillingdon and Perivale so I'm hopeful he can flag anything that was missed in the first investigation. He can still work his old magic once he puts his mind to it. But that's not why I'm here though.' He opened the file, licked his fingertips and began flicking through the pages contained within the folder.

'You know we spoke about the murder up Brentford and the similarities to the one nearly 50 years ago?' Buchanan had leaned in, lowering his voice an octave, despite the nearest person to them sitting more than 10 metres away.

'Yes. While you were away last week I've been doing a bit of digging myself.'

Buchanan's eyes lit up. 'You have. So you agree there's a connection?'

THE CHARRED FOREST MURDERS

'There's similarities, I'll grant you that. What was even more interesting was when I looked into the eight murders. The one in Brentford was supposedly the fifth. The fourth took place a few weeks before and the body was found at Chiswick Mall a few weeks before Barthelemy was discovered in Brentford.'

Buchanan lips curled into a tight smile. 'Go on.' He was evidently pleased that Chambers had decided to take an interest in the case.

'Well I didn't tell you I passed the local police pulling out a body early last month.'

'You what?' Buchanan looked incredulous.

'I know, I know. It sounds stupid. But I didn't know anything about this case at the time did I? It wasn't our patch and I'd just joined the team. I don't know why, I just ignored it.'

'So what you are saying is now you can see that was a direct correlation to the Lockwood bird that was killed April 1964.'

'Yes.' Chambers nodded.

'Well I had come to see you about the dates. It was annoying me that the Tompkins guy they found in Brentford was found on the 22nd while Barthelemy was found on the 24th.'

'Yes and 48 years later. Why be inaccurate to the point of a couple of days? I don't follow.'

'At the moment I can't answer why something has happened 48 years later, but I can explain the dates.' Buchanan pulled a sheet from the file and slid it across the table to Chambers.

'What's this?'

'A copy of the original coroner's report from the post mortem in Ealing. See?' Buchanan pointed to a highlighted line halfway down the page.

Chambers read it. The coroner suggesting time of death to have occurred somewhere between two to three days earlier.

'The body was stored somewhere. Some of the later bodies that were found had been held in storage for various lengths of times before being dumped. Sometimes a few days, sometimes more than a month. They had fine misting of spray paint on them. Led the original investigation to visit numerous garages and spray-painting workshops all over West London.'

'So you are saying Barthelemy was killed on the 21st, stored and dumped on the 24th. While Tompkins was murdered on the 21st and dumped that same night to be discovered the next day?'

'Exactly Chief. What we need to do is get a look at the file on Tompkins. See what the coroner says about time of death. I'll put my mortgage on it being with a few hours of the body being found. If it's the case, then the dates the bodies are found becomes redundant see? It doesn't necessarily relate to the times the bodies were found it's about when they were murdered.'

'I see. OK I'll get on and check it out.'

'I'd suggest getting pally with someone in the MIT team. Have a butcher's at the file. I doubt it's all on the database or if it is you might not be able to get access. But at this stage I wouldn't go stirring up the hornet's nest. Not until we're sure.'

'It might be a bit late for that.' Chambers said with a grimace. 'I've already spoken to one of the investigating detectives about a possible connection.'

Buchanan sat back and folded his arms. 'Let me guess. It's DS Tucker isn't it?' He was no longer whispering.

'Why do you say that?' Chambers said too defensively.

'Cos she's standing right behind you and she's not looking best pleased.'

Chambers swivelled round in his chair almost knocking the tray of cups out of Tucker's hands.

'Careful Detective Inspector Chambers. My wee ears have been burning over there, so they have. Any of you gentlemen care to inform me of what you have been gossiping about?' She gave them both a long and none too friendly stare.

Chambers scrambled to his feet, nearly knocking his chair over in the process. 'Come and join us DS Tucker. Please. We're just talking about the case. The link between your Tomkins and our Barthelemy.' He blurted out.

'Easy John. I'm just pulling your leg.' She said before setting the tray down on the table and grabbing a chair. 'Help yourselves gents.' She said indicated the cups of tea on the tray. 'So what have you discovered?'

'I don't think we should be getting carried away quite yet.' Buchanan said tempering his earlier tangible excitement.

'DS Tucker, what was Tomkins estimated time of death?'

'Nothing like a warm welcome eh? How was your weekend, that kind of idle chitchat among colleagues that builds a rapport, you know? Not us, no, we're straight into the meat of it. And drop the formalities John. You were calling me Jess on Friday night, all night.' She beamed as Chambers blushed and Buchanan gave them both a quizzical look.

'What happened on Friday? Or shouldn't I ask?' Buchanan enquired.

'The usual drinks in The Tap as per normal on a Friday.' Chambers said far too quickly keeping his gaze fixed on the coroner's report in front of him. 'So what was the time of death?' He asked again.

Tucker stifled a laugh. 'OK John, we'll get on with business. The coroner was sure the murder occurred between 6-8 hours before the body was found. So we're looking at late on the Saturday night or maybe the wee small hours on Sunday morning.'

'Making the date?'

'We'd be looking at Saturday April 21st.'

Buchanan nodded. 'And John, when did you see the body of Marshall getting pulled from the water?'

'It was a Monday morning. It was on the foreshore. I wouldn't want to say for definite it had been in the water until we know cause of death. But that Monday was April 9th.'

Buchanan rubbed his hands together briefly before reaching across the table for one of the cups of tea. 'Irene Lockwood was last seen in The Windmill pub on Chiswick High Road on April 7th 1964. She was found on the riverbank at Chiswick Mall the following morning. She was one of the few that wasn't stored somewhere. Looks like she was killed and dumped the same night.' He emptied a sachet of sugar into his tea began to stir methodically.

'So then why the one day discrepancy?'

'Hard to say. My initial guess is maybe the killer did drop the body off at the right time. Just might not have been discovered till the Monday. Could have been dropped off from a boat on the water. Got snagged. Who knows? We need to get on to whoever's investigating it. Do you know which station has it?'

'Chiswick are dealing with it. And now a month has passed my guess is they should have uploaded a lot of the information to the database by now. I can check that when I get back to my desk.' Tucker said.

'For now though I think we should keep this to ourselves. Any problems with that?' Buchanan said.

This perturbed Chambers. If someone was out there recreating a series of murders from nearly a half-century before then surely they would have to pass this up the line to Barlow at least. A taskforce would need to be set up and probably at great expense. If they were wrong about what they thought they had discovered he didn't like to think what the consequences would be for his career that already appeared to be in freefall. For now though he decided to give the experienced Buchanan the benefit of the doubt. He wanted to see where this would go.

'If there is a copycat killer recreating the murders of Jack the Stripper then we need to look at the dates and figure out who's next. Lockwood and Barthelemy. These weren't the first two were they?'

'No. It all depends on whether you count Elizabeth Figg in '59 and Gwynneth Rees in '63 as part of the eight murders or not. There's still a lot of conjecture on that. Regardless of whether they were one and two or not though there was still the murder of Hannah Tailford. She was found at Hammersmith in February '64. That was before Lockwood and Barthelemy. We need to see who or what turned up near Hammersmith Bridge in late January or early Feb of this year. And as I recall, there was some time difference between her disappearance and discovery.'

'If there was anything found around there, it would likely have been dealt with by Chiswick again.' Tucker was taking notes of what she needed to check on the database. Every now and again Chambers could feel her eyes boring into the side of his head. He couldn't bring himself to look at her. He felt an enormous sense of guilt over the way he had treated her, but more so about what he had done to the memory of Lucy. Especially now that he had a slightest belief that Lucy might still be alive. And worse held somewhere in captivity that he had inadvertently prolonged.

'What about going back to look at the others? Figg and Rees?' Chambers asked.

'I can add that to the search in the database. Buck can you email me the dates?' Tucker asked.

'Sure can.'

'But you said they might not be part of the original killer's repertoire? And also that would be assuming that if they are included would we be going back five years to make sure they are all exactly 48 years ago?' Chambers challenged.

'I think it's worth checking for those dates each year. Buck do you recall if those two were stored before being dumped or not?'

'Figg was definitely found the morning after. Rees was dug up on a rubbish tip in Kew, I'm pretty sure she'd been there for weeks. I'll check the files and get you some dates.' Buchanan replied.

'Definitely. Let's not get too carried away yet though.' Chambers took a slurp of his tea. 'What about connections between the two men that have been murdered?'

'Marshall and Tomkins? At this stage I think we are the first people to make a connection so I'll have to do a bit of digging.' Tucker responded. 'You think they should know each other or have something in common?'

'Possibly the later. All of the Stripper's victims were prostitutes. All of them quite short in stature. It will definitely be interesting to see if our copycat has a "type", won't it?'

'What about any leads for the Tompkins killing?' Chambers asked Tucker without taking his eyes from the file in front of him.

'Nothing as yet. No CCTV. No witnesses have come forward. The body was found inside the park but near the gated entrance. The fence isn't particularly high but it would have taken a fair bit of effort to get a body over the metal railings, which would suggest the murderer is in good physical shape. But that's assuming he's working alone and that's how it was brought in to the park.'

'What do you mean?' questioned Chambers.

'Well there's nothing to say the murder didn't take place in the park earlier and the body hidden elsewhere in the park then moved later. We've had the team scour the park but nothing has come to light so far.'

'I see. And what do we know about him?'

Daniel Oliver Tomkins. IC1 male. Brown hair. No tattoos, piercings or other identifying marks. He was single. A 25-year-old barman living alone in Farringdon. Originally from Chichester. We haven't found any links to this area. He was last heard from on Saturday afternoon when he texted a friend to say he was going shopping and would be in touch to go for a drink later. The friend never heard back but as it wasn't a definite plan he didn't think too much about it. He had no criminal record. Nothing obvious stands out from his past.' Tucker responded.

'The victim's of the Stripper as the name suggests were found naked or with very little clothing present. What about our man?'

'Yes naked too.' Answered Tucker. 'Ligature and scratch marks around the neck.'

Buchanan nodded. 'It sounds like a copycat to me. Same cause of death as Barthelemy. Did you find any of the man's clothing?'

'Nothing at the scene or when we searched the park and nearby streets. It's possible something he was wearing was used as the murder weapon. A scarf for example.'

'What about CCTV from the nearest tube station?' Chambers asked. 'What's the closest tube station to there?'

'Now are you sure you don't know the answer to that?' was Tucker's swift riposte. She fixed him with one of her trademark stares. 'There's Boston Manor a few hundred metres further up the main road. Or if you headed up Swyncombe and hung a left you'd be at Northfields in 10 minutes. I'm sure you're quite familiar with Northfields station aren't you John?' She was smiling at Buchanan now who looked even more confused than before.

'I think that's plenty to be getting on with. Don't you?' Chambers said changing the subject. 'Let's reconvene in a day or so and see what we've got.'

'Don't you think you've forgotten something?' Tucker said looking directly at Chambers.

Was she asking for an apology? Chambers froze. Then shook his head feebly.

'If Lockwood and Barthelemy were numbers four and five. Who was number six and when and where was the body found?'

Chambers couldn't think straight. Tucker's relentless pressure had emptied his mind. 'Buck?'

'I'm well versed with this whole case. It's my speciality so to speak. Number six was Mary Fleming. Found in Chiswick, Berrymede Road. July 1964. That gives us a couple of months of breathing space.' Buchanan replied.

'Not necessarily. As you said before it's when was she killed that's critical right? If he was storing the bodies, she must have been murdered before that date.'

'True. But if my old memory serves me correctly I'm pretty sure it was just a couple of days. It was the last two of his victims – Frances Brown and Bridie O'Hara – that were stored for a long time. Both of them for over a month. No, I'm pretty sure Fleming was just a few days. I'll check that but my guess is we'd be looking at early to mid-July as the next planned murder. That gives us the best part of two months before the next one is due.'

'Right, well we've got some time.' Chambers said feeling better that they would have time to do plenty of digging around before the killer was due to strike again and he would have more time to establish a link and decide whether or not to let Barlow know about what they had discovered. As he got up from his chair he scooped up his files and mail. 'Let's meet on Wednesday afternoon in here. That should give us a bit of time to go through the files. Buck I want you full time on this with me. Pass all the files for the Booth/Townsend case to Forster. It keeps him busy and frees you up to work exclusively on this. Potentially we could be onto something big, but I suggest we don't go mouthing off about it quite yet. Not until we know more and establish some clear links. OK Thanks for the tea, DS … I mean Jess.' He nodded quickly in her direction and set off for the exit followed closely, much to his relief, by Buchanan. He didn't look back when he got to the door.

Arriving back at their office, the pair were confronted by Forster holding court to the rest of the captive members of the team. He had drawn several puzzles on the board and was in the middle of cajoling or more accurately harassing the team for not knowing the answer.

'Well, look who has deigned to join us.' He cackled ominously. 'These two experienced coppers will surely be able to educate the rest of you dunces in the art of lateral thinking. Gentlemen.' He rolled a hand out to them. 'Would you mind joining us for a little quiz?'

Chambers did mind. But he was aware that he needed to show a bit of solidarity with the team and also he didn't want to alienate the mischievous old devil any further.

'Sure. Fine. What's the question?' Chambers closed the door behind them, folded his arms and lent against the opposite wall.

'Simple. See this? Just a little quiz to sharpen the grey matter.' Forster said pointing to the words written on the white board next to the where the images of the cold case murder victims had been stuck up.

1. *Island whose capital is Douglas.*
2. *Canis lupus familiaris.*
3. *Units of digital information.*

He looked back straight at Chambers. 'Forms a twist on a common newspaper headline. This shower of shit haven't got the foggiest.' He gestured around the group.

'Easy old man. Not everyone is actually fussed about your quizzes you know.' Adams said with just a hint of anger in his voice.

Forster fixed the younger man with an ugly stare. Chambers saw the old man clench his fists. It was a ridiculous mismatch. Adams, the martial experts could dispatch Forster in one swift move. The stand off was ended only when Buchanan spoke up.

'Chad you're losing your touch. I remember when you used to set proper quizzes. Capital of Isle of Man is Douglas. Canis lupus familiaris is Latin for dog. Units of information would be bits or bytes. So it's "man bites dog", a twist on the common local rag headline of "dog bites man". Now that our impromptu Brentford version of 15-to-1 is over can we stop this larking about get back to doing some proper police work?' Buchanan said without any bravado and stepped quickly back to his desk.

'Hear, hear' said Adams.

Forster broke eye contact with Adams and turned his gaze to Buchanan, nodding briefly, but scowling none the less, before shuffling back to his desk.

Chambers was pleased for the efficient way Buchanan had calmly diffused the situation; his respect for the old copper was increasing daily. He was in no mood to have to confront Forster. Lately, controlling his temper seemed to be getting harder and harder and despite the positive meeting he'd just had with Buchanan and Tucker, the shock of the letter from Hong Kong and the distressing photo had only served to cause him more anguish. He sat down heavily in his chair and rifled through the files and mail he had swept up of the canteen table to locate the envelope with the photograph of Li.

THE CHARRED FOREST MURDERS

He took the photograph out of the envelope and held it up in front of him so he could try and discern any further details from the dark photo. It was definitely Lucy, he was now 100% sure of that. The reflection in the glass showed one side of her face. She wasn't looking into the camera, she was looking away to her left but there was enough in the picture to confirm that it was Lucy. Her long black hair was tied up in a bun, similar to the way he had seen her wear it on occasion. But her face was smeared with dirt. She didn't look distressed but she looked tired and fearful.

Chambers looked away towards the window, tears pricked at his eyes. He felt responsible but deep down he knew it was ridiculous to blame himself for this. She was a policewoman. She was trained and this was the risk she ran as part of her job. But the feeling that he could have at least come to her aid before now ate away at him. There was at least a month of wasted time that was his fault, although he couldn't have known that the killer they were seeking would have made contact this way. He briskly wiped his eyes and looked back at the photo. In the bottom right of the shot near the foot of the mirror was something that looked like a red card. It was partly out of shot and there was a reflection running across it that most likely came from the overhead strip light. On the card Chambers could make out some form of printed lettering. The card in the photo was no bigger than one centimetre. He scrambled hurriedly through the desk drawers until he finally located a printer's glass. He placed the photo on the desktop and the small, round, black-based magnifying glass over the bottom corner of the image. The lettering was quite unfamiliar to him.

"ລຕູ ບາງບາສາ ເ"

The script was cropped by the right edge of the photograph. It appeared to be a printed font. White letters contrasting against a red background. Chambers sat back in his chair and rubbed the stubble on his chin. Whatever it read and whatever language it was in, he at least had somewhere to start his investigation into where Li might conceivably still be. And no matter how small the chance he had to believe she was still alive.

***

Chapter 12.

Half hard nation

Wednesday, 16th May 2012 – 3:03pm

When the group of three reconvened over an afternoon cup of coffee, Chambers was aware that he had done little of any use in the murder case they were investigating. He'd been far too caught up with the worrying photograph he'd received from Hong Kong. He'd called Brian Tang at the Wanchai police station to find out if any other mail had arrived for him and was disappointed to find out that in the hiatus nothing had been received. Once he explained to Tang the contents of the envelope, the Hong Kong detective had demanded that Chambers send back the original photograph to help in their ongoing investigation into the murder of Inspector Pang by Shen and now his definite involvement in the disappearance of Li. Chambers was happy to oblige and once he had photographed the hardcopy photo and the envelope within which it had arrived he had couriered the evidence to Tang later that Monday afternoon.

If, and he was almost definite in his belief, the letter had come from Tomar Shen then there had to be some way of contacting him, unless Chambers figured, the photograph was sent merely to gloat at how he had got one over the police. The perfect crime. Maybe this was a game that Shen was playing. Somehow the madman had got hold of his name, the envelope had his name on the front although his rank was incorrect. Had he been able to get information from Li or Pang? Or had he just been able to glean the information from the media. Whatever the case was, he was sure Li was alive. At least that's what Chambers' ego willed him to believe. Therefore there had to be a way, a trail, and some kind of starting point.

The original envelope had a Hong Kong postmark, but the script in the photograph definitely wasn't either the Traditional Chinese characters used in Hong Kong or the simplified Chinese characters used in the mainland. Chambers had spent time on the internet looking at different scripts and had come to the conclusion that it was likely to be from one of Thai, Khmer, Lao, Burmese or something from that region. He had ruled out anything coming from further west as the Bangladeshi and Indian scripts although somewhat similar lacked the distinctive style that he had seen in the photo.

To be on the safe side, he had contacted Dr Parvati Bhanji, who was the point of contact Barlow had given him for any forensics requests. Dr Bhanji was the Borough Forensic Manager for the South West quarter of the Forensic Services Command Unit also known as SCD4. The 32 London Boroughs were divided into four 'links', with each link covering eight boroughs. Until now, neither Chambers nor his team had met Bhanji in person, as she was located at the Fulham station along with the links' team made up of Assistant Forensic Practitioners (AFPs) who examined crime scenes and other support staff including the Crime Scene Managers (CSMs) who attended to more serious crimes.

Chambers fired off an email to Bhanji attaching a copy of the photograph with a request for information as to the provenance of the script and also a request for her or one of her staff to come and give a presentation to his team from the Development Group, a part of FCD4 that Chambers had recently read about. He knew from past experience that the members of FCD4 were both snowed under with the ever-increasing crime scene demands for their skills, but were also keen to showcase their latest technology. This small team of forensic staff specifically worked to introduce new techniques and processes to help the officers continue to be more efficient and effective with the resources available to them.

He was aware that his request wasn't going through official channels, as there was no crime number or related information, so in the same email he had decided to ask them to come in and present their latest technology to his team. By requesting her and her team come and give a presentation to his team, he hoped that by showing an interest in their work, his team could benefit in the cold cases they were working on, while simultaneously his personal request might be bumped up the ladder.

Picking up the folders for Lockwood, Barthelemy the Chiswick and Brentford murders that correlated to the recent copycat ones, Chambers also brought along the file of Hannah Tailford – the preceding murder according to Jack the Stripper's original timeline – and headed to one of the interview rooms on the ground floor of the Brentford police station as per Chambers email of the day before. He hesitated at the door feeling a wave of apprehension at coming into close contact with Tucker again. Over the past 36 hours he'd been able to avoid all contact. What was it his first boss had warned him in relation to office romances? Don't shit on your own doorstep. A rule he had lived by – until now. He'd seen many careers go off on a tangent because of the acrimonious outcomes of misguided intentions of people being thrust together for long periods of time. After works drinks mixed with a liberal amount of alcohol often resulted in trouble. Anything from the creation of a disruptive work environment all the way to divorce at the other end of the spectrum. Until a few days ago he'd been free from all that crap. But that was then, this was now. A problem all of his own making. He tapped on the door and let himself in.

Buchanan and Tucker were sitting opposite one another at the square wooden table. Instead of sitting next to Buchanan and opposite Tucker, Chambers sat to her left making it harder for her to fix him with that look that unsettled him so.

'Sorry I'm a bit late. Where are we up to?' Chambers said as he slid into his seat avoiding eye contact with either of them.

'Jess here has made some interesting discoveries.' Buchanan replied.

Tucker continued, 'I called a friend of mine who is based at Chiswick police station. Do either of you know DS Pete Manuel?' When both men shook their heads she continued. 'No matter. He's a good mate of mine so I pumped him for a wee bit of information.'

'Did you tell him what it was in relation too?' Chambers butted in.

Tucker retorted sharply, 'Jesus, John. I'm a professional for fuck's sake. Give me the benefit of the doubt for once, would you?' She frowned at him.

Suitably rebuffed he mumbled, 'sure go on.'

'I've had a bit of a chat with Pete and I steered him round to current cases and got him on to speak about Tom Marshall.' She turned to look at Chambers. 'That's the body you saw getting removed from the banks of the river Thames at Chiswick Mall that you somehow forgot all about.' She shook her head slowly before continuing, 'he said the body was found at dawn on the riverbank on the morning of the 9th April. The coroner's report, here,' she pushed two photocopies out into the centre of the table, 'states time of death to be more than 24 hours before.'

'That makes time of death more likely to be late on the 7th or early on the 8th. Same as Lockwood.' Buchanan nodded dragging one of the photocopied pages towards him.

'That's right. Pete thought the body had either been dumped into the river at another location or maybe put into the Thames from a boat.'

'What was the cause of death? Drowning?' Chambers asked.

'If you want to take a minute to read the report in front of you.' Tucker said curtly. Evidently Chambers was not in her good books, which he found quite understandable. Either that or he was being paranoid. Ever since the accident in Africa and the suspicion he was being followed he was finding it harder and harder to get a proper perspective on matters and even what appeared to be the most innocent of social situations.

Chambers skim read the report. The body of a man was found face down parallel to the bank, his head pointing upriver. River water was present in the lungs. There was a 6" post mortem incision across the man's right shoulder and chest. The coroner had reported the cause of death as drowning.

Looking up briefly at Tucker he asked. 'Do you have anything else on him?'

Tucker flicked through the pages of the file. 'Full name Thomas Beecher Marshall. IC1. Aged 29. Paralegal in the city. Comes from Woolwich. Not married. Lived alone. No criminal record. Last seen leaving his place of work at 8pm on Friday.'

'And his body was discovered on Monday, right?'

'Correct. So sometime between leaving work and late Saturday night, early hours of Sunday, our boy Tom here crossed paths with someone who did this to him.'

'Are you sure we can rule out an accident? Few drinks on Friday night and a header into the river?' Chambers enquired.

It was Buchanan's turn to speak. 'It's a possibility that we can't totally rule out. Assuming he was out drinking in the naughty naked nude.' Buchanan chuckled. 'I guess he could have stripped off. Although the poor sod would be a damn sight harder than me, prancing about naked in the middle of the night in early April. We have to believe the coroner's report that he drowned. But I don't buy it. Look at the similarities to Lockwood. Same injury. Found in the same place. OK it's one day out but I've got a horrible feeling that the killer was expecting this to be found on the Sunday and for what ever reason it wasn't but then maybe he wasn't bothered, the key thing is the crime occurred 48 years to the day of the Lockwood murder. I think we can safely say the day the bodies are found is not as important as where the bodies are found. And I think it was very specifically put there. Maybe the tide came up and washed it away.' He wiped his nose with his thumb and forefinger, and then gave a quick sniff. Another of his short, sharp, neat movements. 'I believe he might even have come back. Replaced the body to make sure it was where it was supposed to be as that's the critical thing. He's letting us know that's what matters. The where not the when.'

Chambers folded his hands across his stomach trying to take it all in. 'What was your friend Pete saying about it? Have they got any leads?' His mind drifting to his early morning running route. There were some expensive places along Chiswick Mall that meant there would definitely be CCTV footage.

'They've got no leads at present. He was saying there's a fair bit of conjecture it might've been a suicide. Lonely young man and all that.' She replied.

'Do we know if he had a love interest? Surely they had a look at the angle. Spoken to his colleagues, his family.'

'I'll need to check. On the database I could only get access to the files they had already uploaded. The coroner's report for one. The witness and family statements and transcripts aren't up there yet.' She looked up from the file and fixed her gaze on Chambers. 'I think that from our chat here and the similarities between these two cases and the ones you've got from the sixties, that it's more than enough to escalate this. I feel uncomfortable keeping all this info from Hutchinson. He's the SIO on the Brentford case and if he thinks I'm withholding information from him I might as well start looking for another job if all this comes to light. The DSI, our beloved McKinley is

THE CHARRED FOREST MURDERS

already giving him shit about the lack of movement on the Tomkins case.'

'Have you still not had any leads on that one?' Chambers asked with genuine interest.

Tucker glowered at him. 'Apart from pulling a witness out of my arse what do you want me to do?' She said with thinly veiled sarcasm.

Buchanan stepped in to appease her. 'Hold tight Jess. I think John is just asking the question that needs to be asked. That's all. I think we need to tighten up here a little bit. Seems to be a bit of friction and I don't think we need that among the three of us. Right?'

'Fine,' Tucker snapped, 'as it stands we're no further on than we were earlier in the week. There's a bit of guesswork but it's a fair assumption that unless he was killed in the park then the body had to be dumped there. If that's the case and it wasn't stored in one of the nearby garages then it had to be brought in by vehicle. There's no CCTV footage of that street or in fact anything really within a half mile except the footage from Boston Manor tube looking out onto Boston Manor Road. The closest we have the other way is from the slip road off the A4. The only other way to get there is Swyncombe Avenue and unfortunately there's no cameras in that direction either.'

Buchanan nodded. 'So if he comes from the A4 to the south or from the Uxbridge Road to the north we should have an image of the vehicle.'

'That's right and they are the two main roads coming close to the scene that give good access to and from London. If he comes from the third direction or the murder took place in the park or the body had been stored earlier in the day we're stuffed. That's where Hutchinson is at the moment.'

'Hmmm, that's not great is it? Anything else show up where the body was found?'

'About 20 metres away some charred sticks and ash were found on the edge of the forest that leads back to the water on the other side of the park.'

'Any relevance?'

'Not so far. The ash could have been paper but it was beyond salvation. And anyway, there's no link to the body.'

'Fingerprints? Anything under the victim's nails? Sign of putting up a fight?' Chambers was tapping his pen on the paper in front of him.

'Nothing. No signs of a struggle. No identifying marks. I'd hazard a guess it was the work of someone who has done this before.' Tucker surmised.

'And we know from the reports that the body was found lying on a pile of leaves, face up in the same position as Barthelemy was. Same scratches on his neck that she had and bruising to the face. It begs the question – why is someone out there recreating these murders 48 years on?' Buchanan said clearly bemused by it all.

'I agree. It can't be the same person, can it? I mean even if he was a teenager at the time in '59. Say 18 years old, that would make him at least 71 now.'

Chambers couldn't help glancing at Buchanan. What had he said before? It was this case that had got him interested in being a policeman. He was 16 when Barthelemy was found in 1964. Making him 11 at the time of the first murder in 1959. Chambers hadn't seriously been looking at Buchanan as a suspect, more thinking of his age and whether at his present age of 64 he was fit enough to carry out the work. He seemed in good nick, took care of himself and had a look about him that suggested that lugging bodies about in the middle of the night wouldn't pose him a problem. But for someone to be the original murderer and to be doing this again in his seventies seemed too farfetched, too preposterous to be taken seriously.

THE CHARRED FOREST MURDERS

'It just has to be a copycat killer. But why after all these years? And why men and not women? I don't get it.' Chambers was thinking out loud.

Tucker shook her head. 'I've found nothing so far linking the two recently deceased together in any way, shape or form.'

What about going back to the third of the Stripper's victims. The one that would have preceded these two.' He turned to address Buchanan. 'What are the details again?'

'Early afternoon on Sunday, February 2nd 1964.' Buchanan said, as if reading from a file, but the folder lay closed upon the desk while he looked straight at Chambers, 'two rowers found the near naked body of Hannah Tailford on the foreshore near Hammersmith Bridge. The body was wedged beneath a pontoon at the landing stage.'

'Near naked?' Chambers interjected.

'Naked save for her stockings bunched around her ankles. Also she had a pair of knickers stuffed in her mouth.' Buchanan explained.

Chambers noticed Buchanan had flicked a look at Tucker, as if to gauge her response.

'Which way was she facing?' Tucker asked.

'Same as Lockwood. Same as the recent one. Head facing upstream. Why?'

'I'm wondering if it's important. What the relevance is? Were they placed like that or do you think they have floated downstream and washed up on the bank? That would mean they could have been put in the river at Chiswick, Brentford, Isleworth, Richmond or even further upriver.' Tucker replied.

'Cause of death?' asked Chambers.

'It was the same official coroner, Dr Teare I believe his name was. Same official result. Drowning.'

Chambers turned to Tucker. 'I'm kind of dreading asking you this question.'

'Go on John. You can do it. Don't be shy now.' She said, her eyes twinkling back at him.

'Did you get a chance to look to see if there were any murders, missing person reports around about the first week of February this year?'

'Yes. Nothing.'

Chambers let out a sigh of relief. 'So we can look at these two as possibly being the beginning then.'

'Hang on a minute John. I did what Buck here suggested the other day. I went back to the date Ms Tailford went missing. She was last seen on,' she consulted her notebook, 'January 24th 1964. That was a Friday night. The exact time from her partner and neighbours' witness statements vary slightly. But it seems she was heading off to work her patch around Victoria. There were some other sightings of her over the following few days but there was nothing to corroborate it and I think, most importantly she left her kid at home and if she was alive for another week then surely she would have returned if she could.'

Buchanan shook his head, 'I dunno. These brasses are, or at least were, prone to go off on all week benders. Bloody little good the social used to do back in the day. Kids left at home for days fending for themselves.'

Chambers watched the change come over Buchanan before it seemed to disperse just as quickly. There was definitely more to the older policeman's past than met the eye.

'This is your long-winded way of breaking some bad news.' Chambers said flatly fearing the worst.

'Yes.' She shifted in her seat. 'A man was pulled out of the shallow water at low tide on the 25th of January this year. Naked. Just to the east of Hammersmith Bridge.'

'Shit.' Chambers said as Buchanan shook his head. 'The day after Tailford went missing. Similar location. Similar state of undress. Who's investigating that one?'

'Hammersmith.'

'Do you have any connections along there?' Chambers asked them both.

Buchanan nodded. 'I got an old mate over there. I can bell him this afternoon.'

'Surely Chiswick and Hammersmith must have discussed this.' Chambers looked towards Tucker. 'I mean we're talking a few months apart, same stretch of river. Same appearance. I'm assuming these neighbouring stations talk to each other?'

'Traditionally there's always been a bit of rivalry.' Buchanan acknowledged. 'Used to be a right pain in the arse if I'm honest. But that's just how it was. Now it's not as bad. I'm sure someone must have put two and two together.' He scratched the back of his head. 'But just don't count on it. It's possible the river police would have been involved as well to further muddy the waters, so to speak.' Buchanan looked mildly pleased with his pun.

'Buck can you do me a favour and take a look into this one? Tread carefully but see what you can extract? Could be all detailed on the database. Jess what else did you find out about the victim?'

'Aaron Burr, IC1 male. A 26-year-old ex-soldier. Currently unemployed. He does have a criminal record which makes him different from the other two.' She was reading from her notepad again. 'An ABH charge against a man called Alex Hamilton in June 2010. Burr lived alone in Clapham.'

'What do we know about his service record?'

'Served a tour in Afghanistan in Helmand Province. There were scant details in the record.' Tucker answered.

'And the assault?'

'Brief description in the file sounds like it was a punch up in a pub.'

'Could we be looking at a revenge attack do you think guv?' Asked Buchanan.

'It's a possibility.' Mused Chambers. 'But the MO is just too similar to the others. It would be good to have a little chat with this Hamilton character just to rule him out. I'm guessing the team at Hammersmith must have followed up on that avenue of enquiry already though.'

'I'll check it out.' Buck replied.

'There are a few questions we need to address.' Tucker said. 'Do these young men have something in common, and if so what is it?'

'And' Chambers added, 'we better take a look back at the other murders as well. What were there dates and locations?'

'Rees was found 8th November 1963 on a rubbish tip near what is now Kew Retail Park, next door to the National Archives, the old Kew Records office.'

'I'm not familiar with where that is.' Tucker stated.

'If you head over either Kew Bridge or Chiswick Bridge. It's tucked in between them on the south side there almost on the river front.' Buchanan explained.

'Another river front location then?'

'Yes, but she'd been buried in the nearby tip. I don't know what the relevance to the river is. The tip would have been the ideal hiding ground for a body.' Buchanan answered. 'By the time the body was found, she was already badly decomposed. The post-mortem revealed several teeth were missing and she had in all likelihood been strangled with a ligature. She had been last seen nearly six weeks earlier, getting into a car with a

THE CHARRED FOREST MURDERS

man on the night of September 29th. That made her the victim that was stored the longest.'

'But she wasn't actually stored though, was she?'

'No that's right. But she was the one with the longest gap between murder and discovery. Forty-odd days. But she could have been dumped immediately just not discovered.'

Chambers thought about the condition in which the body would have been found. Buried in a rubbish tip at the end of the summer. He was surprised it had taken so long to find. Maybe the rank smell of the decomposing body was masked by the general smell of the tip. 'Do you think the killer was moving the bodies around by boat? It seems possible.'

But what about the one in Brentford? That's at least a mile away from the river.' Tucker challenged.

'Well not exactly.' Buchanan replied.

'What do you mean? It is a mile away. The Thames goes off west towards Isleworth.'

'From the river Thames it's a mile. Yes you're right. But not from the river Brent.' Buchanan explained. 'The Brent meanders under from the north down under M4 and past the far side of Boston Manor Park where our body was found. Actually the park borders the river. So we can give credence to John's point. It's most definitely possible to move the bodies by river. And Boston Manor Park is heavily forested. I can't see why under cover of darkness you couldn't shift a body easily through there from the river.'

'Does the Brent flow into the Thames?' Tucker asked.

'Yeah sure does.'

'Where about?'

'A couple of hundred metres from where we're sat.' Buchanan gestured over her shoulder in the direction of the neighbouring

Morrisons supermarket. 'Curves round under the road near the Pet Supermarket along by Syon House, then swings back to join the Thames opposite Kew Gardens, right here next to Brentford Dock it forms part of the Grand Union Canal that runs north all the way up to Birmingham.'

'So you think the murders could be taking place somewhere along the river or canal system? Then the bodies carted by boat to their drop off points.' Tucker looked like she was starting to see this as plausible. 'Either using a houseboat or even one of them river islands as a secluded place to commit the murders.'

'Eyots.' Buchanan smiled.

'Eight what?' Quizzed Tucker.

'An eyot or an ait. That's the correct name for the river islands that dot the Thames.'

'Got it. But don't you think they look like the perfect place to commit a crime of this magnitude? They're heavily forested, uninhabited. If you were using one of those as a base, you'd have perfect access to the river to move the bodies about at night and also a secluded place to commit the crimes.

'That's a very interesting point. I think it's a possibility that we really need to consider.' Buchanan replied.

'I've just had a thought.' Chambers interrupted. 'Jess you mentioned there was a limited amount of CCTV around Boston Manor park.'

'Aye that's right. Why?'

'Well there must be buses passing up that road right?'

'Yeah the 195 and E8.' Buchanan responded quickly.

'It might be a slim chance. But I worked a case up in Westminster, where they managed to get some images of a crime that was taking place on the street from a passing bus. All these buses now have a range of CCTV cameras aboard. One of

THE CHARRED FOREST MURDERS

them might have picked up something when it drove by the park. It's not much. But could be worth a look I guess.'

Tucker nodded. 'I don't think anyone's checked that yet so I'll let the team know. Although it's only useful if he didn't bring them in by boat.'

'OK so back to our investigation. We should be looking for any naked males who have turned up dead in Kew around that date she disappeared. And if we stick to the timeline of 48 years it will be late September, early October 2011. Buck can you look into that Hammersmith case of Burr? See what you can dig up. And Jess can I leave you looking into the Kew scenario.'

'What about the Stripper's first murder.' Buchanan asked. 'Elizabeth Figg, discovered by the rowing club at Dukes Meadows near Barnes Bridge. She was found up against a tree overlooking the river. Thing is it was June 1959. So add 48 years to that and the murder we'd be looking for would have taken place in June 2007. As I said before there's always been plenty of speculation this one wasn't linked to the others. It was only done so retrospectively because of the location. It's almost opposite the rubbish tip in Kew.'

'I'll handle that,' said Chambers. 'Jess I know you want to escalate this but I really think we need to establish our facts first. We still got a few months before the next one is due. Let's see what we can find out about the murder of Burr in January and see if anything else appears to correspond to the other murders of Figg at Dukes Meadows and Rees at Kew. Then we can put a more coherent case forward to your boss Hutchinson and then also up the chain to McKinley. I don't know what dealings you've both had with her, but I want us to be 100% sure of what we are dealing with before we go to see her on this. Is that OK?'

Tucker shrugged. 'John, I want you to promise me this isn't going to come back and bite me on the arse. OK?'

'I'll do my best. Buck?'

'All fine with me. So when do you want to reconvene?'

'I'm on a bloody course all day tomorrow and Friday. Who puts MIT on courses in the middle of an investigation? Can we say early next week? Monday or Tuesday?' Tucker requested.

'OK. Let's do Tuesday. Give you a chance to get some work done when you get back.' Chambers said with a sense of relief. Tucker would be gone for a few days so he was free from the risk of bumping into her on his own. Also he knew time wasn't hugely critical on this particular case. If the murderer was following a copycat pattern, which they had every reason to believe from what they had uncovered so far, then they had a couple of months up their collective sleeve until the next murder was due to take place. He would rather take the time than go to see their hard-nosed Superintendent with a half-cocked story. Plus it gave him more time to work on his other investigation. The one playing out half a world away. The mystery of what had happened to Lucy.

***

Chapter 13.

Birth via Japan

Tuesday, 22nd May 2012 – 1:41pm

On the day the three detectives were due to meet up again, Chambers received a reply from Dr Bhanji at the Fulham police station.

Dear DI Chambers,

Many thanks for your email dated 14 May and my apologies for the delay in responding but we are severely understaffed right now and I have to follow protocol and assess cases on a priority basis. As your request comes without a case number or any supporting documentation I would be unable to prioritise this matter usually. However I took a quick look at the JPEG you sent across and I can tell you that the script on the card in the bottom left hand corner is, I am most definitely sure, a Laotian font. There are several reasons I can confirm this. One is that it is clearly an abugida script that is made up of consonantal ligatures, tone marks as well as the usual consonants and vowels. The distinct use of character and the rounded serif style differentiates it immediately from say the Khmer language which itself is an alphasyllabary script that uses multiple levels of character stacking and the vowel system consists of independent vowels and dependent vowels. The dependent vowels have two registers of phonemes to account for the fact that there are fewer vowel graphemes for the vowel phonemes in the spoken language. Khmer also uses diacritics that further enhance the pronunciation of words.

But I feel I have digressed. In layman's terms, although Thai, Khmer and Laotian scripts share a common ancestry there are some clear differences in how they have developed. Another reason I feel I can be sure is that I recently vacationed at Angkor Wat in Cambodia and also to Luang Prabang in Laos in last year and I have checked through my photography and certain characters in the sample appear in Laos but not in Cambodia. The first two characters represent the numerals 9 and 8, and in fact this is what clarifies the script as clearly Laotian, as the numerals are very distinct from written Thai. I have taken the time to try and decipher the next word, as the last is incomplete. I can only translate it as Paksapak in the roman script, which means nothing to me and is not a word that translates into English with any meaning; I hope therefore it resonates with you. It could however, be the name of someone or perhaps a place. The initial character of the third word could be the letter 's'.

As for the writing on the back of the envelope in the second JPEG you sent. If you have the original I can run some ink and paper analysis but before I proceed I need a case number to create a file.

I hope this has been of some use. Also we would be delighted to come and give a presentation of our work. Let me know a good time and we can arrange.

Yours,

Dr P Bhanji

Chambers let out a sigh. He wasn't quite sure about what the good Doctor had been saying for the most part in the email, except that her use of the word 'vacationing' meant she was either American or at least American educated. But she had confirmed the words on the card in the photo with Li were

Laotian. But that threw up a new puzzle. Why was Li being held in a place with a card from Laos but the envelope sent had come with a Hong Kong postmark? It didn't help particularly. He fired off a quick reply to Bhanji to thank her for her help and to organise a presentation for sometime in the following two weeks when her schedule allowed.

Opening his browser he typed 'Pakpasack' into Google and the top two links were for Facebook pages for a technical college in Vientiane. The third was for a restaurant in Vientiane. He looked up Vientiane on Wikipedia. The opening line, after the various pronunciation's explanations stated that '(Vientiane) is the capital and largest city of Laos, situated on the Mekong River near the border with Thailand.' On the top right of the page were the city's coordinates. He clicked on the link and was taken to http://toolserver.org that offered a link to Google maps. Chambers clicked again and the new page was a close up map of the city that told him nothing. He zoomed out several times until he could see the location in relation to the country and those surrounding it. It was completely landlocked. The city appeared to be midway across the beginning of the peninsula that ran south into Thailand and onto Malaysia. Laos was bordered by Vietnam to the east, Thailand and Cambodia to the south, Thailand and Burma to the west, while due north led to China. Vientiane sat almost halfway between Bangkok to the Southwest and Hanoi to the Northeast.

Zooming out again, Hong Kong appeared on the far right of the map. Chambers looked at the scale of the map. It had to be 800 miles in a straight line from Hong Kong to Laos. It didn't make any sense at all. It had to be a coincidence that there was something from Laos in that room. Why would Shen have taken her there? By land it would mean travelling through at least 1000 miles of China before heading south into Laos. And by boat it was impossible to get to Laos – it was the only landlocked country in Southeast Asia. He wished he hadn't sent the original photograph and envelope back to Tang in Hong

Kong. While he thought about it, he sent his ex-colleague in Asia an email suggesting they prioritise getting ink and paper samples tested. It could only help.

Chambers shut the browser and decided for now that there was little he could do save for taking a flight to Laos to go on a wild goose chase. He would wait and see what Tang came back with. He wouldn't rule out jumping on a plane to Asia to find her, but he needed to know whether he should go to Hong Kong or Laos first. For the moment he needed to think. Although it had been raining for five days straight, his plan to run come hail or high water, had ceased for the time being. But when he looked out of the window there were rays of sun poking out from behind a fat grey cumulonimbus cloud. Chambers decided a walk in the sunshine might help him to clear his mind.

***

Back from his walk and his impromptu lunch, Chambers headed to the meeting room to find out what Tucker and Buchanan had been able to find out. This was the first time he had seen Tucker since their meeting the previous Wednesday. He had come to the conclusion that her hostile and aggressive attitude towards him was with good reason. He just hoped today would be easier and that she might be ready to put their ill-judged dalliance behind them as he was clearly trying to do.

The first thing Chambers noticed as he entered the room was Tucker was looking red-faced and there were visible beads of sweat on her brow.

'Afternoon John. How are you? Good weekend?'

'Fine you? You're looking a bit hot and bothered.'

'Do you say that to all the girls?' She smiled at him, flicking her long wavy black hair behind her ear.

As usual she had been able to cause Chambers to blush and make him believe he had a form of dyspraxia simultaneously, as he put his coffee cup down too hard on the table causing some of the boiling contents to lap over the side and scald his fingers. The sudden burst of pain nearly caused him to cry out. He sat down self-consciously as Tucker whipped out a pack of tissues from her handbag on the floor and mopped up the mess. The uncomfortable maladroit moment passed as the door opened and Buchanan entered the room and sat down quickly placing his folders neatly on the desk.

'Hi Buck, First off John,' Tucker began quickly, 'I don't know how long I can stay. Things have taken quite a dramatic turn in the last few hours. Lew Hutchison and Pete Manuel are picking up a suspect this morning.'

'Really? That's excellent news.' Chambers congratulated her although he had mixed feelings. He wanted to be more involved, not merely a spectator, it wasn't his style to be passive on any investigation. It was frustrating working the cold cases. He'd spent most of the Thursday and Friday examining the old case files and in particular the investigation and the range of suspects that the case had thrown up.

'What brought you to this suspect?' Buchanan was asking shifting his chair closer to the table and fixing his gaze firmly on Tucker.

'I got to say it was something John said. We got hold of the CCTV footage from the local bus company. The E8 bus goes up Boston Manor Road. The last bus of the night went past the park at exactly 1:08am. The Fish eye lens in the driver's camera caught a white van sitting waiting to exit Boston Gardens. We managed to get a single frame with the registration plate. Quite a coup. The van is registered to a self-employed delivery driver by the name of Julius Stahel.'

Chambers sat back in his chair with a wide grin on his face. It had to be a chance in a million that the registration plate was legible and the bus had passed at just the right moment. 'Will I be getting a mention in dispatches?' Chambers joked.

Tucker didn't seem to notice the light-hearted angle. 'I'm afraid not. I can't say you or Buck are involved, can I? It will compromise this investigation.'

Buchanan coughed while Chambers felt slightly aggrieved. But in essence she was right. This wasn't their case and in reality he was just happy to have helped possibly bring it to a close.

'Stahel? It's not local. Where's he from?' Buchanan asked gruffly.

'The van is registered to his place of residence in Edgware.'

'And the name? Where's that come from?' Buchanan asked.

'I believe it's Hungarian.'

'Hungary's in the EU is it?' Buchanan asked. 'I can't keep up with all these bleeding Eastern European countries and their splintering and what not.'

'Buck I'm not sure Hungary has even split from another country. Has it? I mean it was part of the Austro-Hungarian empire before World War I.' Chambers replied.

'It's been in the EU since 2005 so it has. I never took you for an old xenophobe, Buck. Where's you sense of camaraderie?' Challenged Tucker.

'A Zeno what? I have no idea what you are going on about darling.' Buchanan winked at Chambers. 'But I'll take it as a compliment all the same. And as for my sense of camaraderie, it is right where I left it. Up the nick in Notting Hill circa 1975.'

Chambers had no idea what Buchanan was alluding to, but what he did know was this wasn't the time or place to be raking up long forgotten issues. 'Do you have any other info on him at this stage? I can see where Buck's coming from. His family could have been here generations or he could have just arrived. There has to be something that links him to the Stripper murders and the other bodies found earlier this year. There just has to be.'

'As far as I know there's still no tangible link between our murders and either the Stripper or those earlier four. I'll have to …'

'What do you mean, earlier four? I thought we only had three bodies.' Buck interrupted.

'Yes I haven't got round to telling you yet. I checked the records and although there was nothing in or around Dukes Meadows that fits with our date on 16th June 2007 for the possible first murder of Elizabeth Figg. There was a body found that corresponds to the Gwyneth Rees murder, when she was found at the rubbish tip in Kew.'

'Jesus!' Buchanan slammed his hand on the table. Chambers hadn't been expecting such a violent outburst and the sudden noise made him jump. Buchanan was up pacing the room. 'I don't get it. But you said nothing for the first victim. Right?'

Tucker nodded.

'Did you check all the other years?' There was a hint of anger in his tone.

'Yes Buck, of course I did, for fuck's sake. Sometimes I wonder what you pair take me for. I checked early to mid-June 2007 to 2011. Nothing. We've got murders for four out of the five. Surely that's enough to prove the link.'

'There's something wrong.' Buchanan returned to his seat. 'I know there's a lot of speculation that Figg wasn't part of it. But I know she was a part of it. I'm 100% sure.'

'How?' Chambers was intrigued.

A sudden calm descended over Buchanan, the flash of anger he had just shown had quickly dissipated. 'Nothing. Just a feeling. S'all.' He said quietly as he bit on one of his fingernails.

Chambers watched Buchanan for a moment but he was now rubbing his palms together and looking fixedly out of the window. 'Go on Jess. You said there's a corresponding discovery for the Kew body.'

'Yes.' Tucker replied slowly taking her eyes from Buchanan to respond to Chambers. 'William Barkley. A 32 year-old IC1 male. Office manager of a travel agency in Kensington. I don't have much more than that at the moment. Save that he was found behind the dumpsters at the back of M&S at the Kew Retail Park on the 30th of September last year. Which correlates exactly to the day after Rees went missing 48 years ago.'

'Do we know if he was found naked?' Chambers asked.

'Not as yet. I'm waiting for info from the station at Kew, but this morning's events have taken precedence.'

'Buck? What about your digging on the Burr murder back in January? Any news you can share?'

'I had a look at the ABH charge for our victim on this Alex Hamilton fella in the summer of 2010. After the case, this bloke did one to Australia, seems he's still down there in Perth, I believe. It looks like a dead end to me.'

The ringtone of Kids by MGMT came from a mobile phone and it was no surprise to Chambers that it was Tucker who responded to the call. He couldn't imagine Buchanan was a big fan of MGMT and their neo-psychedelia form of indietronica. Buchanan was more likely to enjoy the soothing sounds of Neil Diamond, Chambers surmised.

Tucker checked her phone. 'It's Hutchinson. I better take this.' She picked up her handbag and made her way to the door, answering the call as she let it close gently behind her.

***

Chapter 14.

Crablike hand

Tuesday, 22nd May 2012 – 2:11pm

Chambers and Buchanan watched the athletic figure of Tucker leave the room to take the call. Chambers had a good idea it had something to do with the arrest of the suspect in the Tomkins' case.

'Everything OK Buck?' Chambers said eventually.

Buchanan didn't answer for a while. 'Yeah fine, but what was up with her? All red faced and angry? Woman's thing is it?'

'No, I think she must have been doing a bit of lunchtime training. She's a triathlete I think.' Chambers remarked.

'I didn't to be honest. Explains her behaviour on occasion. Too much testosterone pumping around her body. Makes her act like some kind of bleeding alpha male.'

Chambers didn't want to get into discussing Tucker's more masculine attributes. 'What were you saying before about the lack of a body to coincide with the Figg murder in 1959?'

'I just got a feeling about that first one is all. I'm sure that the bird must've missed something. It doesn't add up there was no corresponding body.' Buchanan hesitated before adding, 'something definitely feels wrong.'

'I told Jess last week that I'd specifically look at that one. She must have got caught up with other things. But having said that,

I did look and I didn't find anything either. I went back to 2005 all the way up to last year. Extended the search to the whole of Dukes Meadows and Riverside Lands as far up as Hammersmith Bridge in one direction and Kew Bridge in the other. Nothing at all came up.'

Buchanan just shook his head.

'I don't think we have much choice now anyway.' Chambers said eventually.

'About what?'

'Escalating this to Barlow and inevitably to your best mate, Ronnie McKinley.' Chambers smiled.

'Fuck that.' Buchanan snapped.

'Buck. If this is the man, what choice do we have? Chances are he's also responsible for the other murders this year and this one from late last year. I have no choice.'

'And what if it isn't him? Then what?'

'Then, well, it's out in the open. I got the feeling the longer we sit on this, the more chance we have of getting splinters in our arse. And I for one don't want a splintery backside. Do you?'

S'pose not guv. But let me put this to you right now. There's something amiss in this case. I don't know what it is but something out of kilter.'

'OK Buck. Objection noted. Don't get me wrong. I have reservations too. I had a look at the files like I said earlier. I don't recall there being anyone with a Hungarian name or ancestry in the original investigation. At this stage I simply don't see a connection.'

'So if you read the original investigation then you'd know about the old bloke from the tennis club handing himself in.'

'Archibald?'

'S'right. Kenneth Archibald. He knew Lockwood. Said he'd been with her at The Windmill pub on Chiswick High Road the night she died. Said he took her up Chiswick Mall, strangled her and pushed her in the river.'

'But he retracted it. Didn't he?'

'Yeah, eventually. He used to run an illegal drinking den at the time at the Holland Park tennis club. There were literally hundreds of these places. All you needed was a room, bit of scrap furniture and you could make a pretty penny from the mark up on the booze in these after hours drinking dens. He was running it in the members' room at the tennis club after hours – he was the caretaker there see? Perfect little earner for all involved. Then one night he had a bit of trouble. A couple of punters had a punch up in there, led to a bit of a hoo-ha outside the gaff. Police happened by and he tried to put it down to a foiled burglary. They investigated and found out what was going on and shut the place down. A few connected tasty people would have lost a few quid in earnings when that place bit the dust.'

'You think he felt safer on the inside?' Considered Chambers.

'Of course. Wait till the heat died down and see what trouble might be coming his way. There were some naughty people about back then, just like now. But he was only small fry. He might get a slap for letting the place get closed down. The poor old geezer got himself in a right old state and was plastered by the time he handed himself in, worried himself into a frenzy thinking he was going to get offed by some gangster. Also, the key thing for the police at the time was that he knew Irene Lockwood. He had a business card of hers. Well a card with her name and phone scrawled on it. She'd drink in his place like. These places were common hangouts for prostitutes back then. Lockwood lived up Notting Hill way, not that far from the bar really. But let me tell you back then Notting Hill was nothing like it is today. They had riots up there in 1958. There must have been three to four hundred white lads, Teddy Boys mainly, and a load of coloureds fresh off the boat from the Caribbean. There were some very tasty times up there back then, mark my words. Very tasty.' Buchanan was almost smiling as he recalled the times.

Chambers nodded. Idly wondering if Buchanan and his toe rag mates were somehow involved. But in '58? He would have been too young, not even in his teens.

'You know what they used to call that manor back then?'

'Where? Notting Hill? No idea. What?'

'Rotting Hell.' Buchanan replied shrewdly. 'And that's a fair description. I used to work up there in the mid- to late-1960s. It was still a right shithole. Anything you wanted in the way of drink or drugs or prostitutes, the place was full of it. Hard to believe what a gaff goes for up there these days.'

'So we've got one old bloke scared of getting a beating or worse. So he hands himself in for one of the murders and shortly after he retracts his confession. What about the other suspects? I mean West London must have been gripped by terror back then. Eight murders in West London? Surely there were a few arrests?'

'You're not wrong. It was still resonating years later. The problem was they were all brasses. These girls often worked alone late at night, saw a load of different men, kerb crawling and what not. You know Hitchcock the director?'

'Alfred? Don't tell me he was a suspect.'

'No not all. But he made a film about it.'

'Really?' Asked Chambers incredulously. He wasn't even sure he had seen any Hitchcock films apart from *Psycho*. But he was familiar with the names of a few others, *The Birds, North by Northwest*. 'I thought he was American?'

THE CHARRED FOREST MURDERS

'Hitchcock? Nah, he was a Londoner. Went out to Hollywood during the war. Became a household name but he came back and made this film called *Frenzy*, based on the book *Goodbye Piccadilly, Farewell Leicester Square*. I forget the author. He had a French name though. Anyway the film came out in the early seventies. It's supposedly based on the case. Though in the film Hitchcock calls them the necktie murders.'

'A top Hollywood director made a film that's linked to this case? And it still goes unsolved?' Chambers was gobsmacked. He'd been born in West London in 1967 and grown up around there yet he had no clue about any of this. Not the murders, the book, the film – any of it. 'And I was reading in the case notes that some boxer was supposedly a suspect. Somebody Mills?'

'Yeah. That's right an' all. Freddie Mills. World light heavyweight champion from 1948 to 1950. My old man used to tell me he was a very, very tasty fighter. After he retired he got into a bit of TV work hosting a rock'n'roll show called 6-5 Special in the late fifties. I remember watching him on that as a kid. Then he opened up a club, got mixed up with the Krays and some Chinese gangsters. Found himself in hock and killed himself in his car in a fit of depression in the July of 1965.'

'When was the Stripper's last murder?' Chambers enquired.

'January 1965. Bridie O'Hara in Acton.'

'So it's possible that it was him?'

'I guess so. But from what I can see at the time no one fingered him for it. It was something that came to light much later. I still don't really know how or why the spotlight came to be on him to be honest. Just convenient I guess. The real question for me that involves Mr Mills is this – Was he murdered or did he do himself in?'

'Why do you say that?' Chambers didn't see the relevance.

'He was found dead in his motor out the back of his club. A single shot through the eye. But it was from a .22 rifle. Who decides to commit suicide with a shot to the eye from a .22 rifle? Personally, and I hate guns, can't imagine a worse way to top yourself. But if you were going to do it, surely you'd put a pistol to the temple? I mean there must be even easier ways. Overdose; stick your head in the oven; step in front of a bus or train.'

Chambers shrugged. As the thought of committing suicide had never crossed his mind he wasn't sure. But now Buchanan had mentioned it, and had seemed to have spent more than an idle moment thinking it over, there did appear to be easier ways of doing it. The physical awkwardness of using a rifle and shooting yourself through the eye while sitting in the back of your car in the middle of the night did strike him as somewhat peculiar.

'It's like the other bloke they reckon was Jack the Stripper; he conveniently committed suicide as well. He gassed himself though. The old rubber hose on the exhaust pipe and the other end through the car window, while in his garage.'

Chambers was thinking. 'Who's that one? The security guard?'

'Yes this Scottish bloke, name of Mungo Ireland. The top copper at the time was a guy called John Du Rose. Or four day Johnnie.'

'Four day Johnnie?' Chambers almost laughed at the name.

'Yeah a cracking nickname ain't it? He reckoned he could solve any case in four days didn't he? Well he bit off more than he could chew with this one. He threw everything at it but with no joy. When the last bird showed up dead at the back of the Heron Trading Estate in Acton he interviewed everyone, and I mean everyone who had any business links to the place. That bleeding estate was enormous. He ended up carrying out over 7000 interviews, he had surveillance down Dukes Meadows for months, female coppers dressed as brasses with male coppers as back up. Can you imagine the cost of all those extra hours and the manpower? The whole bleeding operation was costing the Met a small fortune.'

'But if he figured out it was this Ireland bloke, how come the case it still classified as unsolved?'

'Du Rose came out in the press and said he had narrowed down the search to three people. Ireland committed suicide soon after near his gaff in Putney.'

'When was this?'

'March 1965.'

'So du Rose had a valid point then? Ireland kills himself and the murders stop.'

'Yeah, it was very bleeding convenient for four day Johnnie. Even the suicide note helped.'

Why do you say that?'

Buchanan sifted through his files and withdrew a sheet of paper.

'Here's a transcript.' He said sliding the paper across the desk.

"I can't stick it any longer.
It may be my fault but not all of it. I'm sorry Harry is a burden to you.
Give my love to the kid.
Farewell,
Jock
PS. To save you and the police looking for me I'll be in the garage."

Chambers read it through twice. 'It's the PS bit isn't it? I mean it does sound like a confession of sorts.'

'Yeah, at first glance it does. But it turns out he was due in court on a traffic violation that day and he expected a visit from the police when he was a no show. Harry was his brother who stayed with them. And the first part seems to be referring to his marital strife. Read it again from that perspective and it don't seem like a confession at all.'

Chambers read it again, nodded and pushed the paper back to Buchanan.

'And there's other anomalies.' Buchanan boasted.

'Like?'

'He'd only been at the trading estate job for a few weeks for starters. Du Rose believed it was someone who had access to storage facilities there. Some of the bodies had this fine misting of spray paint that had been isolated as coming from one of the sheds on the site. Plus he suggested it was someone who worked nights who could come and go from the estate unnoticed and could dump the bodies around London when the streets were quiet.'

'Seems logical in theory.' Chambers surmised.

Yeah, but then all this stuff came out later about du Rose. All I'm saying is there was a lot of bent coppers back then, and if you get my drift, there's been a lot of similar stuff come out about four day Johnnie.'

'I see. But the bit about having access to storage and working nights. It sounds plausible.'

'Yes but one huge problem was Ireland was back working in his hometown of Dundee, north of the border when O'Hara, his supposed last victim, went missing. He only got back to London the day before her body showed up.'

'It couldn't have been him then. Is that what you're saying?'

'It's possible he could have made a trip down. Murdered her, hid her body and gone back to Scotland. But in those days you're talking about a minimum of 12 hours driving each way. She went missing on a Monday night. If he did drive he couldn't have got back to his work on Tuesday morning, it's not physically possible. He isn't recorded as having taken time off from his work that week. I mean, he might've flown but the cost in those days to fly from Scotland to London would have been pretty prohibitive. And it begs the question why? I mean if he was living in London and bumping off these brasses on his doorstep like, why go to the all the trouble to fly down and back? Why not just get a target up there? It don't add up to me. It seems more convenient for du Rose to ignore the bits that don't fit and say he has solved it to much fanfare and backslapping.'

'But couldn't he have been responsible for the others and not that one? Or maybe he wasn't working alone.'

'The last bodies were all found with this fine misting of spray paint. Whoever did her did some of the others. I'm sure of that. As for the idea that he wasn't working alone, that he had an accomplice or that he was someone's partner. Yes, it's a possibility. But you know as well as I do it's a very rare breed of serial killer that works in tandem.'

'Who else is there that we can take a look at who was in the frame at the time?'

'Well you know what has always struck me as interesting?' Buchanan asked rhetorically. 'The locations. Not so much that they're often near the river. It's more than that. At the time the Met was divided into divisions and sub-divisions. Each body was found in a different sub-division. Now either the murderer got very lucky or he knew where these boundaries were.'

'What? Who would have known that kind of information.'

'That's the thing. Only a policeman would.'

'You're not suggesting it was someone on the force are you?'

'I'm just putting the facts out there as I find them.' Buchanan replied.

'I think we should leave it there for now. I have to speak with Barlow and let him know about the link between then and now. For the time being I'm not going to mention any of this to anyone else. And what you have just told me stays between us OK? I don't even want Jess in on this. It's potentially explosive. In the meantime can you dig out what you have on the link to it being a policeman? And Buck, I'm sure you don't need to be told, please tread carefully.'

Buchanan nodded and gathered up his files.

***

The initial meeting with Barlow had not gone well. After Chambers had left the interview room and his curtailed meeting with Buchanan and Tucker, he went back up to his floor and knocked on the door of his commanding officer.

'Come in.'

Chambers pushed open the door and poked his head round.

'John what a pleasant surprise.' Barlow beamed. 'I trust all is ship shape and you aren't coming in with a complaint about the staff I hope, are you?' The look he gave made Chambers think there was more than a grain of truth to the question.

'No sir. Far from it.'

'Less of the sir business. Sit yourself down. What's all this about then?'

'MIT have just brought in a suspect for the recent murder in Boston Manor.'

'Yes. I heard. What of it? Different department for me now John and you don't forget.'

Chambers took a deep breath. 'Sir, I mean Roger. I have reason to believe that the recent murder of Daniel Tompkins was in fact a copycat killing of one that took place 48 years ago and one that we are investigating as part of the broader scope of Operation Yetna.'

Whatever traces of joviality that Chambers had first encountered when he had entered the room had now completely disappeared.

Barlow took his time to respond. 'You said 48 years ago. Early sixties. Why are you looking so far back? The remit of this unit is supposed to be predominantly focussed on the seventies and eighties.' He let out a long sigh. 'How sure are you?'

'Almost certain.'

'How on earth have you made the jump from then until now?' Barlow seemed genuinely bemused. 'You're not even on the MIT team; you're not even in the same building as them. Hold on. It's that blasted Jess Tucker isn't it? I've seen you two cosied up in The Brewery Tap on more than one occasion on a Friday night. Now I come to think of it, I can't recall seeing you with another detective from the MIT. It simply must be her.'

'I'd rather not say if that's OK Roger. But I have been working closely with Buck and he has an encyclopaedic knowledge of the old cases and in particular this one. It was him that pointed out the similarities.'

'Cases? What cases?'

'You know about the "Hammersmith Nudes"?'

'Oh Christ. Is this that effing Jack the Stripper mess? God help us if it is. You know if the press get hold of this it will be a bloody PR disaster. What was it? Seven, eight unsolved murders in the area? It's always struck me as a miracle no one has ever said anything sooner. Bloody disgrace the way the case was handled then by all accounts.' Barlow stopped speaking and started picking at the varnish on the edge of his desk. 'But basically we don't have the manpower to open this one up again.'

'I'm not sure we have a choice. What we've put together shows a copycat killer is out there and is likely to strike again, and probably multiple times.'

Chambers watched the Chief Inspector who seemed to have momentarily forgotten Chambers was in the room. Eventually he snapped out of his stupor and rubbed his eyes with the heels of his palms. 'I don't know what in hell's name our vaunted leader McKinley will make of this. Who knows about this possible link exactly?'

'Buck and me.'

'And Jess?'

Chambers nodded slightly, feeling guilty for acknowledging her part.

'OK let's keep it that way for now. I'll talk to McKinley. How long have you three been working on the connection?'

Before Chambers had a chance to answer, Barlow continued. 'In fact, I don't want to know. At the end of the day I'm sure the less I know about all of this the better, for now anyway. Tell the others to keep schtum. Basically let's see what comes of this suspect and I'll work it into the conversation with McKinley when I see her later on. I'll bring you up to speed as soon as I can. That'll be all John.' Barlow sounded exasperated. Chambers guess was Barlow would be trying to factor in the impact on his imminent retirement.

Chambers took his leave. He was surprised how Barlow had reacted. Where was the man who was desperate to clear up the old cases? Or was it something to do specifically with this one? There seemed to be more questions than answers at this stage. It would be interesting to see what the Detective Chief Superintendent's take on it all would be and what the fallout would mean for the both the MIT and Cold Case units.

***

Chapter 15.

Why green nets?

Friday, 25th May 2012 – 9:07am

Chambers had resumed his jog/walk to work as the inclement weather of the past week had given way to something mildly more hospitable. What he hadn't been expecting on his arrival at the office was to see Chad, although he was sometimes in on a Friday it wasn't common.

'Alright,' the old man said gruffly without looking round. There was no one else present.

'Morning Chad.'

'Oh it's you.' He mumbled something that Chambers couldn't quite catch before slowly rotating his chair.

'Hey, I got a riddle for you.'

Chambers rolled his eyes as he made his way to his desk; he had his back to him until he sat down. Feigning interest he said, 'come on then. Let's have it.'

'What's got two legs, one wheel, about 27 teeth and is red all over.'

Genuinely puzzled, Chambers mind was blank. He flicked on his PC and ummed and aahed for a bit.

'You want a clue?' Forster said as if he was talking down to a child.

'Sure thing.' Chambers said, ignoring the tone of the comment, as he opened his email and browser.

'Takes its meals through a straw.'

Chambers was non-plussed and looked up from his screen at Forster who was sitting looking mightily pleased with himself.

'I've no idea. Put me out of my misery.'

The old man started his ugly laugh. It sounded like this throat was choked with phlegm. 'The answer is an Irish bird.'

'An Irish bird with one wheel? I don'…' Chambers tapered off.

'Your current ride. Although I doubt you or her will be much in the saddle for a while.'

'Chambers jumped to his feet. 'You sick fuck. What's wrong with you?' He demanded. The door opened and Pierce and Polk came in.

Chambers ignored them. 'I asked you a fucking question! What is your problem? If I find out Jess has been hurt in any way and you are sitting up here taking the piss I will fucking kill you.' Chambers stormed out past the two men and made his way down the stairs to the front desk. He could feel the veins in his temples thumping. It was a miracle he hadn't gone and laid out the facetious old bastard with one punch. He certainly had it coming and if it wasn't Chambers there was a queue of other people waiting to do it, he was quite sure of that.

There was a young uniformed officer on the desk that he didn't recognise.

'Have you seen Jess Tucker this morning?' Chambers demanded.

The young officer looked a bit taken aback at the aggressive manner in which he was being questioned.

'Er, no. Not yet.'

THE CHARRED FOREST MURDERS

'Do you know if she is OK?' He demanded acidly.

'Let me call her desk for you.' The officer replied pleased he had something to do to divert the attention of visibly angry detective standing in front of him.

Chambers was standing close enough to hear the ringing tone that was answered on the fifth beep by a man's voice although he couldn't hear what the answers to the young policeman's enquires were. After a minute the desk officer hung up.

'Appears she won't be in today. Seems she had an accident on her bike last night. Sideswiped by a car. That's what DC Black says anyway. She was in West Mid hospital last night but he thinks she will be sent home today at some point.'

Chambers thanked him, his rage turning to concern over his injured colleague. Also the realisation of what he had just said to Forster in front of witnesses was starting to dawn on him. And not just any witnesses, one of them was Forster's nephew. Chambers needed to get out of the station. As he opened the front door and walked down the steps he saw Buchanan coming the other way.

'Leaving already?' Buchanan said with a grin as he removed his headphones.

'No, just had a bit of a run in with Chad. Seems like Jess has had an accident and the old prick seems to think it's funny.'

'John, easy mate. You mustn't let the old fella get a rise out of you. That'll give him a right old buzz this morning knowing he's got the better of you. Do you know what's happened to the bird?'

'I'm going to try and call her now.'

'Alright you do that. I'll go up and sort things out up there. He listens to me. At least I think he does.'

'Cheers Buck.' Chambers said moving away towards the kerb and looking for a break in the traffic before he crossed towards

Goddards Removals and Storage facility on the other corner of the Half acre. He stopped on the opposite side in the shade and dialled Tucker's number. It rang out and went to her voicemail. He left a short message asking if she was OK and to call him when possible. Then he sent her a text message saying pretty much the same thing.

   Chambers was still seething at Forster and decided to walk along the High Street towards the Grand Union Canal and take the opportunity to calm himself down before he returned to the station. The time it took him to make the five-minute walk showed him another side of this often forgotten corner of West London. The one thing that he had noticed when he had ventured out before was the sheer number of pubs that seemed to be dotted on every corner. Up along the High Road from The Beehive was The Magpie and Crown and just beyond that The Six Bells. Back on the left was the team's new local The Brewery Tap, while tucked up behind the Brentford Magistrates' Court was the Weir Bar that Chambers discovered by accident when he veered right up Market Lane. He had taken the impromptu turn as the facades presented to him along the High Street were making him more miserable the further he travelled. The dismal looking greasy spoons and bargain shops seemed to reflect the equally worn out and run down countenance and appearance of the people he passed loitering about the wide pavement. The turn brought him to another part of Brentford. This was like the developments taking place at nearby Kew Bridge. New, modern looking apartment blocks overlooking the calm waters of the Brent river and seemingly miles away from the grim offerings to be found on the nearby High Street. He doubted the developers would be including a photograph of the depressing High Street in their promotional material, more than likely focussing on the nearby Kew Gardens, Syon Park and the Thames and Brent rivers. Chambers turned left at the pub and found himself at an open expanse of water near a recently developed area grandly entitled 'The Island'.

THE CHARRED FOREST MURDERS

Near here, he found a series of wrought iron benches overlooking the water and where more apartments were getting built on either side of the stretch of the River Brent where it had been canalised to make it wider and more easily navigable. Chambers sat and slowly began to relax as he watched an old couple further along the bench feeding bread to a variety of waterfowl including imposing white swans, graceful Canada geese, pale brown and grey Egyptian geese, red-crested pochards with their distinctive red bills and orange heads and the more common mallards with their dark, metallic-green heads and yellow bills. A slight vibration in his pocket alerted him to an incoming message. It was a reply from Tucker.

'Thx 4 asking. Crashed on a training ride. Lucky. Only Broken jaw. Lost a few teeth, nothing else broken. Cut and bruised. Will b back in the office next week.'

Only a broken jaw? Chambers had to respect her optimism when she considered herself lucky with those injuries. He texted back. *'Take your time and get some rest. Are you at hospital or home?'*

'Home. U no the address! Don't disappoint.'

When he'd left her place a few weeks before he had been too hungover to take much notice of the house number. He had just been desperate to slip away before she returned. But he was confident he could find it again if he had to. He was caught in two minds about going round to see her to make sure she was OK or heading back into the toxic environment that his office had become. Also he was keen to find out more about the Hungarian suspect that MIT had brought in a couple of days before. Information available to those out of the loop was proving elusive. But had she meant come round? Maybe she just meant send a card or something? As usual recently when it came to women he had no idea of what he was supposed to do. In the end, Chambers decided to face the music and head back to the office rather than grab a cab to see Tucker. But before he went back he decided to stay in his new peaceful location a little while longer.

Despite the occasional noise from the construction of the apartments the scene itself was quiet and relaxing. The sun had poked through from behind a solid bank of grey cloud and for a while he felt a world away from his job, the station and the growing strain he was feeling about almost everything. Whatever had happened since he'd been in Hong Kong, his life felt more and more like it was spinning out of control. There'd been the trouble in Scotland and his nighttime flit to Africa where he'd run into even more trouble. The car crash, the police harassment, the murder charge. Ever since the traffic accident he'd begun to feel a growing sense of paranoia. In addition he was finding it harder and harder to control his temper. He began to wonder whether he had received some kind of brain injury. The demotion at work, the loss of Li had come at a time when he desperately needed consolidation in familiarity. Not this. The strain was becoming too much. He had seen a body on the riverbank at Chiswick and he hadn't even batted an eyelid. That wasn't right, surely. Now he had just had a meltdown at Forster in front of witnesses. Who knew where that might lead? He was starting to think he needed a break, not just a holiday but also maybe, a change of careers. But he'd been with the Met over 20 years, what else did he know? One thing was for sure – he couldn't go on like this, it would lead to a breakdown or worse if Forster kept provoking him.

***

It was with some trepidation that he opened the office door. About half an hour had passed since his contretemps with Forster and he was relieved to see the old man wasn't in the office. Pierce and Polk stopped their banter when they saw him come in and both appeared to be suddenly very interested in items on their respective screens. Hayes and Adams were not at their desks, the pair of them were spending most of their time on door-to-door work or up at Ealing police station.

THE CHARRED FOREST MURDERS

As soon as Chambers sat down he saw a new email come in. It was from Buchanan.

'Heads up. Chad's gone home. Said he had a bad turn. He was grumbling about your verbal assault and how you'd overstepped the mark and how sick it had made him. He was making threats to take it to Roge, and the two idiots you see in front of you were egging him on. It's all a game I know the old fox too well. He's just trying to make your life difficult. That's all he's got left. Sad bastard. I just told him to get some rest and come back Monday.'

Chambers nodded but didn't say anything or reply to the email, he just deleted it. Hopefully Chad would let it lie. For now Chambers had other things to think about. Li for one, and the second was how he could keep tabs on the ongoing MIT investigation now that Tucker was recuperating at home. That reminded him. He Googled Interflora and jotted down the number of a local florist. He would send her flowers once he got her exact address. It would take a little delicate investigation to glean the information from a colleague of hers in the MIT.

***

Monday 28th May 2012 – 9:46am

Chambers arrived at his customary time on a Monday morning. Buchanan, Pierce and Hayes were already in. Automatically he checked Forster's desk, the old guy wasn't there. Chambers brief sense of relief was tempered when he noticed a steaming mug sitting by the keyboard. His gaze shifted to the whiteboard and he cringed. Another of Forster's ridiculous quizzes was scrawled on the board.

'Morning all.' Chambers announced generally to the room, then turning to Pierce he asked 'Paul, where's Russell this morning?'

'Off sick. Messaged me to say he got a concussion at football yesterday.' At the same time he said this he made a drinking gesture with his right arm and turned back to his PC.

Chambers mood hadn't been the best when he arrived. It was Monday morning which always meant a run-in with the belligerent Forster, Li was still missing with scant information on where she might be; Tucker was smashed up which was a major set back for his investigation into the Jack the Stripper case and now Polk was on yet another sick day on a Monday. It was his fourth in eight weeks since Chambers had joined the team. Until now Chambers had turned a blind eye, hoping the wayward young detective would appreciate his leniency but enough was enough.

Sitting down heavily at his desk, he flicked his PC on and as it was booting up he looked over at the latest and now inevitable Monday morning conundrum courtesy of Forster.

2+3=8
3+7=27
4+5=32
5+8=60
6+7=72
7+8=??

Solve it.

Chambers was pleased to see it was a maths puzzle with no obvious inference to any of the team either absent or present or at least as far as his non-mathematical brain could work out. Hopefully the old man had got the message and decided to wind his neck in.

Opening his email he sifted through the usual admin messages and routine circulars. The latest email was from Barlow at 9:46am. As Chambers opened the email, the office door opened simultaneously and in came Forster. The heavy set man stopped briefly and stared at Chambers. The familiar scowl remained in place, and for several seconds the pair stared at each other before Forster plodded slowly back to his desk.

The email was brief. Simply asking for Chambers to come to Barlow's office when he had a moment. Seizing the opportunity to put himself anywhere that was away from the poisonous influence of the old man, Chambers made his way down the corridor to Barlow's office, rapping his knuckles on the door.

'Enter.' A voice came from inside.

'Morning Roger. How's things?'

A brief smile flashed across the Chief Inspector's face before his features settled into a frown. 'John, come in, come in. Please take a seat.' He sounded stiff and formal.

'I'm hoping you've got some positive news for me regarding the suspect and our case. How did the Super take it?' Chambers asked.

Barlow looked non-plussed for a moment. 'Oh that? Yes, well, hmmm. We can get onto that in a moment. That's not why I've asked you in here this morning.'

Barlow paused and when it became clear he wasn't going to add anything Chambers eventually said something, 'OK. So what's this about?' He couldn't think there were any reports on the team's current investigations he had failed to send the previous Friday.

'How should I put this? Basically it's a little awkward. I've just had one of your team in here making an official complaint against you.'

Chambers felt an immediate rush of blood to the head. That arsehole Forster. No wonder the time he had returned to the office coincided with the time of Barlow's email. 'It's Chad isn't it?' Chambers almost shouted, struggling to maintain his composure.

'Now hold your horses John. I think we should be focussing on the seriousness of the allegation and not who made it for the moment. When all is said and done, it's been alleged you threatened to kill a colleague and in front of witnesses too.'

'This is absolutely ridiculous. Chad was taking the piss out of Jess's accident and I won't stand for it.'

'Jess Tucker, I see, that's interesting.'

'No, I don't think you do actually.' Chambers could feel the blood pumping in his ears. 'I won't stand for any of my team or any colleague to be talked about in the despicable manner in which he spoke about Jess. She could've been killed and that old dick is in there taking the piss. I simply won't have it.'

'But John, he's alleging you threatened to kill him.'

'He's a cancerous, conniving, shit of a man.'

'Oh John, that's pretty insensitive, considering his illness. You're trying to portray this old man as something akin to the devil, it's not on.'

Chambers regretted his choice of wording, but it was true. Forster appeared to have no reason for coming to the office other than to undermine the work that the majority of the team were trying to complete. He took a few deep breaths and tried to regain his composure.

'I'm not taking sides here John, you understand that? But I simply need to get to the bottom of this. Basically I have to take his allegations seriously and let me reiterate, I need to follow procedures. Now did you make the threat or didn't you?'

Chambers nodded. 'It was a poor choice on my part,' he admitted, 'I lost it. At that point I didn't know Jess had been in an accident and what Chad hinted at it sounded very severe.'

'How is she?' Barlow asked.

THE CHARRED FOREST MURDERS

'Broken jaw, lost some teeth. Lucky to be alive from what I can gather. She had a bike accident.'

'I see. I see.' Barlow scribbled something on his notepad.

'So what now?' Chambers asked.

'As I just said to you. This is a very serious allegation and off the record you have just admitted to making the threat. My first thought is to get Chad in here and see if we can sort this out man to man.' He shook his head.

'Or?' Chambers prompted, he was still seething.

'Or if he decides he wants to pursue a case it will need to be investigated internally and it could end up in a suspension.'

Chambers sat for a moment looking stunned at how the whole affair had been turned on its head. After some time he said, 'you know what Roger?'

'What?'

'I quit.'

Barlow looked flustered. 'John. What? Please. This is no time for rash decisions. We have mechanisms in place. We can talk to Chad and sort this out amicably I'm sure.'

'No, my mind is made up. I've been thinking about this for a while and this is the final straw. I'm through with the Met. I'll go back and write up an official 728 resignation form now and have it on your desk, as you're my line manager, later this morning. Then I'm going to go home.'

'John you can't simply get up and walk out.'

'Really? Will you try and restrain me? Tie me to my chair?' Chambers said sarcastically. 'When you pass my 728 form to McKinley you can tell her I've gone home on sick leave for a week and if she needs to know more I'm sure you're more than well versed in coming up with a load of crap to appease her.'

'You mean you will be back in next week to work notice?' Barlow asked incredulously.

'Probably. Let's see shall we?' Chambers got up and opened the door.

'John.' Barlow called after him. 'Please, keep this quiet for now. I'll cover for you with the team. Just have a few days to think about it. Please don't do anything stupid. No rash decisions. We can discuss it when you cool off.'

Chambers closed the door firmly behind him and went back to the office and sat down at his desk. He needed to find the right form from the HR drive on the network. After a few minutes searching he found it and printed it to the office PC. As he walked over to the printer to collect it he saw someone had solved the puzzle.

2+3=8
3+7=27
4+5=32
5+8=60
6+7=72
7+8=??

Solve it.

Underneath in handwriting unfamiliar to him was written:

98

(a*(a+b))-a

It brought a flicker of a smile to his face. Anything that annoyed the old man could only be a good thing. Once he had filled out the form, he slipped it in an envelope, picked up his jacket and sports bag and stood up. Leaning forward he switched off his PC and turned and walked back out off the office without acknowledging any of the team, although he was sure he could feel Forster's beady eyes watching him.

***

Chapter 16.

Mule kazoos

Monday, 4th June 2012 – 9:29am

A week had passed since Chambers had slipped the envelope containing his resignation letter under Barlow's door, in which time he had spent the week moping about at home watching Jeremy Kyle and other car crash daytime TV that had done little to improve his miserable mood. He had thought about slipping off to one of the local pubs to soften the edges of reality, make time disappear, but he dismissed the idea as detrimental to his fragile mental and physical health. Somewhere in the back of his mind he knew it would only make matters worse. He cut himself off from all contact with the outside world, friends and family. The only person he saw was the bloke who ran the local convenience store on the Goldhawk Road. His time had been spent half in regret at his spontaneous action and half in nervous excitement that he had done the right thing and about what the future may hold.

He hadn't heard anything from Barlow that caused him to feel distinctly uneasy. On the Wednesday he had received a text from Tucker saying she was back at work and that Buchanan had told her that he was off sick for the week. For a few minutes after her message, he had wanted to call her and ask her what was happening with the suspect they had picked up the week before. But in the end he decided it was none of his business anymore. He had resigned and now just had to work out his four-week notice period. His last day would be Friday, 22nd June, and it was probably a good idea to start looking for another job. The only problem was he had no idea of what he wanted to do.

Eventually the time came to return to the office and the week off had only added to Chambers' sense of apprehension at what he might be facing on his return. He could barely get out of bed on the morning he was due back and seriously considered calling HR to prolong the inevitable. Eventually he struggled downstairs and caught the bus avoiding eye contact with anyone. Somehow he found the mental fortitude to enter the station and pulled himself together to put on a brave face when he saw his colleagues. Arriving at his usual Monday time he found it was business as usual. There was, surprisingly, a full team busy at work and the now customary quiz question on the board from Forster. Chambers nodded to Adams and Hayes who looked up in his direction, both looking slightly surprised, as he entered the others didn't seem to notice or care.

Turning on his PC he instinctively looked towards the board and Forster's new challenge. This time it took the form of a riddle scribbled in the old man's ugly handwriting on the whiteboard in a green marker pen.

A dark winter's night – a Brentford detective is at home. All of a sudden a snowball comes crashing through his window. The detective got up and looked out the window just in time to see three kids who were brothers run around the corner. Their names were John Smith, Mark Smith and Paul Smith. The next day the detective finds a note on his door that read –

? Smith.

He broke your window.

According to the evidence, which of the three Smith brothers should the detective question about the incident?

Chambers, as usual, didn't have a clue. He opened his email and saw over 100 new mails in his inbox. He sorted quickly through the admin and circulars and was able to delete more than 70% of them without opening any of them. There were a few from Buchanan and Tucker that seemed to be a conversation he was CC'd on. One from Dr Bhanji and another that caught his eye was from Brian Tang in Hong Kong. Li was his priority so naturally he opened this one first; it was dated Thursday, 31st May.

'John,

Thanks for your mail. I have the ink and paper test reports. The original documents are in Traditional Chinese so I didn't attach. In summary, the envelope has been traced to a batch from a stationary company based in Savannakhet, Laos. The ink sample comes from a standard Bic pen. Not much to go on and so far our investigations here are at a dead end. Anything you can share on this would be very helpful.

Brian'

Chambers drummed his fingers on the desk. There was the Laos connection again. It couldn't be coincidence. But the envelope was postmarked Hong Kong. Either Li was in Laos or Shen had gone out of his way to put evidence in the photograph that would lead the investigation down the wrong path. The ink told him nothing. At some point he was going to have to make the call and head East. What confused him was why after the first clue that Shen had sent, had the trail gone cold? If he wanted to make a game of this why hadn't he been back in touch? Chambers could think of no way to get in touch with Shen.

Chambers replied to Tang thanking him for the assistance and enquiring as to whether any more mail had arrived for him. Then he opened the email from Dr Bhanji who was suggesting a date of Monday, 19th June for the presentation to his staff. For a while Chambers considered cancelling it. The presentation would take place in his last week at work and would be of little use to him. But he relented thinking that at least Buchanan,

Adams and Hayes might gain something from it, even if the others were unlikely to be particularly interested.

That left him with the emails from Buchanan and Tucker. The ones from Tucker came under two different titles. One was clearly the email chain conversation with Buchanan while the others had titles 'Where are you?', 'Where are you?1', Where are you?2' and on and on.

He looked at these ones in the order they were sent and the tone had started off friendly enough. Just giving him a head's up on her injuries and that she was back at work, and over the five emails the tone got less affable and more irritated. The last one demanding him to respond and let her know that at least he was safe.

Chambers flicked an email to her.

'All good. Back in office now. Free to talk. Will check your con with Buck now.'

He moved on to look through the email conversation that he'd missed from the week before. The emails began on Wednesday with Tucker's return to the office. She was bringing them up to speed. The original suspect, Julius Stahel, the Hungarian van driver had been released without charge when he provided an airtight alibi that he was in Budapest at the time visiting his family. Stahel had been released on the 25th May. The investigation had moved on swiftly though and on the 28th May – Julius Stahel's brother, Godfrey, had been brought in for questioning.

Despite Chambers resolute feeling that he was no longer involved in the two cases, he was intrigued as to how this Godfrey Stahel character linked the two cases together. Chambers flicked through the other mails. The one's from Buchanan were characteristically short. On the previous Friday, Tucker had emailed to say Chiswick police had arrested a man for the murder of Thomas Marshall at Chiswick Mall. Tucker had included the suspect's name. A Polish man by the name of Samuel Zook. How could this be? It clearly had to be a mistake. Either the Brentford or the Chiswick MIT had made an error. At this stage Chambers was favouring the mistake to have come from Chiswick. The Brentford MIT had a number plate of a vehicle seen at the site the body was discovered. But he also knew he was only receiving scant information.

He fired off an email to Tucker and Buchanan requesting an immediate meeting in their usual room. Without waiting for a response he grabbed his files pertaining to the Stripper case and made his way to the door. Halfway there he turned sharply to the whiteboard picked up a blue marker pen and wrote – "Mark". Followed by the letters NFO just for good measure. Then he turned smartly on his heel, a broad smile across his face as he walked purposefully towards the door, not waiting to see Forster's response to his solving of the old man's riddle.

Buchanan wasn't long in entering the room after Chambers.

'All OK guv? You've been out of radio contact for a week. I was starting to fear the worst.'

'You've not heard?'

'There's been a bit of banter in the office that that you were suspended due to the incident with Chad the other week, but it has been mostly from Tweedledee and Tweedledum so I've not given it too much credence. Don't go telling me it's true. Surely Roger's not that bleeding daft. Is he?'

Chambers raised his eyebrows and let out a long sigh.

'It's worse. I ...' He broke off as the door opened and Tucker came in.

Chambers was shocked by her appearance. It was 10 days since her accident but the left side of her face was still swollen, an ugly greenish-purple bruise and several deep scratches marked the side of her face.

'OK, done staring?' Tucker said through clenched teeth. 'Get it all out of your system now.' She sat down and used her fingers to pull her lips apart so they could both get a good look at the wiring that had been put in to help her jaw knit back together.

'Shit.' Buchanan said. 'Looks painful.'

Tucker just opened her eyes wide and stared back at him.

'Sorry Jess.' Was all Chambers could muster.

'So you bloody should be. Not coming to visit me.' She feigned being hurt.

Chambers shook his head. 'I'm sorry,' he mumbled again.

'I know just what you need.' Buchanan said with a smile.

'Tea? Coffee? Something stronger?' Tucker responded. 'Any of those would be great.'

'No I think you need an Orville.'

'What? Is that some bloody rhyming slang for something?' She looked nonplussed.

'Not at all. You know Orville. Keith Harris and Orville! A dummy, cos you're doing a bloody good impression of a ventriloquist.' He started laughing much to the chagrin of Tucker. Chambers joined in. He couldn't help himself. It felt like a long time since he'd had a laugh, even if it was at poor Tucker's expense.

'Go on you bastards. Get it out of your systems. Have a good laugh. I just hope when one of you has an accident I'm on hand to point and laugh at your misfortune. So I will.'

'I'm sorry Jess. I really am. Too good an opportunity to pass though. I'll go and fetch you a coffee now.' Buchanan was up and out of the chair in an instant. 'Guv?'

'Cheers Buck, yeah a coffee would be great.' Chambers said, an uneasy feeling settling over him as he realised this was the first time he'd been alone with her since their impromptu night together.

When Buchanan left the room, Tucker turned to him. 'What the feck's been going on? Where have you been? Buck's saying there's rumours flying about that you got suspended.'

'I had a run in with Chad. Said a few things I ought not to have said.' He didn't want to tell her the specifics right at this juncture.

'Why didn't you reply to my emails?' She sounded mightily pissed off.

'I don't have access to work emails at home.'

'What about the messages I sent? Don't bloody tell me you left your phone here as well.'

'No' Chambers shook his head in embarrassment. 'I just needed a bit of time to myself.' He changed topic. 'Jess I want to apologise for my behaviour towards you recently, it has been very disrespectful. I'm sorry about everything the other night.'

Tucker leaned back and gave him a quizzical look. 'You big eejit!' She laughed loudly. 'Is that what all this shite is about? I bet you don't know even know what happened do you? I knew you were drunk but …' she tailed off.

'I don't recall a lot. But when I woke up you weren't there.'

'John, you were drunk, you demanded to walk me home and then invited yourself in for a nightcap. Luckily you passed out in the spare room. When I came back from my run you had slunk off and have been avoiding me ever since.' She almost laughed, but her wired jaw prevented her. 'I bet you think we slept together don't you? Good to see you still have a sense of humour. Chance would be a fine thing.'

'You mean ...' he tailed off. Chambers nodded an overwhelming sense of relief and shame washed over him simultaneously. 'I thought ...' He stuttered.

'More fool you then. Explains why you've been skulking about like some bloody embarrassed teenager. Act like the man you are supposed to be. What's up with you?'

'Nothing.' Chambers replied testily.

She shook her head. 'For Christ's sake John, we're up to our necks in a bloody big murder investigation, in case you've forgotten.' She said acidly.

'No Jess,' Chambers corrected her, 'you are.'

'Is this what all this moping has been about? All this feeling sorry for yourself? Is your nose out of joint cos your not the lead investigator on this? I asked you the first time we met if you are level headed or if you're a bloody glory seeker and now I know what you really are.' She shook her head. 'Or is it that I didn't give you any credit for the CCTV on the bus? Poor little diddums.'

'No not at all. I've been out of sorts for a while. This crap with Chad was the final straw.'

'Final straw? What do you mean?' She looked confused.

Chambers hesitated, fiddling about with the corner of one of the old files.

'John?' She demanded.

'I've quit. As of the 25th of May. I'm working my four-week notice now. My last day is 22nd of this month.'

'John, are you shitting me? What the hell are you playing at?'

The door swung open and Buchanan came in carrying a tray of cups.

'Buck do you know about this?' She turned to face Buchanan.

THE CHARRED FOREST MURDERS

'Hold up.' Buchanan replied placing the tray on the table. 'Know about what?'

'That John's bloody resigned.'

Buchanan looked genuinely shocked as he turned to stare at Chambers, who in turn could do little else than raise his palms to the sky and give an awkward smile.

'For fuck's sake.' Was all Buchanan said as he retook his seat. 'Is there any point you being in here then? I mean why did you even call this meeting? Just to announce that you quit? Well now you've done it can we all sod off back to work?'

'Yes I've quit. But it doesn't mean to say I'm not committed to what's going on here.' Chambers sat up straight in his chair. 'I'm serious. I'm going to give it everything before I go. Buck what did you find out about the old cases and the link to it being a copper?'

Buchanan didn't answer immediately, he just looked at his clenched fists on the desk. Eventually he relaxed his hands and looked up at Tucker then back at Chambers, raising his eyebrows. 'You sure guv? Right now? That's what you want?' He asked.

Chambers cottoned on quickly, he had forgotten he wanted Tucker kept out of it, but now the cat was out of the bag he might as well continue. It was unlikely that Tucker would be involved in anything or connected with the old guard. He nodded his assent.

'Right, well I'm still digging about. I need to get access to the HR files from those days, it's a bit before my time. There were apparently a couple of coppers who were in the frame. One was a detective who was suspected by a colleague of du Rose. A senior copper name of Detective Superintendent Baldock had his suspicions that it was a former copper. This alleged policeman had been kicked out of the force in the early 1960s. Seems he had an accident early in his career when he'd got knocked out. From that time, according to colleagues, he started acting strangely. Things went missing from stations he worked at, so he got moved about, caused him to feel more isolated and bitter. Over time his crimes escalated to burglarising houses on his beat. He would then sabotage the investigations of his fellow officers by hiding evidence.'

'What was his name?'

'That's the problem. I can't find it anywhere in any file. But Baldock mentions the bloke worked in West London stations, so I'm hoping there will be an HR file on him somewhere. But it shows he would have been familiar with the subdivisions of the area. The theory is that he killed the girls to humiliate his former colleagues as they couldn't solve it cos he was interfering with the evidence and he knew the subdivisions would cause a lot of problems as the stations didn't communicate too well back then. But this bloke was out of the force by 1963, so I'm not sure about how he would have got the inside track into the investigation for the later murders.'

'It's possible he could have done all of them. Just adapted his methods.'

'Exactly. After he left the force he moved away down the coast somewhere. He was a car salesman so it gave him plenty of chance to be driving around London.'

Tucker interjected. 'But then why did he stop?'

'Good question. Could have been that there was such a big police presence by early '65. You see du Rose had flooded the streets with beat coppers, female police officers dressed as brasses. Our man might still have had contacts in the Met who he could have got that info from. Also the police sub districts changed in April 1965, which could have been a factor, as he would have been out of the loop by then. It's not unknown for serial killers to stop as well. Look at Dennis Rader.'

'Who the hell is Rader?' Asked Chambers.

THE CHARRED FOREST MURDERS

'He was the BTK killer in the US in the seventies.' Buchanan said as if that was enough of an explanation.

Tucker looked at Chambers who shrugged.

'BTK?'

'That was his moniker. Blind. Torture. Kill. It was his signature like. He used to tease the local police with letters about the murders. He killed 10 people. Started with four in '74, had a break of a few years, couple more in '77, a hiatus until '85 and '86, then another break, then he did another in '91. He only got caught cos he started his letter writing again in 2004. He made some mistakes and forensics had made some advances. He included a floppy disk with one of his letters and they could trace it via the metadata in the Microsoft Word document.'

'I hope you don't mind me saying Buck, but you appear to have a bit of a morbid fascination with serial killers.' Tucker said. She had meant to smile to soften the accusation but her wired jaw meant the grin was more of a grimace.

Buchanan chuckled. 'We've all got hobbies and interests ain't we? I guess mine is serial killers. This guy Rader, he worked for a home security company. He installed alarms as a part of his job, and many of his clients had booked the company to stop this crazy BTK from ever entering their homes, unaware that it was the BTK himself that was installing them. He was a devout Christian and cub scout leader. Bloody frightening isn't it?' Buchanan stopped to take a sip of his coffee before continuing. 'But my point is that he stopped killing, sometimes for a few years but when they caught him he hadn't killed in 13 years. People's situations change. How do we know that this copper wasn't suffering from a change brought on by the head injury, but he might have recovered. His situation might have changed or maybe he was just that smart he knew when to get out.'

'You're right Buck, the thing is we just don't know. Can you keep digging see if you can get a name for this guy. You say he moved away?'

'Sure, I'll see what I can find. I'm sure it was along the coast somewhere.'

'Great, let's see if we can get an address and we'll go and pay him a visit.'

'If he's still alive that is.' Tucker added.

'True.' Chambers nodded. 'Jess what's going on with your case. I see from you emails that your original suspect was released and his brother brought in.'

'That's right. Julius Stahel was released when he provided an alibi. Took us a couple of days to get hold of his brother Godfrey. He had access to the van when his brother was in Hungary.' Tucker explained.

'You charged him yet?' Asked Buchanan.

'Hopefully in the next day or so. Just working with the CPS now to finalise a few details.'

'Has he confessed?' Chambers prompted.

'No, but he's said a few things. He's not the sharpest knife in the drawer. At this stage he is saying he went into a bar in the city on the Saturday night and that's where he met Tompkins. His English is pretty bad and he's reluctant to say much. So it's been slow to get anything from him even with a translator.'

'So what was it? A bar fight that escalated?'

'We're not sure at this stage. We've interviewed a few people up at the bar. They met in a place called Comptons of Soho.'

The name rang a bell with Chambers. He had been based in Chinatown just around the corner. The original murder case that took him to Hong Kong had taken place in a nearby road,

Rupert Street just off Shaftesbury Avenue. 'That's on Old Compton Street? It's a gay bar isn't it?'

Tucker's eyes flashed. 'Anything you want to share?'

'Yeah guv, you're secret's safe with us. We won't tell anyone outside these four walls.' Buchanan sniggered.

'Bugger off you two. I used to work around the corner, that's all.'

Tucker continued. 'Yes it is a gay bar. No one from the bar recalls any incidents that night. Thing is, it's packed with skinheads and Godfrey is a skinhead so he would have blended in. He says he's not gay and he didn't know it was a gay bar.'

'Is he a Neo-Nazi?' Chambers asked, trying to think of whether it was possible that Stahel had been drawn to the place thinking it was a hotbed of Nazi sympathisers and got himself mixed up in a completely different scene entirely. He added. 'Maybe he had been approached by Tompkins in the bar and that had been the catalyst for what happened later.'

'He denies he's a Nazi and he's got no tattoos or literature at his brother's flat that would back that up. But it's a possibility he was in there by mistake.'

'Would be good to get a look at the CCTV of that night.'

'Hutchinson's already on it.' Tucker said abruptly.

Chambers felt suitably rebuked. As if Tucker was warning him to stay within the bounds of his own investigation. He moved swiftly on. 'OK. What about this email on Friday? The arrest of this bloke for the Chiswick murder.'

'I got a call from my mate Pete at the Chiswick station late in the day on Friday. He mentioned they had picked up a Polish guy, Sam Zook, for the murder of Tom Marshall, the one you saw at the Mall.'

'Are they sure? Is it an arrest or just someone in for questioning?'

'He seemed pretty confident. One of the security cameras at the nearby apartments that face the river caught it all on tape. He's pretty sure this is their man. Apparently they have footage of him over two days. Coming over by boat from the other bank and dropping the body off. Then coming back on the same boat the following morning at dawn and repositioning the body.'

'But how good is the footage?' Asked Buchanan. I mean it's some distance from the nearest flat to the water's edge, plus it would have been almost dark. Seems a bit far fetched to me.'

'Buck, I don't know.' Snapped Tucker. 'I'm just the messenger. I'm only telling you what he told me. Maybe he had on some distinctive clothing. Who knows?'

'The problem is,' Chambers began, 'what do a Polish bloke and a Hungarian have in common and what's the link back to our murders from the sixties? I just don't see the connection.'

Eventually Buchanan spoke up. 'Jess, have you checked out with your mate Pete whether this Marshall guy was gay? I think it might be an angle worth looking at. I recall you saying some of the victims lived alone and we've got proof that Tompkins was in a gay bar in town. Could be something in it.'

'I don't think they have. I'll call him after this and it's probably worth us doing a bit of digging into the victim at Hammersmith and Kew as well. You might be on to something there Buck. I just think we need to tread carefully on the links to the current Brentford case and the old one for now.'

'Yes but we need to find a link between Stahel and Zook. There has to be one. Are they working together. What do we know about their pasts?'

'I can't speak for Zook. I mean I can try and find something about him from Pete at Chiswick. But as for Stahel. His immigration records indicate that he came to the UK last year.

He's been living with his brother up in Edgware. We've not been able to find any record of where he's been working but he's probably been here doing some cash in hand stuff.'

'OK, well for now we know what we have to do. Jess, get on to Pete and see what you can find out about Zook. Buck, keep digging on this ex-copper. Let's see what if anything is in it. I'll look into the backgrounds of the other victims Burr and Barkley see if there's any connection between them.'

'John.' Tucker said.

'Yes?'

'Are you really committed to this? I mean you've resigned right? I'm not sure I want to risk my career helping out on this and possibly jeopardising my career if it gets found out and you leaving us in three weeks' time.'

'Jess. All I can say is I'm 100% in until then.'

'No change of heart then guv?' Asked Buchanan.

'No.' Chambers said abruptly. 'Let's keep in contact via email. But I suggest deleting your mails regularly OK?' And with that Chambers stood up. He felt re-energised. He also felt that maybe he had made the wrong decision. This is what he was born to do. But it was too late now. He was already a quarter of the way into his notice period. All he could do was ensure he would go out on a high and he believed he had two people alongside him that could make that happen.

***

Chapter 17.
Notes harm

The treatment Li received had so far been brutal. Left in the bottom of the boat in the murky water soiled with engine oil, rotten fish and, worst of all, at least one human eyeball. The gnawing hunger and desperate dehydration she had suffered had indicated to her that she had been there more likely a matter of days than hours in her initial place of captivity. Rarely, she had seen the figure of Shen or possibly another man moving about on the small deck above. The occasional shaft of light that illuminated her squalid surroundings suggested she was being held on a small craft, possibly, judging from the violent rocking, something as diminutive as a sampan, the small boats that littered Hong Kong Harbour hardly eliciting a second glance from the array of huge cruise and cargo ships that ploughed the South China Sea, the swift dual hulled catamarans that ferried passengers to the outlying islands and as far as Macau. All sorts of craft inhabited the busy port city from industrious tug boats to sombre Mainland Chinese battleships and gunboats, tourist junks and gaily coloured floating restaurants. A near invisible sampan could pass unnoticed through the organised mayhem of the bustling harbour.

But it was the mental torture that had been the cruellest. During her confinement she had been desperately trying to piece together those horrific last moments in the derelict house by the water's edge on the tiny island of Peng Chau near Lantau Island. Her body trembled as she recalled those last seconds as

Shen counted down – three … two … one. It had been her gun that Shen had raised and levelled at her head. She had been about to be killed with her own sidearm. There was something faintly ridiculous about it she remembered thinking as the terrific explosion of sound reverberated around the small room. The accompanying flash of light blinded her. The force of something or someone slamming into her and sending her reeling back into the concrete wall behind, cracking her head firmly against something solid and unyielding. The feeling of being winded, bewildered and confused all at the same time as she sank to the floor. The terrible cry of pain from Pang as he too crashed simultaneously to the floor. The sound of footsteps as Shen rushed over to her and clamped something over her nose and mouth, her inability to hold her breath, the overwhelming fumes. Dazed, she had been unable to put up a fight. The next thing she recalled was the escape, the freedom that had appeared so real. The vivid dream of that beautiful, exotic beach and the awkward, confused, awakening that led her to the nauseous and current, terrifyingly real nightmare.

How long she had been unconscious was anyone's guess. Her current thirst and hunger told her it had to be at least a day, maybe more, maybe less. The violent movement of the boat meant it took most of what little energy she had not to vomit. She spent a great deal of her time lying on her side. Her hands were tied behind her, making any attempt to sit up inside the violently rocking vessel a near impossibility. And for what use? The more upright she sat, the more the movement, the more it made her gag.

What she did know was it was dark when she was unceremoniously dragged up and out onto the narrow deck. She could see lights on the shore, maybe a mile away, but not the impressive light-polluting luminosity she associated with the hectic Hong Kong skyline. This was much more low key. A few lights from a village or maybe some boats moored up in a smaller harbour somewhere. The almost pitch black sky revealed the faint outline of the top of tall hills and a smattering of stars above. Li took this in during the brief moment she was on deck. The night breeze was cold against her damp skin. She was wearing only her jeans and a T-shirt, she had remembered at some point she had a jacket, but it was now long gone. There she enjoyed a few precious seconds of relatively clean air. She sucked in long breaths through her nose allowing her diaphragm to relax and extend her lungs' capacity. For too long she had been surviving on shallow breathing and the rush of blood to her head was intoxicating and almost overwhelming. She stumbled and nearly fell over the edge. If Shen hadn't grabbed her it would have been a distinct possibility.

'Don't try anything stupid. Where do you think you can swim to with your hands and feet bound? You'd be a fool to try.' He snarled.

Her gag had slipped off hours before meaning it was possible to converse with this monster but Li declined the opportunity. She wanted nothing to do with him. The burning questions of where she was and what had happened to Pang would only serve to allow Shen to assert his authority over her. She looked away back to the shore, the light wind blowing her damp hair about her face.

Shen looked disappointed at her stoic reaction. He wanted sport but she wasn't giving him the satisfaction. He dragged her to a small wooden ladder that stood up against the steel hull of a neighbouring ship.

'I'm going to untie your feet. Don't try anything. If you are foolish enough to, I'll shoot you dead and throw you to the sharks.'

Pushing her face against the ladder, she felt the rough sawing of the rope that bound her feet together.

'Climb.' He ordered when he had severed the rope.

Li put her right foot on the first step but without being able to use her hands and the pitching of the boat made it hard to lift her left leg off the deck. Suddenly a violent blow to the small of her back caused her face to smack hard against one of the steps of the ladder. For a moment the pain blinded her. She could taste the metallic blood as it dripped from her nose into her mouth.

'I said go.' Shen barked.

Li felt a hand push against her back allowing her some sense of balance to climb. The ladder was about 12 feet high with a rough step about every foot. The angle of the ladder was almost vertical making progress on the lurching boat more perilous the higher she climbed especially when after the fourth step she was out of reach of Shen's outstretched arm. A thought flashed across her mind.

Without looking she raised her right foot as though moving up to the next step, leaned close to the ladder and with all her might thrust her foot down in the rough direction of where she guessed Shen's head might be. Her unshod foot cracked painfully down on something hard. Shen let out a cry and reeled back, caught unawares by this sudden aerial attack. The force Li had used to kick Shen in the head caused her to lose her balance on the single narrow step and she toppled backwards, trying desperately to free her hands from the bindings to break her fall.

She landed heavily on her back on the wooden deck a sickening pain shooting up her arm that had broken her fall. As she looked around to see where Shen was, she heard an almighty splash from over the side of the narrow sampan, he must have lost his footing and stumbled over the edge. Despite the liquid fire in her right arm she had for a moment the briefest sensation of excitement. With Shen overboard there might just be a chance she could escape.

***

Chapter 18.

No to slime!

Friday, 8th June 2012 – 3:33pm

The week had flown by for Chambers and the rest of the team. Outside of work he had taken the positive step of booking a flight to Thailand. It was based on the evidence from the photograph and the envelope analysis. He had looked at flying straight to Vientiane but flights had been scarce and Bangkok seemed a much more convenient and considerably cheaper jumping off point with a number of travel options north to Laos. The outward journey was booked for 25th June departing Heathrow at 12:30pm on Thai Airways flight TG911. He'd booked a return for two months later. If it was necessary he could always extend his trip. Once the flight booking had been confirmed, Chambers felt a weight lift from his shoulder and his guilt begin to assuage. At last, although now several months since Li disappeared, Chambers had now finally taken a positive step in the search to discover her fate.

In the office, the investigations appeared to be gathering momentum. Buchanan was in and out of the office, calling in favours from long retired ex-colleagues. For someone who enjoyed being at his seat, it was a rare sight to see him out and about so often. His activity had caught the eye of the ever-watchful Forster. Chambers had noticed that Forster was in again that Friday and had even made a surprise appearance on the Wednesday as well. As usual he was sticking his beak into everyone's business but thankfully had spent most of his time hanging about with Polk and Pierce. The only good thing about his increased presence was that he had seemed to have been having a positive influence on the pair and now the three of them seemed to be progressing on their case with the added input from Forster. Chambers felt relieved. It was good to be back among a proactive team and even he didn't mind the presence of the old man if it was having a constructive effect on the most inefficient element of the unit.

Most of Tuesday afternoon had been taken up with the presentation from two Crime Scene Managers sent by Dr Bhanji who to Chambers disappointment, for he wanted to thank her for her help decoding the script, hadn't come along. The team had found the presentation enlightening and it was no surprise to Chambers that Adams and Buchanan had the most questions. He was surprised that the normally effervescent and ebullient Hayes had appeared somewhat subdued, he would have thought this would have been an engaging topic for her and one that she would have joined in with her usual gusto.

On Thursday Chambers had received a call on his office phone from Buchanan, who was out of the office, to inform him that his mate at Hammersmith police station had contacted him regarding an arrest in connection with the body that had been found near Hammersmith Bridge back in January. A man by the name of Milo Stone from Stockwell had been arrested the day before on a charge of drug possession with intent to supply by members of Operation Trident, Eddie Adams' old team. The Fingerprint Bureau, part of SCD4, had entered Stone's fingerprints into the system. The search had resulted in an exact match with those found on the body of Burr. The scant information Buchanan had was that according to what Stone had told police, he had come to the UK four years previously, originally he was from the Saint Ann parish in Jamaica.

Again the news was confusing to Chambers. This was the third separate arrest for three out of the four so-called copycat killings. All the arrests were from relatively recent immigrants with disparate backgrounds. So far a Hungarian, a Pole and a Jamaican, it sounded like the beginning to a joke, and one that Chambers needed to find out what the punchline was. All of the arrested men were living in different parts of London with no obvious links to one another. Chambers had asked Buchanan to keep digging to see what he could come up with. Surely all three of the recent spate of murders couldn't just have a coincidental relationship with those from nearly five decades before. But if there was something linking them it remained elusive and the relative MIT teams still weren't looking at a connection between the three. Having informed Barlow, his senior officer, there was little more that Chambers could do without gaining access to interview the suspects.

Chambers was still sitting at his desk in the middle of Friday afternoon, musing over the latest twist in the case when the afternoon mail arrived on his desk. There was one plain white envelope addressed to *'kold kase cheif. Brentford Stayshun.'*

Thinking it was some kind of joke, Chambers opened it, reached inside and pulled out a single sheet of almost rigid, rust coloured paper. Flipping it over, he saw a note written in particularly messy handwriting that at first he was unable to decipher. It took him a full five minutes to get to grips with the old fashioned style of writing complete with ink smudges and stains. In the end Chambers managed to transcribe it onto a separate sheet as best he could. It was hard to believe the spelling mistakes could have been made accidentally.

From Rotting Hell

Sor

I sent you my kondolensis. Avin not had no luk in findin me – act on impuls.

I'll joke n sing tonigt in yer onor. Keep your eyes peeled.

I may sen you the bloody clue if you only wate a whil longer.

THE CHARRED FOREST MURDERS

Signed

Catch me when you can

Mister detectif

Chambers carefully put the original back in the envelope trying not to contaminate it any further than he already had. He placed the envelope in his jacket pocket and quickly left the room. When he got found an empty interview room he closed the door behind him and called Buchanan who was out of the office.

'Guv.'

'Buck, I've just received the oddest piece of correspondence.'

'What is it?'

'Can you speak? Are you on your own?' Chambers asked.

'Yes sure am. Why? What you got?'

Chambers read him the transcript. Explaining the spelling mistakes as he went. When he finished he heard a sharp intake of breath.

'What is it? Does this mean anything to you?'

'Yes. It sure does. It sounds like a bastardisation of the "From Hell" letter that Jack the Ripper is supposed to have sent to George Luck, the Chairman of the Whitechapel Vigilance Committee back in the 1880s. The last line sounds exactly the same but the beginning has been changed. Was anything sent with it?'

'No. Just the letter. Why?'

'The original letter had a box with it containing a kidney purportedly of one of the Ripper's victims and he promised to send the knife that he had removed it with. He never did though. There's a lot of speculation about that letter. There were so many fake letters sent at the time but the authorities thought that one was real. What's the postmark say?'

Chapters flipped over the envelope. 'Nice touch,' he almost laughed. 'Says Whitechapel.'

'Date?'

'Yesterday. Thursday.' Chambers clarified.

'That makes sense I guess. What we need to see is which of our three current suspects are still in the nick. None of them made bail right?'

'As far as I know Stahel and Zook are still in custody. Your fellow Stone though, was he out when the letter was posted?'

'No I think he was picked up on Wednesday and he hasn't been out since.'

'Strange right? What the hell is going on? Why are there so many spelling mistakes in it?'

'I don't know. I suggest you do an internet search for the original. Make some comparisons. My first thought is it's definitely someone who knows a bit about both Jack the Ripper and Jack the Stripper. I mean the copied style of the letter. All the original typos. But that reference at the top. The original says "From Hell". We have "From Rotting Hell." I told you before, that was the old nickname of Notting Hill. Well Jack the Ripper had no connection with that area, not as far as I know, but we know a few of the victims that the Stripper killed either lived up there or were regulars in the illegal drinking dens and Ska clubs around there. He's toying with us that's for sure.'

'But how does he know that we're investigating it? The envelope is addressed to the cold case chief, Brentford.'

'Good question. But if he knows Stahel was arrested and taken to Brentford it seems like a logical starting point to me. What now?'

'I'll photograph it so you can take a look later, but I want to get it over to Dr Bhanji ASAP. Top priority. See if she can get anything off of it apart from my fingerprints. I hope I haven't spoiled it.'

'OK guv. I'm out for the rest of the day. So no drinks down the Tap for me tonight. Have a good weekend and I'll see you on Monday.'

'Sure thing. Have a good one.' Chambers cut the call and this time emptied the envelope onto the table and using his phone took several photographs before carefully sliding the page back in and heading to his desk to get an official envelope to send the evidence over to Fulham. He also sent Dr Bhanji an email letting her know he had a critical piece of evidence that would need handwriting analysis and testing for ink and paper chemical analysis and this time he had a crime number as this was part of a cold case investigation and officially nothing to do with any ongoing MIT investigations.

Once he had dispatched the email and the envelope over to Fulham, he Googled the original 'From Hell' letter. Whoever had made the recent copy had worked hard to match the old fashioned writing as accurately as possible, the faded colour of the paper and the bizarre spelling errors. Whether an ill-educated person or at least someone who wanted to appear that way had written the original, the modern reproduction had attempted to faithfully follow the style. The only missing thing was the lack of accompanying kidney. But as none of the Stripper copy murders had involved mutilation there was little the author of the modern letter could have said. Chambers got the overall feeling someone was playing games with him, if indeed he was the intended recipient of the letter and Chambers had no reason to believe he wasn't.

Later in the afternoon, Chambers slipped off home missing the regular drinks at the Brewery Tap. He wasn't in the mood for socialising or getting caught alone with Tucker and having to further justify his resignation. Not that he was looking forward to being home alone all weekend. He would have preferred to come into work and continue his research into the other victims of the modern killer. There had to be links that they were missing. However due to the recent controversial changes made by the London Mayor Boris Johnson, Brentford police station, along with many other stations across the capital would only be open Monday through Friday, 9am–5pm, and would be closed on Bank Holidays and weekends. There was no other alternative than to head home and try again on Monday. Before he left he happened to look over at the whiteboard. Forster was still putting up his little challenges for the team. This one had gone unanswered all day.

Apples & Pears

Paul has three boxes of fruit in his barn: one box with apples, one box with pears, and one box with both apples and pears. The boxes have labels that describe the contents, but none of the labels have been put on the correct box.

*How can Paul, by taking only **one** piece of fruit from **one** box, determine what each of the boxes contains?*

Looking at it for a while and finding his thinking was getting confused, his mind began to drift back to Lucy. It made his stomach tighten at the thought of what, assuming she was still alive, she would be going through. He was torn. Part of him wanted to fly now to try and find her. The rational part of his brain told him it was ridiculous. He would need to spend time researching Laos and find out what Pakpasack meant if anything and if it was important. He would be leaving in a few weeks until then he needed to focus on the case and do his best to find out what was going on.

Unable to solve the puzzle and realising it was currently the least of his worries he switched off his PC and headed home.

***

Chapter 19.

Any bell break?

Wednesday, 13th June 2012 – 9:29am

Chambers was now half way through his penultimate week at the Met police. The place he had worked for over two decades. The thought of what he would do once he had finished had been pushed to one side. The gnawing feeling of being out of work had taken a back seat to what he would do when he touched down at Bangkok's Suvarnabhumi Airport in less than a couple of weeks' time. He had spent the weekend buying equipment for his trip and getting the necessary jabs from the nurse at the local health clinic as well as a two-month supply of anti-malarial tablets. He had no idea what he might encounter in Laos and thought it better to err on the side of safety.

The only thing of note that had occurred earlier in the week had taken place on Monday morning when without warning Sandra Hayes quit. As her line manager she had asked Chambers to go for a coffee in the canteen and in the relative anonymity of the hustle and bustle of the usual Monday morning caffeine call, Hayes had slid a letter across the table and explained that she had decided to pursue a sea change as she had referred to her decision. Chambers had tried to ascertain a reason why but all she would say was that it had been a great opportunity to work with Adams Buchanan and him but it was just the right time. The conversation had stalled and Hayes had made her way back to her desk. Chambers sat bemused, unsure as to whether she knew of his imminent departure and whether that had anything to do with her decision. What it meant was he would need to go and speak to Barlow and let him know what was happening. But when Chambers had got back and emailed a meeting request to Barlow, he had immediately received an automated response stating Barlow was out of the office for two days. Chambers followed up asking for a meeting at 9:30am on the day he returned.

Forster's had replaced his previous week's puzzle with a new Monday puzzle that was still on the board. Chambers was annoyed that Forster hadn't put up the answer to his earlier 'apples & pears' riddle from the week before, but he refused to give the old man the satisfaction of asking him for the solution.

His latest quiz question was the shortest yet:

'What work can no one finish?'

Unfortunately the conciseness of the quiz afforded Chambers no easier solution and he was stumped as usual. He checked his watch – it was now 9:30am and time for his meeting with Barlow.

'Come in.' The disembodied voice said after Chambers had knocked. 'Oh it's you John. Take a seat.' Barlow's normal effusive, happy-go-lucky personality seemed to have disappeared now that Chambers had resigned, and there was no need for Barlow's pretence of positive energy or motivational techniques.

'Roger. I thought you should see this.' He passed over Hayes' letter of resignation.

Barlow took the envelope and read the enclosed letter, occasionally tutting. He carefully replaced the letter when he had finished reading. After placing the envelope carefully on the desk he took a moment to look out of the window to the grey and windswept Brentford High Street. Eventually he turned back to Chambers. 'Anything you want to add?'

Chambers shook his head.

'Has she been acting strangely recently? Basically what I mean to say is, have you seen a change in her personality?'

Chambers shook his head again.

'I'm shocked to be honest. Before you came in she seemed to be very happy here.'

Chambers thought he heard an emphasis on the word you' but ignored it and said, 'she's been working closely with Ed, mainly out on the street or over at Ealing. I've not noticed anything odd in her behaviour. She'd been out at drinks most Friday nights. Always seems fine to me.' He paused, 'last week though, I recall she was a bit quiet at the Forensics presentation we had. Apart from that I can't say I've noticed anything. Maybe it's worth you having a chat with Eddie.'

'Interesting John. I was with her in The Tap on Friday night for a drink. You know what she told me?'

'No idea.' Chambers said, shaking his head.

'In a nutshell she said she's been subjected to continual bullying in your office. That there was a clear culture of sexual and racial discrimination that made her and Eddie Adams feel particularly uncomfortable and that was why the pair of them were out of the office so much. Also that they received no assistance from you as their direct line manager. You had been absent from the office for a week without letting any of the team know your whereabouts.' He stopped to rub his nose. 'At the end of the day, it's a bloody mess John, that's what it is. We spoke when you started at about working with integrity.' He shook his head. 'Let me reiterate, it's a bloody mess.'

Chambers was completely taken aback. He thought he had a good relationship with Hayes, this had blindsided him. But if Barlow mentioned integrity one more time then he was likely to boil over and lamp his commanding officer.

'Just how the hell do you think I'm going to explain this away to McKinley? First you drop the ball and quit and now our only female team member is quitting and hinting to me about sexism, racism and bullying in the workplace. And she's bloody disabled.' He rubbed his eyes. 'It's a bloody nightmare I tell you John. I'm this close to my retirement.' He held his finger and thumb an inch apart.

'Roger. There's nothing in the letter about bullying or sexism.'

'Yes and we should bloody well thank God for that. Basically you and I are damned lucky she's had the decency not to sink to the levels of some others eh? I gave you carte blanche to run that department how you wanted as long as you got results. I expected you, a Detective Inspector with an good reputation to reach out to the less experienced members of the team, mentor them, train them, mould them, so to speak into a crack team. I'm starting to think I should have listened more to what your old boss Asbury said about your attitude. I saw warning signs. But I'm too bloody soft that's my problem. So far it's only our retired consultant Chad whose come up with anything! No one else on your team has done anything. Have they?' He jumped up from his chair. 'Been bloody made a fool off.' His cheeks were red and he was visibly angry.

Chambers had been ready to react, but seeing the genuine distress of the inefficient and ineffective Barlow, he now just sat quietly and took the admonishment. What was the point in arguing when he only had seven and a half working days left? The mention of Chad being the only productive member of the team showed just how out of touch Barlow really was when it came to the actual day to day workings of the team. What was it Buchanan had named him of the first day? Roge the Dodge? It summed him up perfectly. Bloody useless, just like half of his team.

'Nothing to say for yourself, have you?' Barlow was demonstrably annoyed. Chambers reticence to speak was further antagonising the Welshman. 'And your idiotic suggestion that this murder in Brentford was linked to the new one and the ones in Chiswick and Hammersmith. Now they have three different suspects under arrest. Basically I'm just thankful I didn't believe you or your crap and put this to McKinley. I'd be the bloody laughing stock of the whole of the West London policing community.'

Chambers only nodded, he'd never seen Barlow so animated. His behaviour on any other occasion would have been quite amusing. It begged the question of how people like him got promoted to these positions. He didn't know whether to be pissed off or relieved that Barlow hadn't backed him on the suspicion of the link between the old and new murders. It showed a distinct lack of belief from Barlow in his theory, but also it probably saved Buchanan, Tucker and himself from coming under intense scrutiny from the Superintendent.

'Before you leave next week John, I want a bloody report on my desk about this alleged bullying and the prehistoric work environment you've allowed to become established in the department. Do you understand? I trust you can do that?' He said sardonically.

Chambers nodded. Trying not to smile. If he'd had any doubts about resigning, they had dissipated in this brief meeting. The Met, like many other organisations, was now run by bean counters, pen pushers and yes men, and Barlow epitomised everything that was wrong with the force, an ineffective dilettante, hopelessly out of his depth and elevated to a position beyond his ability. What was it that he had heard about the public service? Managers promoted until they were found themselves in a position beyond their limited ability and too proud to admit it, so department after department doomed to fail due to under qualified, inept leadership. It didn't bode well for the future of London's police force. No wonder the respect the public held it in was now at an all time low. Common sense had gone out of the window. All that mattered now were Key Performance Indicators, Return On Investments, other pointless initialisms, plus a host of hollow numbers for arrest figures and budget cuts that had no impact on the real world outside of some government spreadsheet or meaningless white paper. Real policing would soon be a distant memory. The sooner he was out of it all this nonsense the better.

'That's all John.' Barlow waved his hand dismissively towards the door.

Chambers got up and pulled the handle.

As he was about to exit Barlow spoke up. 'At the end of the day, you've really let me down John. You really have.' Barlow barked at him.

Chambers closed the door quietly behind him, stopped and took a deep breath. Some part of him was desperate to open the door and give Barlow a piece of his mind and now he was leaving what was the worst they could do to him? But he thought better of it.

He wanted to get back to his investigation into the murdered men – William Barkley, Aaron Burr and Tom Marshall. Danny Tompkins who had been found in Brentford was last seen in a gay bar in Central London. The initial feedback they had received in relation to the others was that they were all single men living alone. There was nothing particularly uncommon in that but Chambers had been digging about. He'd already been to visit Mr Barkley's work colleagues at the travel agency where he worked on Kensington High Street. Chambers thought it best not to speak to his parents for fear of alerting them to a separate investigation. He'd spoken to three colleagues who confirmed Barkley lived alone and was well liked. Chambers wanted to tread carefully and it was only the third colleague, an older woman who responded to his question about whether Barkley had a girlfriend with something more than a shake of her head. Not one to gossip, the woman had gone on immediately to say that Barkley was indeed a homosexual and quite extrovert about his sexual persuasion. Maybe the fact that two of the men killed were homosexual was more than a simple coincidence.

THE CHARRED FOREST MURDERS

His successful trip to Kensington had taken place on Monday afternoon. The new lead in the case had begun to cement itself on Tuesday when Chambers called the solicitor's office where Thomas Marshall had worked. He had quickly got to the point with the receptionist who had taken the call. There was no point escalating the enquiry further than it needed to go at this early stage. After he had introduced himself he came straight out with it. Asking the young lady if Marshall had a girlfriend or wife as he was trying to trace them to get some background information. The woman had gone quiet. Chambers had reassured her that she wouldn't get into trouble and she had explained that as far as she knew Marshall didn't have a girlfriend as she believed he was gay. Now there were three from three and surely a connection.

Aaron Burr, the soldier with a conviction for assault, was proving harder to get information on. He spoke to Buchanan who was still out of the office following his own investigation. Later on the Tuesday, Buchanan had got back to him with an email address in Australia for Alex Hamilton, the man Burr had assaulted a few years ago.

Chambers had sent him an official looking email requesting him to get in touch on a formality in the case and when Chambers returned to his desk from his meeting with Barlow there was already an email response from him, asking what the request was to do with.

Quickly Chambers had emailed to ask for clarification about the assault. Within a minute a reply came in. Stating they had been mates for a while and had been having a drink and he had made a flippant comment about Burr being gay as he didn't want to take the lead in chatting up any women when they were out. Burr had flipped out and hit him with a glass. He realised when it went to court that Burr was actually gay and had suffered mercilessly at the hands of bullies in the army that had eventually led to him leaving the armed forces.

Chambers fired off a thank you email. He now had the link. All of the four men who had been killed were gay. It was a starting point. But what did it mean in the wider scheme of things? It could just be four random hate crimes. Unfortunately it was still all too common for crimes like these to take place on the streets of Britain. While he was thinking about this he called Buchanan to find out where he was. His colleague informed him he was in Hammersmith but would be back in the office in the following morning. Chambers hung up and emailed Tucker to see if she was free for a meeting the following day for an update.

***

Chapter 20.

A lemming fry

Thursday, 14th June 2012 – 10:15am

Tucker, Buchanan and Chambers met once more in the interview room on the Thursday morning with their coffees already in hand. Although it was only just over a week shy of the Summer Solstice it was a cold and miserable day in West London. The temperature was down in the low teens centigrade and whether because summer was supposed to have started two weeks previously there was no central heating on in the building. Chambers had a shirt and sweater on, Buchanan was obviously made of stronger stuff and was only wearing one of his trademark short-sleeved shirts, but they were both surprised when Tucker entered wearing a knee length coat with leather gloves. Chambers put her show of ostentation down to a woman's inbuilt love of fashion. But he was taken aback by how good she looked. Her swollen face had returned to normal and the bruising had all but disappeared. The only fly in the ointment was when she tried to speak and both men could see her jaw was still wired firmly together.

Chambers got the ball rolling. 'I've made a few "hands on" enquiries at their places of work and I'm confident now that all four of our recent murder victims are gay.'

'How did you find that out guv?' Buchanan winked at Tucker.

'Yes John? You been hanging out up Old Compton Street? Don't you think that's taking your "hands on" approach too literally?' Tucker flashed her smile back at Buchanan who started laughing.

Chambers was still smarting from the dressing down he had received from Barlow the day before. Maybe the prig of a boss had a point, but it was just a bit of banter in the end, wasn't it? He smiled briefly to show he was a good sport. 'Seriously, apart from what you might think about my methods we have a serious link. I don't think this is a subject to be taken lightly. All four murdered men are homosexual. What do you make of that?'

'I think we need to look at the fact we have three people in custody for three of the four murders. No one outside this room is linking them together and possibly with good reason. Don't you think?' Tucker said removing her gloves and placing them neatly on the table in front of her.

Chambers deflected. 'Buck, any news on the copper from the original case? You got a name yet?'

'Nothing. It's like I've hit a brick wall. I've had nothing out of HR I've been asking around a few of the old school brigade. Not a sausage so far. I went up Notting Hill yesterday for a bit of a snoop about at the station there but it's all changed. Anyway I got a couple of irons in the fire so let's see what comes of it. They should be getting back to me by the end of the week.'

'Jess, what about the murder at Dukes Meadows in '59. Did we get a link to anything yet in the records?'

'Still nothing. I've read through the case notes on her. I just don't think she's involved. She was found with most of her clothes on, it wasn't the Stripper's MO. That's clear just from his nickname and it was several years before the others. It's only the location and her occupation that makes it relevant. I mean the place was famous in those days for prostitutes and their clients. So, of course if something gets out of hand down there, it's going to be a prostitute that gets it. Right? Could have just been a trick that went wrong. He might have been a nutter, or maybe she tried to rob him and came off worst.'

'I'm sorry Jess.' Buchanan said. 'I know this case inside out. I just know it's him that done it.'

'But what proof do you have?'

'I just know OK?' Buchanan's voice was slightly raised, the tone was defensive. 'Can we not leave it there?'

Chambers could see his older colleague was never going to let it go. 'OK well whether she was or wasn't one of the Stripper's victims, what we do know is there is no corresponding recent murder to align with it more recently. I don't know what that means. We know the new murders have taken place relative to the times the others were killed not discovered. Maybe it's something to do with that. Where the body was found.'

'What do you mean?'

'In one of the files. I think it's the murder of …' he hesitated, trying to recall the name, 'Fleming is it?'

'Mary Fleming.' Buchanan added. 'What about it?'

'In the report it says there were three workmen doing a shop renovation on Chiswick High Road late one night when they saw a vehicle pull up and the driver acting suspiciously as if he was looking to dump something out the back of his van. Eventually they shouted some obscenities and the driver took off in a hurry. A couple of hours later Fleming's body is found in a dead end road a few hundred metres away.'

'And your point is?' Tucker pressed.

'I see what you are getting at.' Said Buchanan. 'You think the first victim Figg was meant to be put somewhere else. Maybe he got spooked. His first time and all. So he goes somewhere safe. Somewhere out of the way like Dukes Meadows. So we need to look at where the body was intended to be dumped, not where

Figg was found. But we have no idea where he wanted to put her. So that doesn't help much.'

'So what are you saying? We need to extend the search? How far do you want to spread the net? Jesus this could take days or weeks to cover.'

'That's the spirit.' Chambers joked. 'I know it's not ideal but we need to give it a go. Let's spread the search out to a two-mile radius from where she was found. That just about covers the range where the other victims were found. We must get some kind of hit.'

'Interesting though isn't it?' Tucker said pointing vaguely out of the window.

'What is?'

'It's mid-June now right? Figg was killed on the 17th June. That's four days short of midsummer's night. It wouldn't have given him a lot of wiggle room. I mean, it's still light until about 10pm and dawn is around 4am. He would have been taking a few risks carting a dead body about with only a small window of darkness at night.'

'That's right. So if he did get scared off his first plan to dump the body he must have been close by. I still think we search a two mile radius to be on the safe side.'

Tucker shrugged her shoulders. 'Fine. I'll get on with it after this. Hey Buck, you said these workmen got a good look at the man acting suspiciously. How come there was no photo fit of the suspect made?'

'As I recall they never reported it at the time. The shopfitter came forward much later. They were working in a shop that at the time backed onto a service road and pedestrian passageway. Sort of where the Sainsbury's is now, back then it was a brewer's bottling plant and storage depot for Whitbreads or Charringtons, I forget which. You know the supermarket tucked behind the main street next to Chiswick Park Tube going up towards Acton. Time had passed so he was vague about specifics. Youngish bloke, mid-twenties, maybe thirty, 5' 10", medium build, clean-shaven, office type. I mean you can't get more vague than that, can you?'

'What time was that?'

'Between 2 and 3am if I recall correctly. Whatever the specific time was, neighbours in Berrymede Road heard a car revving at the same time. But no one got up to investigate and the body was found at the dead end of the road a few hours later.'

'Sounds plausible. That he got scared and bolted. Dropped the body off down a quiet street.' Proposed Chambers.

'Yeah but how did he know that was a quiet street? Surely he must be local or knew the area. Imagine you're panicking with a dead body in the back of your car. The last thing you want is to be driving around without a clue where you are.' Queried Tucker.

'What about the car? The workmen must have got a good look at that.'

'Yeah but they couldn't agree on the colour. One of them thought it was a Hillman Husky.'

Chambers and Tucker looked non-plussed.

'It was a type of estate car at the time. Plenty of room in the back if you put the seats down.' Buchanan nodded. 'Perfect for ferrying a body around in the boot anyway, let's just say that. Throw a tarp over it and no one would have been any the wiser if they happened to peer in.'

'OK, well it gives credence to the fact that not all his murders or disposals went to plan. I mean the ones in the river. They possibly could have been put in Dukes Meadows and floated down or, or we just don't know. But it's interesting that after the first four are found near to the Thames and the fifth is close to the Brent, the final three are found a distance away from any rivers. It makes me think our early idea about the killer using a river island as his base and ferrying the bodies around doesn't hold water.'

'Maybe he just changed his method. The last ones all had the fine misting of paint. Maybe he just had a better place to store bodies. He got concerned during a previous murder. There's a lot of reasons.' Tucker suggested. 'As Buck said, maybe he invested in a car and realised it was a damn sight easier to drive a body hidden in the back than dragging them on and off boats.'

Chambers nodded. It made sense. 'I tell you whatever we might find out about the multiple killers of these modern murders, they are somehow tied in to the old ones. I'll stake my reputation on it.' Chambers surmised grandly.

'Hmmm. That doesn't really mean a lot right now when you're quitting next week, now does it?' Tucker said, quickly popping his balloon.

Chambers took a sip of his coffee and winced at the sharp pain in his tooth. He would need to get it looked at.

'You OK? I hope you're not that sensitive to a bit of messing about? I can send you some concrete if you'd like. Toughen you up a bit.' Tucker said sarcastically.

Buchanan sniggered into his coffee.

'Spot of toothache is all.' Realising it wasn't the most sensible thing to say to someone who had a wired up jaw, several missing teeth and a future that involved many painful and expensive trips to the dentist.

She nodded. 'This might not come as a shock to you. But I've got the name of a good dentist if you need one.'

Buchanan snorted again, this time mid sip, causing coffee to come out of his nose he laughed so hard before descending into a fit of coughing. 'Sorry all,' he said when he got his breath back. 'I'll leave you two to it. I got places to go, people to see.

THE CHARRED FOREST MURDERS

Catch you later.' He turned to John. 'I'll be out and about looking at these leads, but I'll be back tomorrow afternoon. Let's catch up then or if not, I'll definitely be in the Tap after work. OK?' As he moved to the door he looked back at Tucker. 'You coming for a drink? I mean your whole intake is through a straw right now so you might as well inhale something a bit more fun right?' He didn't wait for an answer but went out of the door chuckling to himself.

Chambers was up quickly. 'OK Jess. Keep me posted on your search, the latest on your case or if not I guess I'll see you in the Tap on Friday?'

'Is that a date?' She winked at him.

Chambers shuffled awkwardly towards the open door, closing it carefully behind him. He was sure he could hear Tucker laughing as he made his way down the corridor.

***

Chapter 21.

Rash reflectors

Friday, 15th June 2012 – 9:15am

Chambers had come to work earlier than usual on Friday, but not for any case related reason. He'd woken from a bad dream in a cold sweat at 3am and had been unable to return to sleep. In the nightmare he had been walking with friends through fields on a beautiful summer's day. They had walked part of the South Downs Way and were walking along the banks of the river Arun to a riverside pub they knew called the Black Rabbit. Not far from their destination they had passed a group of Friesian cows, all of them in the far corner of the field. As soon as Chambers had looked over at them they had slowly formed into a herd and begun to walk in his direction. His group had sped up at his urging and made their way via a small wood into the pub's car park and then on into the relative safety of the bar. They had ordered pints of the local Tanglefoot brew, and sat at a table. Suddenly from nowhere the herd of cows had surrounded them and were closing in, squashing the group, they were enormous at least six feet to the shoulder, lowing aggressively. Chambers had jumped onto the wooden table and leapt into the nearby river. As he hit the surface of the freezing cold water he had woken with a start covered in sweat.

What the dream meant was beyond him. But whatever it was it prevented him from returning to sleep so he had got up, breakfasted, showered and, as it was a nice day, he decided to walk to work. He had arrived just before 9 and was disappointed

THE CHARRED FOREST MURDERS

to see Foster was the only one there. The old guy was still coming in most Fridays and the occasional Wednesday as well.

'Morning,' he said in an almost pleasant tone. Chambers wondered if maybe today was one of the old boys rare affable days as he closed the door behind him and walked to his desk.

'Morning Chad. How's it going?' Chambers knew he had a week left in the office after today. What was the maximum number of times he would have to deal with him? Two? Three? He was sure he could handle it.

'Not bad, you know. As good as it can be when you have a death sentence hanging over your head.' Forster said coldly.

Chambers braced himself for a blow-by-blow description of his latest round of invasive tests or the graphic description of the passing of blood when the old man went to the toilet, but today it wasn't forthcoming. 'How you getting on with the Jean Bradley case with Paul and Russell?'

'They're good kids but they got no idea about proper police work. I wonder what they teach up Hendon these days. It's all about tiptoeing about the community, not pissing anyone off. Where have the real detectives gone? That's what I want to know.'

'Good point. I feel the same. But what about Bradley, any new leads?' Chambers was sitting now, waiting for his PC to boot up.

'I've had a word with a bloke who used to be along at Acton. I'm hoping he might shed some light on it.' Forster turned to look at Chambers. 'A little bird told me you quit.' Forster had an odd grimace on his face that Chambers could discern wasn't actually a gargoyle-like smile.

What the hell he thought. 'Yes it's true. I've been with the Met over 20 years and it's time for a change.'

'I hope it weren't nothing to do with what I said.'

'No.' Chambers lied. 'I see you haven't got a new quiz this week.'

'I'm just about to write it up now. No one guessed Monday's quiz yet.'

Chambers looked back at the question.

'What work can no one finish?'

'Well?' Chambers prompted.

Forster's ugly face cracked into a broad smile. 'Their autobiography.' The old man gave a throaty laugh. 'So bleeding simple ain't it?' He boasted.

Chambers shook his head. While they were enjoying a rare moment of camaraderie he asked, 'what about the apples and pears one from the other day?' The answer still eluded Chambers.

Forster stopped laughing. 'He takes one from the box marked apples and pears. If all the labels are wrong then if he picks an apple he knows that it can't be the pears box or the apples and pears box. So it must be the apples box. Then he just switches the other two labels see? Easy.'

'You love your little quizzes don't you?' Chambers said in an affable manner.

Forster who had had moved over to the whiteboard shot him a sharp look. Ignoring his question. 'What you working on with Buck and that Tucker bird? I seen you three thick as thieves.'

Chambers didn't like the tone but after consideration he felt the old guy might actually be able to help. 'Why? What's Buck told you?'

'Bugger all. He's a sly one that one, mark my words. I'd be careful working too closely with him. What with all that stuff up Soho you want to watch your back.'

THE CHARRED FOREST MURDERS

'What stuff?' Chambers recalled Barlow alluding to something the first time they'd been to the pub. 'The Vice scandal?'

'That's right. Who told you?'

Chambers shook his head. 'Just heard rumours that's all.'

'Don't get me wrong, I like him. He's a stand up bloke in some regards as a mate like. But he's your absolute classic example of a bent copper. He always had his hand in the till up Soho way. And if his hand wasn't in the till it was somewhere else it shouldn't have been if you catch my drift.' Forster leered. 'He loved the whores he did. Could never get enough of them. His first wife bailed on him cos of it.'

Chambers nodded and tried to not show any surprise at these revelations. He couldn't quite believe that Buchanan had such a past. Although he'd seen flashes of anger on occasion from Buchanan, he'd not seen or heard any suggestion he was on the take or looking to take advantage of his position. But there was the original comment from Barlow so maybe there was something in it.

'Has he spoken to you about that old case. The serial killer in West London. I forget the name.' Forster asked.

'The Jack the Stripper murders, you mean?'

'Oh yeah, was that the name? Is that the one with them prostitutes getting killed?'

'Yes.' Chambers nodded his attention now fully focussed on Forster who was busy writing up his new puzzle.

'He was bleeding obsessed with it he was. I remember when we first worked together he was always banging on about it.'

'Really?'

'Yes. Talk about a man with a one-track mind. It was his favourite subject. Prostitutes. Drone on about it all day. The ones he'd had his end away with, or those murders and how come they'd never been solved. Drove the station up there crazy. Eventually he got shifted out of there cos he was nicking birds and letting them off for services rendered, shall we say.'

Chambers was shocked. He picked up a pencil and jotted down 1964 on a post-it note on his desk. That was the year of Barthelemy's murder in Brentford. Buchanan had said he was 16 at the time. That was old enough to have committed the crime. Rees in Kew in 1963? At 15? Maybe. But surely Figg in 1959 when Buchanan would only have been 11 wasn't possible. It just couldn't be unless, Chambers paused, was it a possibility that Buchanan was involved working with someone else. Someone older? There was something in Buchanan's past that Chambers had a feeling he might need to investigate.

Looking back to his screen to enter his log in, Chambers was surprised to see once again Paul Pierce's login name where Chambers' name should have been. He deleted the name and put his own name and password in. As the home screen appeared so did a thought. Maybe Buchanan was desperate to link the murder of Figg to the others as a diversionary tactic. Not everyone was in agreement that she or Rees were part of the Stripper's portfolio of murders but with Buchanan pushing hard enough it might be enough to remove the scent from him for a while..

Chambers shook his head, surely it was too farfetched? 'When did you first work with Buck?' He asked Forster.

Forster stopped writing and turned to face him, still waving the blue marker pen about in mid air. 'Oh I would have to say late sixties. Buck had just married, er, bloody hell what was her name. Little blonde bint she was. He liked them shorter than him see? Always did.'

Something sparked in Chambers' memory. All the victims of the Stripper were less than 5'5". Why was Buchanan so interested in getting him involved in the old case? It was Buchanan, and Buchanan alone, that had made the connection with the new case. No other investigation team were even considering it.

'You OK? You've gone all pale.' Forster asked.

'I'm fine. What happened to his first wife?'

'Angie! That was the bird's name. Marriage lasted till about '71 as I recall. She left him and went back up north. Rotherham or some other shithole where she originally came from.'

'Do you remember her maiden name?' Chambers had a sick feeling in the pit of his stomach.

'Nah, not off the top of my head. Memory like a bleeding sieve these days with all the medication I'm on.'

'Not to worry. What about your case? The one you took over from Buchanan. How's that going?'

'Gloria Booth? Not a lot to be honest. I'm looking at the links between that and the 1954, murder of Jean Mary Townsend. She was found murdered on what was then wasteland near to where Booth was found. The post-mortem report stated that she had been strangled with her own scarf, much like Booth was.'

'But wasn't Booth much later?'

'Yeah '71. Big jump I know, but the MO was the same. Location was the same. Got to be worth a look right?' Forster cleared his throat noisily and returned to writing the remainder of the question on the board.

Chambers wasn't sure if it was a question or a statement. If it kept the old guy busy and out of his hair for the remaining week then it could only be a good thing. 'Sure. Go for it.' At the moment he was distracted by Buchanan's possible involvement in the Stripper murders which begged the question – what, if any, was his connection with the contemporary murder scenes?

Forster looked over his work before shuffling back to his desk. 'There you go.' He said as he sat down.

D B1
N B2
A B3
T B4
S B5

After a cursory glance, Chambers ignored the latest quiz question. There was more going on than he first thought. Lost in thought, he began gently biting on the pen top considering what Buchanan's involvement might actually turn out to be. What had Forster just told him? Buchanan divorced in 1971. The same year Booth was murdered in Perivale. Had the Stripper stopped because he had got married? And then started again in the 1970s? He would need to begin an investigation into the other unsolved murders and even those that had supposedly been solved. This case looked to have got a whole lot larger. He accidently bit down too hard on the pen top and nearly let out a yelp as it struck a nerve. First though, he would get his troublesome tooth fixed.

***

Friday 15th June 2012 – 4:04pm

It was just past 4pm when Chambers called it a day. Although he wasn't normally one for an early mark a 4:30pm appointment with the dentist down at nearby Strand on the Green was the only one he could get at the last minute. Tucker had made the recommendation, as it was this dentist who was responsible for her extensive dental reconstruction. The office hadn't exactly been a hive of activity. Buchanan was due back in any moment as he had arranged to go for a beer with the rest of the team, but this was something else Chambers was keen to avoid after the revelations he'd heard from Forster earlier in the day.

Some of the things had begun to resonate more and more with Chambers as the day progressed. Buchanan himself had said it was suspected it was a policeman. But how come he had been unable to come up with a name? No wonder he was so heavily involved with their investigation and looking after that particular line of enquiry on his own. What Chambers needed to look into on Monday was where Buchanan had been at the time of all the recent murders. The one in Brentford had taken place over the weekend, the same as the one at Chiswick Mall. It wasn't going to be easy to extract the information from him without raising suspicion. He would have a think as to the best way to approach the delicate subject.

As he left he said a quick goodbye to the team that were left: Pierce, Hayes and Forster.

Reaching the door, Forster called out to him, 'taking an early mark John? I'd do the same if next week was my last week before I quit.' Then he heard the low rumbling of what was the Forster laugh.

Chambers felt himself flush and quickly stepped out of the door closing it firmly behind him.

Standing for a moment on the other side of the door he could hear them inside but they couldn't see him.

'Chad what on earth you talking it about?' It was Hayes.

'He quit, didn't he. Don't ask me why. Maybe Brentford weren't exotic enough for him. Good riddance I say.' That was definitely the dulcet tones of Forster.

Just when he thought he was getting on better with the old man, all his attempts at developing a better working relationship gone in a second. Now the whole team knew he was leaving. He was angry at himself for not taking the time to explain to the rest of them that he was leaving. It had been too easy to put it off for different reasons. It was always a case of he'd do it tomorrow or the whole team were never in attendance. Maybe it was because he wasn't ready to leave the force, or it was easier to deny it was happening if he didn't admit it in public. Whatever the case was, the decision had now been taken out of his hands. Again Forster had put one over on him. Chambers set off to walk the mile or so towards the dentist at Strand and not in the best of moods, while his destination hardly filled him with excitement.

An hour and a half later and considerably lighter in the pocket, Chambers walked back along the tow path by the river back towards Kew Bridge where he could catch a 237 bus home. After 50 metres he came to the Bell & Crown pub, one of three along the Strand on the Green riverfront. It was coming on for 6pm and it was a lovely June day just before midsummer and he'd spent an age in the dentist's waiting room. There was a crowd of people spilling out of the bar and sitting on the low concrete wall that ran along the water's edge. The tide was high and beginning to lap over the towpath. Chambers decided to have an impromptu drink and stepped into the crowd, up the metal steps and into the dark interior of the bar, emerging a couple of minutes later with a pint of Fullers Chiswick Bitter.

Finding a gap on the low wall, he took a seat and put his pint down. He was facing towards the direction he had just walked from looking towards the railway bridge that crossed the Thames from Chiswick to Kew with his back to Kew Bridge. The north side of the railway line ran between the two other Strand riverside pubs, The City Barge and the Bull's Head. The wrought iron bridge culminated on the far bank near the Kew Records Office and the Kew Retail Park. Chambers looked over at the far bank that was lined with trees. Somewhere in that vicinity a body had been found nearly 50 years before and her murderer had never been found. He shook his head, it was all quite unbelievable that so many bodies had turned up in this peaceful part of West London.

Closing his eyes, Chambers enjoyed the warm rays of the evening sun. It was a substantial change in temperature to the more winter-like day they had endured the day before. In a week this would all be over, he could expend his energy on finding Lucy. He felt vaguely worried about what he would be letting himself in for. At this stage he had no idea what he would do when he stepped off the plane in Thailand. He opened his eyes and watched a couple of swans glide over the surface of the water, the sun dancing on the ripples in their wake as they silently motored to where an old man was throwing in pieces of bread.

Still looking downriver towards Hammersmith, Chambers took a sip of his beer and immediately realised his error as some of the liquid spilled down on to his trousers His bottom left jaw, cheek and lip still numb from the anaesthetic. Quickly he wiped away his embarrassment. It had put a bit of a dampener on his plan to get half cut and for a while at least, leave his worries behind him. Several boats and small craft were making their way up and down the river but the general water traffic was very light. Chambers couldn't help but think of the contrast to Hong Kong's bustling harbour and of course his thoughts turned to Lucy once more. He tried to snap himself out of it, wondering what the Thames would have been like in its pomp. Surely it would have been solid with all manner of boats and ships plying their trade up the capital's main transport artery of the time. In the distance he could hear something that at first he thought was a roll of thunder that struck him as odd on such a perfect, cloudless summer evening. He looked downriver and saw a train powering noisily across the bridge. In the middle of the river half way between himself and the train bridge was a heavily wooded, leafy river island. The trees in full bloom gave the impression of a huge green turtle lying solemnly in the middle of the river. Chambers continued to look at the pleasant relaxing scene. Occasionally the water birds would take to the air with great difficulty or come flying in to land on the water at high speed only to flare at the last moment and plop comfortably into the water or land on the low wall looking for scraps from the empty plates of earlier diners.

At this point a young blonde woman, that Chambers recognised as one of the barmaids, came out from the conservatory at the rear of the pub and began collecting glasses.

As she came close to him to pick up a few empties Chamber said to her. 'Excuse me, do you know what that island is?' He said pointing down river.

The woman gave him a strange look.

'Sorry,' he slurred in apology wiping saliva from his mouth. 'Just back from the dentist.'

'Ah, no worries,' she said in a thick accent. Australian or New Zealand he couldn't be sure. 'I thought you'd been hitting the grog too hard.' She laughed. 'That over there? Isn't that Oliver's Island? I can ask inside if you like. I'm not a local.' She said stating the obvious.

'No it's fine. Thanks.' Chambers smiled up at her. It raised the question again that they hadn't resolved. If the original killer had a boat, then one of these river islands that dotted the Thames would make the perfect place for hiding bodies and transporting them unseen at night along the river. The first two bodies were found on the riverbank at Dukes Meadows. From a boat that could take less than a minute to pull up and dispose of the body. The one at the rubbish tip had access from the river and the site would have been deserted. Three and four were found on the riverbank at Hammersmith and Chiswick Mall, again much easier by boat. He thought back to his riverside runs in the morning. There were more islands up river at Brentford and beyond. Most of them to his knowledge were uninhabited. One that was inhabited and was well known was Eel Pie Island at Twickenham. It had been a musical venue for over a century but was probably best known as one of the first venues played by local band, the Rolling Stones among other well-known rock and roll acts including The Who, The Yardbirds, Pink Floyd and David Bowie through the sixties.

But these other islands that dotted the Thames, whatever they were formerly used as, most of them to his knowledge were almost certainly uninhabited and probably had been for decades since road and rail had surpassed the Thames as the main

THE CHARRED FOREST MURDERS

transport route. It would make for an ideal hiding place. He decided to call Tucker to find out what she had discovered from her enquiries to the river police, and also because he decided he didn't want to drink alone on such a lovely evening. Standing up he fished about in his trouser pockets as the realisation dawned on him that he had left his phone in his jacket pocket on the back of his chair.

He quickly looked at his watch. It was coming on for 7pm. Under the ridiculous new rules the station would be closed. Chambers let out a sigh. There was little he could do about it now. It was probably for the best. Draining the last of his pint he put it back on the low wall and made his way back towards Kew Bridge and the 237 bus stop. He could always do a little bit of research on his laptop over the weekend and talk to Tucker about the river island theory on Monday. What he was going to do about Buchanan was another matter. He needed to think carefully over the weekend as to how to handle this tricky matter.

***

Chapter 22.

Pic cleared up

Monday, 18th June 2012 – 9:16am

Despite his usual tardiness on a Monday morning, Chambers was actually keen to get in the office and confront Forster. Partly as he was now beginning his final week as a Metropolitan Police officer and partly because until now he'd tried to be nice, but the old man was playing him for a fool and Chambers was keen to give him a piece of his own medicine. He was sure Forster had forced Hayes' hand in quitting. The constant snide remarks from Pierce, Polk and Forster were responsible for all the negativity in the office and Chambers was more than happy to comply with Barlow's request for an investigation and name the three reprobates as the source of all the animosity. Also it was about time someone brought the old man down a peg or two and Chambers was happy to oblige.

When he got to the office door he took a few deep breaths, he needed to be calm when he entered into the fray. Pushing the door open he was disappointed to see that apart from Paul Pierce the office was empty.

'Morning Paul. Your uncle not in yet?' Chambers asked.

There was no response from the young detective who was looking slightly away beyond his PC.

Chambers walked past and sat down at his PC and booted it up. While he was waiting for it to load he saw the quiz question had been answered but there was no new one written up.

THE CHARRED FOREST MURDERS

D B1
N B2
A B3
T B4
S B5

Stand up and be counted.

Chambers nodded, another simple solution that had somehow eluded him.

When the screen opened on the password prompt, it reminded him that on more than one occasion he had seen Pierce's log in name appear there when it shouldn't have.

'Paul.'

No response.

Paul!' Chambers shouted this time, he was pissed off at Forster not being in and now his stroppy nephew was ignoring him.

Pierce turned round 'What is it?' He said moodily.

Chambers could see Pierce's eyes were red-rimmed as if he had just been crying.

'Are you OK?' Chambers voice mellowed.

'Fine.' Sniffed Pierce.

'Really? I mean, you don't look great?' Chambers suddenly smiled. 'Big night out with the football team was it?'

'What? I don't even play football. That's Russell.' Pierce now looked really pissed off.

'Yeah sorry. So were you out with a young lady? Or just had one over the two?' Chambers tried to make a joke out of his earlier error.

'No.' Then after a considerable pause. 'I just had some bad news that's all.'

Chambers felt a sick buzz of excitement. 'Is it Chad? Is he OK?' he said slightly too eagerly.

'No that old bastard is fine. Just something personal that's all. I'd rather not talk about it if you don't mind.' Pierce looked like he was about to start crying. At least that explained his red eyes.

'I'm sorry to hear it. If you need to chat about it, I'm here.'

'Thanks John.' Pierce said reluctantly. 'Maybe later.' He turned back to staring off into space.

Chambers decided it wasn't the most appropriate time to talk about the login issues. At that moment the door swung open and Polk came in. He really did look the worse for wear but considering it was a Monday it was more of a miracle that he was in the office at all.

'Hi boss.' He gave Chambers a friendly wave. Chambers nodded back at the dishevelled young detective.

Taking this as his cue to go and get a coffee, Chambers left the two mates alone, he just stopped to dip into his jacket pocket and was relieved his mobile was still there. He'd had a horrible feeling over the weekend that a light fingered cleaner might have had it away and then he felt guilty for casting aspersions on the hard working cleaning staff.

When he got to the canteen there were a couple of officers in front of him he didn't recognise. While he was waiting he checked his phone. There were several missed calls and a few text messages. Eventually he got his coffee and retired to a corner table of the canteen.

In between sips of his scalding coffee he listened to his messages.

Friday 4:58pm – Buchanan. 'Alright guv. Tried you at your desk, you must already be in the Tap. See you in 30.'

THE CHARRED FOREST MURDERS

Friday 5:34pm – Buchanan. 'Guv. At the Tap. Can't see you. Maybe you're having a heart to heart with Roge. Lucky boy! Hopefully see you in a minute.'

Friday 7:13pm – Buchanan. 'No idea where you are. I'm at the Tap with Jess. Roge is here as well with Sandra. They looked well pissed off when I asked them if they had seen you. Hope all is well. Jess has a very interesting theory that I think you should hear. Ok catch you later.'

Friday 9:41pm – Buchanan. 'John answer your bleeding phone. Drinking with Jess is not good for the liver. I got to do one out the back door or I'm doomed. Have a good one you old bastard.'

Friday 11:49pm – Buchanan. 'Johnny boy. I'm onto something. I think I've got it all figured out. I'll tell you when you pick up your bloody phone. You ain't going to believe it! Call me back when you get this. It's urgent.'

Chambers let out a sigh. Judging from the sound of his voice and the noise in the background the party was in full swing in the penultimate message. In the final one Buchanan sounded absolutely hammered his words were badly slurred. As Chambers went to check his text messages he saw Polk enter the canteen and order a drink.

The first text was from Tucker at 5:35pm. *'R u up for a drink?'*

Chambers flicked through to the next text when he heard a voice.

'Can I join you guv?' It was Polk.

Chambers nodded and put his phone down on the table. 'Everything OK Russ?'

'Sort of. Bit hungover like.' Polk took a sip of his coffee. 'Is it true then?'

'What?'

'Everyone in the pub was talking about it on Friday night?'

Talking about what?' But Chambers had a good idea.

'That you quit?' Polk's Birmingham accent sounded particularly strong this morning.

Chambers nodded. 'I wanted to tell the team. I was just trying to get everyone together.'

'Where you off to?' Polk asked. 'I mean I'm guessing you have something lined up like? Security work, something like that?'

Chambers shook his head. 'No, just taking a break for a while. I've been here over two decades.'

'Shit. Shoot me if I'm still doing this in another 20 years.' Polk acknowledged.

'What's up with Paul this morning? I've never seen him like that.'

Polk shrugged.

'Come on Russ. You're his best mate. I'm not asking for any other reason that I'm concerned, that's all.'

'He called me last night,' Polk said taking a mouthful of coffee, 'he was in a right two and eight. But I was in the pub with the lads so I couldn't really speak. It was too noisy and I was a bit pissed up. I told him to keep it together and I'd speak to him today.'

'So what was it? Did he tell you this morning?'

'Seems like a good mate of his was killed at the weekend. He was a bit vague on details.'

'Like what? Chambers was suddenly engaged. 'What did he tell you exactly?' Chambers urged.

THE CHARRED FOREST MURDERS

'He just said a good friend of his, a bloke called, er, Henry Wilson, was killed on the weekend.'

'Killed? Murdered? What?' Chambers was struggling to keep his voice down.

'Murdered.'

Do you know where this took place?'

'Not that far from here. Chiswick somewhere I think.'

Chambers felt his stomach tighten. He had a horrible feeling he knew where. 'Can you be more specific? The High Street? Strand? Grove Park.'

'Nah. He said up near the rugby club at Riverside Lands.'

Chambers knew exactly where that was. He'd run past it in the mornings on enough occasions, it was just near the train line at Barnes Bridge. It was on the riverbanks at a place on the border of Dukes Meadows the two places names were synonymous with each other. 'What was the date on Saturday night?'

'16th. Why?'

'Shit.' Chambers replied, rubbing his face with his hands. What had Tucker been saying just a few days ago? About the original killer looking for a place to leave the body nearly at midsummer's night 53 years previously. It was the same day Elizabeth Figg had been found sitting upright against a tree overlooking the water at the same place as the body of Mr Wilson. She had been strangled. But why was this one 53 years and not 48? The next chronological Stripper murder was supposed to be the one that correlated to Mary Fleming, found in Chiswick on July 14. Why the change in order? It didn't make sense.

'You OK boss? It's just you've gone white as a sheet.'

After a moment Chambers responded. 'Yes I'm fine. I just need to make a quick phone call. You'll have to excuse me.'

Chambers grabbed his phone as he stood up and made his way swiftly to the door.

When he got outside the building he jogged across the road and called Tucker from outside the Goddards store.

'John. I see you've finally remembered what your phone is for.' She said in her now usual sarcastic manner.

'Hi Jess, sorry left my phone in the office on Friday. Look something has happened. But first I want to hear what your new theory is.'

'OK. I'll let you off as that explains your lack of radio contact over the weekend. Did you get my messages? Apologies in advance if you haven't listened to them. As they might have got a bit cheeky as the night went on. I'm going to have to get a breathalyser installed on my phone so I stop sexting people. Anyway what's all this about a new theory?'

Chambers hadn't checked the rest of her messages yet but at least he was forewarned. 'I don't know. Buck called me and left a message on Friday night saying you had a new theory, but he didn't elaborate on what it was.'

Tucker laughed. 'Poor Buck, now I know why they call him the Toucan. What a lightweight. He was way out of his league drinking with me. The theory? Hmmm, we did talk an awful lot about the case so I might have expounded a few of my more complex ideas.'

'Such as?'

'Bless him. He's still adamant that the first one in Dukes Meadows was one of the Stripper's victims. I think we should rule it out. What I think …'

'Let me stop you there. You haven't heard have you?'

'Heard what?'

THE CHARRED FOREST MURDERS

'They found a body by the river at Dukes Meadows. A man. He was found Sunday morning. Same day as Elizabeth Figg but 53 years ago not 48.'

'Dammit.' There was silence on the other end for a while. 'That might have been the other theory I told Buck about.'

'Can you expand on it?' Chambers urged.

'I just had a thought on Friday night the murder might not be doing them in the same order necessarily. I was trying to think why there was no corresponding victim now for the first one. I was thinking it was because Figg wasn't one of the Strippers'. But at Buchanan's insistence that she was, I started looking at other ways the modern killer could incorporate it and it made sense.'

'How do you mean?'

'It would be much harder for a copycat to do them like that. He would need more than five years to recreate the murders in the same sequence. So instead, I thought maybe he just decided to do them in chronological order by month rather than by year if you follow me. It kind of made sense to me when I was drunk on Friday.'

Chambers nodded to himself. It was a possibility. 'But did you tell Buck that?'

'Yeah.'

'What did he say?' Chambers wanted to know Buchanan's precise reaction.

'He said I must have been drunk and laughed it off.'

'Are you in the office now?' Chambers was trying to think back to the dates. The last six had taken place between January '64 and January '65. 'I think we need to look at the dates of the other murders.'

'Regardless of what you just told me, I was already following up on that.'

'And what have you found?'

'Nothing yet. I only just got in. Where are you?'

'I'm outside the station.'

'OK let me get on and I'll call you when I have anything.' She hung up.

Chambers crossed the road and made his way quickly back to the office. Hayes, Polk and Adams were in, but there was no sign of the others. Something was nagging at Chambers. He had received the anonymous letter but there seemed to be no reason for it. So how did their version of the 'Rotting Hell' letter fit in to all of this? He unlocked his drawers and removed the printout he had made from photo and placed it on the desk in front of him.

From Rotting Hell

Sor

I sent you my kondolensis. Avin not had no luk in findin me – act on impuls.

I'll joke n sing tonigt in yer onor. Keep your eyes peeled.

I may sen you the bloody clue if you only wate a whil longer.

Signed

Catch me when you can

Mister detectif

Chambers read it and reread it. There had to be some clue contained within otherwise why would the killer send it to him? He fired off a quick email to Dr Bhanji to chase up the tests he

THE CHARRED FOREST MURDERS

had requested from her team before returning to reading the letter again. He found it easier to read his transcript version rather than the hard to read original version. Buchanan had told him before that the last line was almost the same as the original 'From Hell' letter. He Googled it and read the original.

From hell

Mr Lusk
Sor
I send you half the
Kidne I took from one women
prasarved it for you tother piece
I fried and ate it was very nise. I
may send you the bloody knif that
took it out if you only wate a whil
longer.

Signed

Catch me when
you Can
Mishter Lusk.

Chambers compared the two. Buchanan was right. The last line, save the superfluous reference to the knife, was almost the same as the original. Therefore, whatever the reason the person who sent it had been trying to tell them, it had to be something in the amended previous two lines. But what?

I sent you my kondolensis. Avin not had no luk in findin me – act on impuls.

I'll joke n sing tonigt in yer onor. Keep your eyes peeled.

Nothing. He looked at the photograph of the envelope. The name and address riddled with typos. The postmark was dated Thursday, 7th June and the letter was posted in Whitechapel, the scene of Jack the Ripper's ghastly deeds. Surely that was a sick joke. Chambers stopped. Where had Buchanan been on that day? He'd spent most of that week out of the office, chasing down leads in Hammersmith, but Chambers had no proof that's where he'd really been. He could easily have taken a tube to Aldgate East from Hammersmith on the District line and posted the letter and no one would have been any the wiser. Chambers felt a wave of nausea pass through him. Everything was pointing to Buchanan. At some point he'd have to share his theory with Tucker.

As a last resort Chambers read it out loud. Drawing strange looks from the other three in the office.

'What's that guv? Your resignation letter. I think it needs a bit of work.' Joked Polk.

'Sounds more like a chat up line to me.' Adams joined in. 'Act on impulse. Like one of them cheesy seventies ads for cheap aftershave.'

'Say that again.' Chambers demanded suddenly.

'The cheap aftershave bit?'

'No the first bit.'

'Act on impulse.'

That was it! 'Thanks Eddie.' Chambers beamed over at the non-plussed detective.

Act on impuls. Acton! So what else was the letter telling him? He sifted through the words. Nothing. On a second look he saw it. *I'll joke n sing tonight.* There it was! *I'll **joke n sing ton**ight.* Kensington!

He dialled Tucker's number.

'Jess' he said when she picked up. 'There's definitely two more bodies. Who did the Stripper murder in Kensington and Acton in '64?'

THE CHARRED FOREST MURDERS

'Hello to you too John. Hang on. His seventh victim was er, Frances Brown I think.' It sounded like she was reading from a file or maybe her notes. 'What was left of her was found by some bins near Kensington Church Street across from the tube station. She'd been missing for a month.'

'Date?'

'Hold on. Went missing 23rd October, found 25th November 1964.'

'Shit we need to get on to the station at Kensington see if they have a body found on or after 23rd October last year. What about the eighth and final victim?'

'Let me see. Bridget O'Hara. Went missing around 11th January 1965, found near the Heron Trading Estate in Acton.'

So he was right. Acton and Kensington. The killer was playing with them. Telling them they had missed two bodies. But how did he know they had made the link with the other four? Everything was pointing to Buchanan. Chambers looked over to the empty seat next to him. Hadn't Buchanan said he would be back in at the office on Monday? And why did Heron Trading ring a bell?

'Jess, what did Buck say about his whereabouts for this week. It's just that he's not at his desk.'

'Last thing he said was he'd be in the office on Monday morning to talk about the case. That was shortly before he tripped into the door on his way out.' She laughed.

So where was Buchanan now? Chambers wondered. He was a creature of habit, known for his punctuality and he never missed a day of work. Something seemed wrong.

'Jess, can you get on to your pal at Chiswick. See what you can dig up on this latest murder. My money's on him being found naked up against a tree.'

'I wouldn't count on it. Check your files. That's why it's always been questioned that Figg wasn't part of the Stripper's victims. She was found fully clothed, remember? Hardly a good fit for a killer known as the "Stripper", right?'

'OK well let's see what you come up with and we'll talk this afternoon. I've got some digging of my own to do.' Chambers hung up and immediately called Buchanan, but his mobile diverted straight to voicemail.

***

Chapter 23.

Violet morn

Monday, 18th June 2012 – 2:19pm

After trawling through the database and making a few calls to the Kensington Police Station during the rest of the morning, Chambers had found some pertinent information. The naked body of a man, Levi Morton, had been discovered on November 24th the previous year. As he had been found near some torn bin bags by a charity collection station in the pedestrianised plaza between Kensington Town Hall and the local library, it had been hard to ascertain if the man had been found clothed or naked. The scant information he could get was that Morton was aged 24. He would need to do some more digging into the young man's background to see if he fit the profile of the others.

Chambers had the file for the corresponding murder of Frances Brown in front of him. Tucker was right; Brown had gone missing on the 23rd November and was found near some bins. But it was 47 not 48 years before. However it did fit with their month rather than their year chronology theory. But was that the only reason the killer was working on this new pattern? Was it to do with a shorter time frame? Chambers could only speculate at this stage. The news he received from Kensington was that until now there had been no arrests in their case.

Was the 'From Rotting Hell' letter indicating this point to the police in general or was it specifically for their investigation into the Stripper killings? It was clearly indicating there had been two other murders that had been overlooked. He needed to find out more about the O'Hara murder in Acton and the one that had taken place on the corresponding date in January, five months previously. It meant that again the 48-year gap that had been consistent for the first few murders would be incorrect. This time, like the murder in Kensington, the difference was 47 years. Again suggesting that the killer had wanted to recreate all the murders in one calendar year rather than the Stripper's original timeframe of just over five and a half years.

Picking up the phone he dialled Tucker's number. She picked up on the second ring.

'Hi Jess. What have you got on the O'Hara linked killing in Acton?'

'I have a match. A man by the name of George Dallas was found naked, strangled to death. His body was hidden in the undergrowth by the train tracks near the back of the Heron Trading Estate found by some railway workers on 13th January. The initial reports were that it had been there for a couple of days which would be a fit for O'Hara who went missing on 11th January 1965.'

'A gap of 47 years. It must confirm your theory.'

'I think it's looking more of a possibly.'

'Jess. Any word from Buck? He's not been in this morning and he's not answering his phone. I've got a bad feeling.'

'About what? Buck? What do you mean? Is he sick or something?'

'I'll explain later. Can you do me a favour and sign out one of the unmarked police cars from the pool. I doubt they'd be keen to let me take one in my last week.'

'John. What's all this about?'

'Jess, just trust me. Get the car and I'll explain it all when we're on our way.'

'Fine. But it better be good. Give me ten minutes.' She sounded annoyed as she hung up.

Chambers put the receiver back down. It was now or never, he hated himself for what he was about to do but what were his alternatives? His concentration was broken by the sound of raised voices. He looked up to see Forster had returned to the office and was in a heated disagreement with his nephew, Pierce. There was the sudden screeching of metal as Pierce jumped up causing his chair to fall backwards and it was only the timely intervention of Adams that managed to keep the two from exchanging blows. Pierce was clearly very upset, his fingers clenched into fists and his breathing was rushed.

'You're just a sick old fuck.' He said as he stormed out of the office, slamming the door behind him. Polk went after him.

'Get your dirty hands off me.' Forster snarled into the face of Adams.

Chambers leapt up from his desk. 'Sandra, do me a favour and take Eddie for a coffee will you?' He said to Hayes a she went past. 'Thanks Eddie, I'll take it from here.' He could see Adams had not responded well to Forster's comments and looked ready to lamp the old guy himself. And for a moment Chambers thought he'd be too late to intervene. But Adams kept his cool and allowed himself to be led away by Hayes.

'Chad, come over here. Let's all calm down. Take a seat in Buck's chair.'

Forster shuffled over to the desk and sat heavily on the corner of it as the others left the office. The old man's bravado had disappeared. He looked deflated and much older than his 70 years.

'What's all this about? I've never even seen you have so much as a cross word with Paul.'

Forster shrugged, he was still breathing heavily. It appeared his recent confrontation had got his wind up and given him a scare even if he was trying not to show it. 'He's supposed to be my own flesh and blood. You saw that? He wanted to knock my block off!' Forster sounded incredulous that anyone, especially family might want to harm him. 'Kids these days, got no respect. That's the problem. All I've done is try and help.'

'What was said? I mean, something got him all fired up.'

'I was just messing about with him and Russell. You know Russell right?'

Chambers nodded. 'What about him?'

'He's married. Got a kid. That's normal right?' The old man's eyes bored into Chambers. Was it a question or an accusation?

'Loads of people aren't married these days or don't have kids. Sandra, myself.'

'Sandra? That ugly spastic?'

Chambers couldn't believe what he had just heard. Was Forster for real? Did he realise what an antagonistic old bastard he was? 'Calm down Chad.' Chambers said through gritted teeth. 'Times have changed. Look, I know you must have a lot of anger inside you. It's understandable with everything you're going through.' Chambers was struggling to keep a conciliatory tone.

'Bugger off! You have no bleeding idea what I'm going through. Anyway, it's not that. I want the best for Paul that's all. He's the last of the line. I don't have kids, due to that miserable old bag I made the mistake of marrying. My sis, Paul's mum, only had him.' He stopped and started scratching the grey, day old stubble on his chin that made him look older and more destitute than he really was.

'Just you and her is it?' Chambers prompted.

'No I had an older brother. But he's dead now. He never had kids neither. So it's all down to Paul and he's not doing what he should.'

THE CHARRED FOREST MURDERS

'He's still young. People get married and settle down a lot later these days. What is he 28?'

'He'll never marry, that one. You mark my words.'

'OK.' Chambers shrugged. 'But while we're all working here together do you mind not winding him and everyone else up so much? Let's try and have a more harmonious environment.'

'Yes of course.' Forster said sarcastically. 'All this bloody namby pamby, touchy feely, crap. Bollocks to that. Why not call a spade a spade and be done with it? Then everyone knows where they stand, right? That's why this country is in the mess it's in. People too bloody scared to say what they really feel.'

'I'm not saying you don't have a point. But that's not how it works these days. You got to adapt.'

'No thanks. I think I'll just agree to disagree with you on that.' Forster shuffled over to the window. 'I see you are still looking at that old case.' He said eventually. 'How you getting on with it?'

Chambers was pleased Forster had changed the subject. 'We've been making some very interesting discoveries. In fact I think an arrest is imminent.'

'Really?' Forster turned to face him. 'Bloody hell. And there's me thinking you've just been sitting over there filling out expense sheets and overtime forms.' The old man cackled, clearly over the recent incident.

Chambers ignored the snide comment. 'How come there's no quiz question this week. I've come to look forward to a little bit of a challenge to the old grey matter.'

'Oh that?' He sniffed. 'Yeah I'll get round to it later.'

Chambers' desk phone rang. 'Hello?'

It was Tucker. 'I'm downstairs. Hurry up.'

'Coming now.' He hung up and turned to Forster. 'OK, I'm out of here. Do me a favour and try not to rock the boat while I'm out. I should be back in an hour or so.'

Forster was rubbing his palms together. 'OK I'll try. I'll put a question up on the board as well. I'm glad someone appreciates my little quizzes. Makes it all worthwhile.' The creased face broke out into his trademark ugly smile.

***

Chapter 24.

Device lit cutely

Li wriggled her way a couple of feet to the edge and looking over into the matt black water but she could see no sign of her captor. On the edge of the deck was a rusty cleat. It was possible that Shen had tripped on the small device used for mooring the boat securely. Some of the rust had eroded to form an almost serrated edge. She awkwardly positioned herself with her back precariously close to the edge and worked her hands slowly against the sharp, corroded metal all the time expecting to see the outline of Shen appear over the side of the vessel.

The pitching and rolling of the boat combined with her desperate fatigue and pain was making it a ponderous affair. More than once her hands slipped and she felt the jagged metal tear into her soft wet skin. The pain from the jagged rust was almost an irrelevance to the throbbing sensation coming from her arm, which she was beginning to believe was broken somewhere near the wrist. After an inestimable amount of time she felt the last threads of the rope snap apart and for the first time in days she was able to pull her arms around in front of her. The pain in her shoulders was incredible and she could do little more than lie on her back and lay her bleeding and smashed arms gently across her stomach.

After she regained a little strength she sat up and using her stronger left arm she managed to push herself up to her feet. There was still no sign of Shen. She could only hope he couldn't swim and had drowned or had been unable to climb back up the sharply curved sides of the sampan.

Now all she needed to do was untie the sampan from the other vessel, push herself off and somehow manoeuvre herself to the small village and raise the alarm. For the first time in a long time Li, despite her violent shaking against the chilly evening, finally allowed herself to believe her nightmare was coming to an end.

Li moved quietly over to where the sampan was joined onto the larger vessel. Her small boat appeared to be held in place by two ropes attached to two cleats on one side of the small craft. She bent over the first one gently cradling her painful right wrist against her chest. Slowly she unwound the rope and let the end plop into the sea before she shuffled across the narrow deck carefully taking her time and using her less damaged left arm for balance. Li stopped momentarily as she heard an odd splashing sound coming from the bow of the boat. Watching intently the place she had heard the noise and expecting to see the outline of Shen silhouetted against the dark blue night sky, but there was no sign of him.

As she began to unwind it, she heard a scrapping noise above her coming from the other ship. The deck of which was 12 feet or so above her. When she looked up there was nothing to be seen, the sharp black outline of the boat and the contrasting night sky. The two craft bounced together and the rubber tyres groaned mournfully as Li refocused her attention on freeing up the last coil of rope. Then she would just need to find someway of guiding the sampan to safety.

She completed her task and dropped the second rope over the side. This time she was sure she heard the sound of someone laughing above her and she looked up just in time to see something falling from the deck above. Instinctively she put her hands above her head as a heavy sheet of tarpaulin, weighted down with something, smacked into her, knocking her to the deck. Her injured right arm had taken the brunt of the impact from the incoming object. She lay momentarily stunned until she heard a loud thump on the deck. She dragged the heavy canopy from over her to see standing a few steps away on the deck was Shen, soaking wet and looking far from happy.

***

Chapter 25.

Legal dogears

Monday, 18th June 2012 – 2:58pm

The plain, silver Mondeo with Tucker at the wheel had clearly seen better days. Chambers clambered into the passenger seat and directed her up the Half Acre towards the A4.

'So what's this all about then?'

'I want us to go and visit a suspect.'

'Suspect in which case? The old one or the new one?'

'Both.' Chambers said cryptically, looking out of the window as they sped up past Brentford library and over the hump back bridge by the Brentford railway station and left onto the Great West Road.

'Any chance of elaborating?' Tucker said as she put her foot down and gunned the car up the incline towards the traffic lights at Syon Lane. She eased off the accelerator as they closed in on the red traffic light.

Chambers was still looking out of the window as they pulled up alongside the large Homebase DIY store that occupied the corner plot. He was still unsure of how to break the news to Tucker and took his time answering, thinking about what Barlow had told him about Buchanan's exemplary attendance record. The old copper hadn't missed a day in over ten years, but now there was no sign of Buchanan and he wasn't answering his phone. Something didn't feel right.

THE CHARRED FOREST MURDERS

'What do you think? Is there anyone who you think we should be questioning?' Chambers tried to deflect the question back to her as the lights turned green and Tucker accelerated away.

'I haven't a clue. I mean we have three different people under arrest for the recent crimes. Two more murders we have just discovered today. You said yourself, the one in Kensington hasn't been solved yet. The one I took a look at in Acton appears to still be open. No results have come through in the Kew case either and the last murder only happened in Chiswick a couple of days ago. As for suspects in the original murders no idea. Why don't you put me out of my misery.'

'What did you find out about the victim in Acton?'

'Mr Dallas? You won't be surprised to know he fits the MO. Young, white male, found naked.'

'Take the next left.' Chambers interrupted as the three-lane A4 narrowed into two lanes. Tucker swung the car down Thornbury Road, they were now in Isleworth, the next suburb to the west of Brentford.

Pointing to a side street, Chambers directed her to take a left down Church Road and halfway along he indicated a space on the left in front of a 1930s semi-detached house.

'This is it.' He pointed up towards the cream coloured building set back behind a neatly manicured garden.

'Are you sure?' Tucker said as she exited the vehicle.

'I hope not.' Chambers said cryptically just out of Tucker's earshot.

The pair of them walked past the neatly trimmed bushes, shrubs and the flowering mauve petunias and orange and yellow gladioli that lined the concrete path, towards the front door.

Chambers leaned in and gave the brass doorknocker three sharp bangs then stepped back and while he waited he turned and looked back, past the garden resplendent with assortment of red and white roses in full bloom, towards the road. It was the picture of a quiet suburban London street.

'Are you not going to give me a name?' Tucker asked.

'This is Buck's house.' Chambers turned back to face the door. There was no sign of movement from inside.

'Oh, OK. I didn't realise we were picking him up first.'

Chambers lent in and banged again. This time five slow, loud knocks.

'No, this is our final destination.'

'John.' She gave an awkward laugh. 'What are you talking about? Stop messing with me.'

Chambers had moved to his left and was trying to peer through the bay windows. But the curtains were drawn and he could see nothing of what was inside.

'John? What's this all about? Tell me what's going on.' Tucker demanded. She did not look impressed.

Chambers ignored her and returned to the door. He took a moment then hurled himself, shoulder first against the door.

'Christ John!' She looked surprised. 'What do you think you're doing?'

'Just help me get this door open will you?' He charged it again and this time the lock gave way and the door crashed open.

'Buck. It's us. John and Jess.' Chambers shouted into the house. 'Now don't do anything stupid OK?' He stepped through the doorway and stopped in the hallway. There was a small table by the door with a telephone and set of keys on it. A couple of paintings showing tranquil countryside scenes faced each other in the narrow corridor. Directly in front of him was a set of stairs. All he could hear was the faint ticking of a clock coming from somewhere further inside. At that moment he was struck by how peaceful it was. The tranquillity of solitude he thought, there was something comforting in the feeling.

He turned to Tucker and gestured for her to look upstairs. She still looked stunned, but moved past him, shaking her head and carefully began to ascend the carpeted staircase. Peering to his right through the open doorway into the living room Chambers could see no sign of life. The room was neatly furnished two identical brown fabric sofas lined two walls, a 42" flat screen TV that stood silently in the corner, near the bay window with the drawn curtains, was the only contemporary item in the room.

He moved cautiously back into the hallway. The layout of the house was similar to many thirties style houses. He guessed the kitchen would be at the back of the house and probably led out into the garden. The next room on his left was more than likely to be the dining room. The door was closed. Softly he took hold of the doorknob and twisted. Gently easing the white wooden door open. Quickly he poked his head around the door. Nothing. Just a large polished rosewood dining table covered in neat piles of Brentford FC match programmes. Chambers was just exiting the room when he heard an ear-piercing scream come from the floor above.

***

Chapter 26.

Jet suckers

Monday, 18th June 2012 – 3:31pm

Bounding quickly up the narrow stairs, taking them two at a time, he stopped briefly at the top to get his bearings. Directly in front of him was an open door to the bathroom. He darted back along the corridor past a closed door on the left and came into the main bedroom facing out to the front garden. Tucker was sobbing in the corner. Turning to look at the bed he saw what was the bloodied remains of what he guessed was Buchanan. It appeared he had killed himself with a shot to the head. The body was sitting on the bed lying slumped against the headboard in the middle of the bed. A SIG Sauer P226 in the man's open left hand, the head a bloody mess. Chambers battled to overcome his shock and revulsion at the scene and moved towards the body. He was reluctant to touch it and further contaminate the evidence but leaning in there was a clear entry point visible under the chin towards the right side of his jaw. Powder residue could also be seen. The blood that had gushed out of his nose onto his crisp short-sleeved white shirt, had also matted in his short beard but as the head had lolled forward the bullet's entry point was surprisingly clear of congealed blood, just leaving the small neat hole. Judging by the brain and bone tissue spattered on to the headboard and further up on wall, the bullet had exited at the crown. In the middle towards the back of the skull there was a hole roughly the circumference of a golf ball, much bigger than the neat entry point under the chin that was no larger than a pea. Somewhere in the mess behind would be the remains of the bullet. Buchanan's head leaned awkwardly forward. The residue on the wall looked dry and a dark burgundy in colour, indicating it had been some hours since Buchanan had killed himself.

Chambers estimated the suicide had happened between midnight Sunday and the early hours of Monday. Sometime after Buchanan had killed and disposed of his last victim and when his conscience had finally got the better of him.

'Jesus.' Sobbed Tucker. 'What the fuck is going on?' She was clearly shaking.

Just as Chambers was going to walk towards Tucker to comfort her. He noticed a torn piece of paper lying on the bed. He leaned over to take a closer look. Against the patterned duvet was a strip of paper that had Buchanan's distinctly neat and compact handwriting:

I can't stick it any longer.

It may be my fault but not all of it.

Farewell, Terrence

Chambers grabbed his phone and took a photograph of it. Then quickly he moved to console Tucker, making sure he turned her so that she couldn't see the bloody remains of her erstwhile colleague. He needed to get her out of the room, then he would have to call Barlow and explain what he had just discovered.

***

Thirty minutes later and all hell had broken loose in this little corner of Isleworth. The quiet suburban street was now vivid scene of noise and activity. The garden had been cordoned off with Police tape. The inside of the house was swarming with SOCO's and several detectives Chambers recognised from the

Brentford MIT including Rob Black and Lew Hutchinson were already at the scene. Standing aloof in the front garden away from the investigation officers, Chambers looked up towards the ambulance and three police vehicles with their lights flashing and the small crowd of neighbours that had quickly gathered. It was going to be difficult for him now, he knew that, as he looked back to his phone and the image of the letter. He had zoomed in so he could read it more clearly.

I can't stick it any longer.

It may be my fault but not all of it.

It was clear to Chambers it was Buchanan's suicide note. How had Chambers worked alongside the killer for so long and missed all the clues? His encyclopaedic knowledge of the case for one. The insistence, against all other evidence, that the first murder, the one of Figg, was the work of the Stripper was another oddity that had failed to resonate with him. Of course Buchanan knew about Figg, because he had done it or at least been involved.

It may be my fault but not all of it.

Chambers wondered if Buchanan was admitting he'd had an accomplice. He certainly had some help with the latest series of murders, that was why three different nicks held three different suspects. Buchanan must have been referring to the earlier ones or was it just an attempt, even in his final act to try and push the blame on to others? Somehow he had been pulling the strings. All the time laughing at the investigation. Surely, Chambers decided, the policeman Buchanan had referred to being suspected in the Jack the Stripper cases was none other than him.

Chambers had little sympathy for Buchanan after what he had done. Murdering eight women decades previously and no doubt coordinated the recent spate of killings. But the whole thing had left him feeling decidedly uneasy. Chambers was due to leave

THE CHARRED FOREST MURDERS

the force in a matter of days and technically now, he could probably take credit for solving the decades-old mystery as well as putting a plausible case for the modern killings to have been masterminded my one man. But the sentiment remained. He had worked alongside, and very closely with Buchanan for the best part of 10 weeks. How had he not made the connection earlier? He'd heard about Buchanan's nefarious past from several different sources, and he'd seen the moments where Buchanan's rage had appeared to take over – his fist clenched, veins throbbing in his forehead. The signs had been there, the other side of this madman. No one had his intricate knowledge of the case, because they couldn't know the murder scenes like Buchanan did. Hadn't he admitted to being at the scene of the Brentford murder in 1963 and he knew everything there was to know about all of the murders.

Of course there were questions. There always were when a murderer killed himself without ever owning up or explaining his actions. No one would ever find out why, after a hiatus of nearly five decades, Buchanan had decided to start killing again. And why the slight changes to his MO? Why young gay men rather than female prostitutes. Unless the men were male prostitutes? It was something Chambers hadn't considered before and he quickly dismissed it now. For the most part they all had relatively good jobs. It just didn't add up. What had happened to Buchanan in the past year that had caused this derailment, this reversion to a previous life as a serial killer. Even when Buchanan had given him the biggest clue of all, he had ignored it. Chambers shook his head as he recalled Buchanan telling him it was a former policeman who was responsible for all of it. No wonder he had been dragging his heels when he was supposed to come up with a name. He'd been too busy obnubilating. Chambers smiled, that was one of Buchanan's words. To obnubilate. He had needed to explain the meaning to a perplexed looking Chambers when he had first uttered the word. 'You know', and he had put on his mock version of the Queen's English. 'When one wants to make things unclear, indistinct, or blurred. From the Latin obnūbilāre to cover with clouds, from nubes cloud.' He reverted back to his thick London accent. 'Maybe I should just bleeding well say "to muddy the waters". Or my attempts may be seen as me obnubilating.' Buchanan had laughed. He had another word like that. Obfuscation. But that one he saved for Forster. He used to say Forster was a master of the art of obfuscation. The other elaborate word he used was mendacious. Buchanan often used it to describe Forster, but Chambers had never got round to asking him what it meant. It was clear Buchanan was a shrewd, manipulative and capable individual who, more often than not, kept a lot hidden from public view, only occasionally hinting at his intelligence and the rage that dwelt somewhere just below the surface.

Chambers felt hollow inside. Buchanan was an enigma, that much was certain. Chambers had liked him, felt drawn to him for the most part. He was quiet, but open to a few people including himself. Chambers wondered if he had been used by Buchanan, drawn to the flame like a moth only to be ultimately destroyed. Taken into the older policeman's confidence, and rewarded for his loyalty. He had been tricked, outsmarted into believing what he was being told, lapping it up like the fool he was. Buchanan had almost been too smart for him. Almost.

There was something else that didn't make sense, but attention was drawn to the approaching figure of Barlow who had just got out of a police car and was making his way towards him.

There had by Chambers reckoning only been seven recent murders. One was missing if his calculations were correct. His mind went blank. He needed to speak to Tucker to confirm it, but she had disappeared. He'd last seen her getting assisted into the back of a police car. Now he was unsure if she was still around or had been taken back to the station for a reviving cup of hot, sweet tea. She had been as close to Buchanan as much as Chambers. And now he felt guilty that he hadn't warned her before. She hadn't had a chance to adapt her thinking to the fact that Buchanan was the madman, the serial killer then and worse, the serial killer now. But it begged the question – why had he killed himself at seven when he needed eight? Had things got on top? Did he know he was about to be caught? Or had they missed a murder? Maybe something had pushed him over the edge. Something had made him confess in a suicide note and kill himself. Maybe he was a coward after all. Maybe he couldn't face the music. He wouldn't be the first to take easy way out, and he certainly wouldn't be the last.

'John. What in God's name is going on here? The press are all over this? You've got some explaining to do.' Barlow spat venomously.

When he received no response he carried on: 'Why didn't you tell me you thought Buck was in on all of this?' Barlow, ruddy-cheeked, was in Chambers personal space, his hot breath all over his face. 'I've got a good mind to …' Barlow was so mad it rendered him speechless.

Chambers just shrugged. Where should he start? Was there any real point to explaining? Buchanan was dead. The murders would stop. The case of Jack the Stripper could finally be closed. He was finishing at the Met in a few days. It was time to walk away from this life. It was time to start over. Time to find Lucy and hopefully begin again. Chambers turned away from his superior and walked towards the street.

***

Chapter 27.

Gig blaze thief

Tuesday, 19th June 2012 – 9:47am

Chambers was at work in body if not in spirit. He was busy staring out of the window and watching the comings and goings on Brentford High Street that was currently dappled in early morning summer sunshine and the rare sight of short-sleeved commuters boarding the bus.

Turning back to his screen he saw a mail from Dr Bhanji had just come in.

'Dear John,

Sorry for the delay. I have attached the forensic examination but I can give you a quick summary of the From Rotting Hell letter you sent to me.

Ink analysis –The result showed strong alkaline results and the presence of the solvent isopropyl alcohol indicates the ink is Parker Quink, a relatively common fountain pen ink.

Paper analysis – 80gsm A4 printer paper. Standard office copier variety. This is from a batch produced by 5 Star Paper Manufacturers in Slough. The colouring has been created by soaking it in acetic acid (CH_3COOH) in this case malt vinegar and left to dry. It has a distinct smell that is particularly hard to obscure.

As I say reports are attached. I do hope this is of some help.

THE CHARRED FOREST MURDERS

Dr Bhanji'

Chambers closed the email. It was almost irrelevant now. The Brentford MIT team were investigating Buchanan's suicide, and inevitably, he would be questioned in due course, but for now there was little to do other than pass the hours until his leaving drinks in a few days' time.

Pierce and Polk were the only other detectives in the office. Forster was never in on a Tuesday and Adams and Hayes were over at Ealing. The whole place felt like the morning after the night before. When he had come in earlier he had made it perfectly clear he wasn't allowed to discuss the case to prevent the others from asking too many questions. Then he had taken a leaf out of Buchanan's books and put his white iPod headphones in his ears to further stop any unwanted conversation from the others.

Opening his browser he typed in Trivago.com. He might as well use the time he had left to book a hotel room for when he got to Bangkok, he'd be there in less than a week and he still didn't really know what his first step should be. Straight to Laos was probably the logical thing to do. There was just one thing was bothering him though. He stopped his online search and began flicking through the files until he got the one for Elizabeth Figg. The Stripper's first victim in June 1959. He flipped open the folder and began reading it again.

Police had patrolled Dukes Meadows at 12:45am, past an area well known as a spot frequented by prostitutes and their tricks. It was lewdly nicknamed Gobbler's Gulch. When the police car returned at 5:10am, a time just after dawn the patrolling PC saw a woman sitting against a tree on the riverbank 200 yards west of Barnes Bridge back towards Chiswick Bridge.

Chambers looked up from the notes. In his mind west of Barnes Bridge would be Riverside lands not technically Dukes Meadows which was east of the bridge. And it was Riverside Lands where Polk had told him that the body of Pierce's friend was found a couple of days before. The copycat killer was right. The location description of the first murder was wrong. That had to prove another link between then and now. He returned to reading the file notes.

The woman was found dead against the tree facing out over the river. Her navy blue and white dress was torn open and there were scratch marks on her neck. Her handbag, underwear and shoes were never found despite extensive searches of the river the banks and the nearby playing fields and allotments.

Why was Buchanan so insistent that she was a part of the killer's portfolio of murders? The body was almost fully clothed. It just didn't seem to fit the MO or the dates. Only the location was convenient. Also Buchanan would have only been 11 at the time. That didn't sit comfortably with Chambers. It wasn't impossible that an 11 year old could have murdered someone, but it did lend weight to the theory that Buchanan must have had an accomplice at the time. Maybe that was what he was alluding to in his suicide note. Chambers took out his phone and once again looked at the photograph of the note.

I can't stick it any longer.

It may be my fault but not all of it.

Farewell, Terrence

The lined piece of paper was torn on three sides. Top, bottom and right. Only the left edge had been left intact, near the margin with its faint red vertical line. Running perpendicular to the light blue feint lines. It was only just big enough to contain the two lines of copy. Chambers had read it hundreds of times now since he had first seen it and the more he read it the more familiar it was becoming. Chambers had an odd sense of déjà vu. There was something that wasn't quite sitting well with him. He stood up and walked to the next desk. Buchanan's desk. The contrast between his own desk that was an unruly sea of files and notepads and post it notes scattered across it making it impossible to guess the colour of the desktop hidden underneath, while Buchanan's was impeccably neat.

It made Chambers wonder if the man didn't have OCD or some other affliction that meant everything in his life had to be perfectly structured. A killer of his obvious cunning would need to have a mind that operated so precisely. Chambers thought back to the organised piles of football programmes on Buchanan's dining room table, the perfectly colour coordinated garden and the orderly, controlled home. The slumped figure of Buchanan in the bedroom against the headboard, the large mottled dark red bloodstain on the otherwise perfectly made bed. It struck Chambers as weird, this sharp disparity of Buchanan's final gesture. This way reeked of chaos and was completely at odds with the orderly manner in which he had run his life. Despite how controlled the act may have been, he must have known this final act would leave a dreadful mess. Did he realise that the last image people close to him would be left with was one that was so unlike the person that they knew, or at least thought they knew? Maybe that was his point. His final act was an admission as to who he really was. That he wasn't the neat and tidy person they believed him to be. In reality his mind was in complete disorder. Chambers was thinking all of these things as he sifted through the folders in Buchanan's intray until he came across a notepad filled with Buchanan's handwriting. He took it back and compared it to the photograph.

Admittedly he was no graphology expert but to his untrained eye the writing on the suicide note and in the notepad were one and the same. They had similar line and word spacing, the slant of the letters and Buchanan's distinctive style of writing the letters 'g' and 't' were exactly the same. Chambers concluded that whoever had written in Buchanan's notepad had also written the suicide note, the author of both was one and the same person.

And then he noticed it.

Something looked odd about the name at the end. The way Terrence was written. The letters appeared ever so slightly larger. The three 'e' letters in the name seemed more closed than in the rest of the note. Would someone print their name on a suicide note or sign it? He wasn't sure. But this printed name just seemed slightly different to the rest of the note. Chambers sat back and sighed, maybe something deep down inside him wanted it not to be Buchanan. Maybe it was just his ego at work that he didn't want to know he had been tricked. Made to look a fool so easily.

Picking up the phone he wanted to dial Tucker, primarily to see if she was OK, but he had another reason, he still had unanswered questions. Since they had discovered Buchanan's lifeless body he hadn't seen or heard from her and he still needed to find out about the missing eighth murder. At the last moment he checked his email and dialled Dr Bhanji instead.

'Hi Doctor. Chambers here from Brentford.'

'Hello, I trust you received my email.' Chambers noted she had a North American accent. American maybe Canadian.

'Yes I did. Thank you, but actually I'm calling about the death of my colleague – Terry Buchanan.'

'Oh yes. How sad. It's been given a top priority, so the team here are on it right now.'

'Can I ask you to take a look at the suicide note. Particularly at the name. I saw it at the scene and I just thought it looked a little odd. There's probably nothing in it but I thought I should follow up.' I'm sure it would have made its way over with other evidence to you. Chambers mobile phone began to ring. He reached across and declined the call. 'Would that be OK?'

'Not a problem. I'll check it's here and I'm happy to have a look but I doubt I'll have anything for you today. Is tomorrow OK?'

'Fine. Many thanks Doctor.'

THE CHARRED FOREST MURDERS

'Call me Parvati please.'

'Thanks Parvati and also thanks for sending your team over here the other week, it was a very insightful presentation.'

'Glad you found it useful. That's what we're here for. OK bye for now.'

Chambers placed the receiver back down and picked up his mobile and called his voicemail. It was an odd sensation listening to his saved messages from the deceased Buchanan from the previous Friday night. The last two stood out.

Friday 9:41pm – Buchanan. 'John answer your bleeding phone. Drinking with Jess is not good for the liver. I got to do one out the back door or I'm doomed. Have a good one you old bastard.'

Friday 11:49pm – Buchanan. 'Johnny boy. I'm onto something. I think I've got it all figured out. I'll tell you when you pick up your bloody phone. You ain't going to believe it! Call me back when you get this. It's urgent.'

Buchanan had seemed in good spirits leaving the pub just after 9:30pm on the Friday night. It was hard to reconcile the man who made that call would be committing a murder within 24 hours and killing himself with 48 hours. Maybe he was feigning being drunk. With everything that happened in the past day surely anything was possible, Chambers reasoned.

The last message he played over again. Buchanan sounded heavily intoxicated but the lightness and frivolity of the previous message had gone. This time he sounded deadly serious. But what was he alluding to? He said he was on to something, he had it figured out and he had wanted to tell Chambers what it was. It didn't sound like he wanted to admit to something. It sounded like he had solved something. Chambers felt a distinctly uneasy sensation pass over him. There was a gut feeling that he should go back to the house and locate Buchanan's study to see what he had been working on when he got back from the pub on Friday night. But he knew he wouldn't be able to get access. Unless he could take someone from MIT with him.

Picking up the phone he dialled Tucker's office number but it rang out. He tried her mobile and this time she answered.

'Hi Jess. How are you?'

'John,' she said quietly, there was none of her usual flirtatiousness or cheekiness, 'I'm OK you know. Just trying to come to terms with it all. I just wish …' she tailed off.

'What?'

'I just wish you had told me Buck was a suspect. The whole thing was just such a bloody big shock.'

'I know and I'm really sorry. It was way out of order. I hadn't really thought of him as a suspect until the very end. It was all very sudden. Are you in the office?'

'No. Hutchinson sent me home yesterday. Told me to take a day to get my head together. I'm just heading out for a run.'

'OK well I just wanted to see if you were OK. Will you be back in tomorrow?'

'Aye, more than likely.'

'Take care and call me if you decide to come in. Bye.' He hung up.

There was no point pushing her today, he'd wait until she came in tomorrow. Then he'd test the delicate matter of getting her to take him back to the scene of Buchanan's suicide if that's what it was. For now he would see if he could find a link between the three suspects in the recent cases.

***

Chapter 28.
Clerks dull ops
Wednesday, 20th June 2012 – 9:47am

There was a full team in the office when Chambers arrived late on Wednesday morning. It made the absence of Buchanan all the more obvious. Even Forster was in for one of his rare midweek appearances. But as Chambers entered he could sense the tension in the room. No one was speaking or looking particularly pleased to be there. Chambers had been running late as he had stopped by at the doctor to pick up a prescription for an extra pack of doxycycline for his trip. The travel nurse on duty had supplied him with a helpful list of do's and don'ts for his travels.

He checked his email but there was still nothing from Dr Bhanji about the suicide note. Picking up the phone he called Tucker. She answered almost immediately.

'Jess it's John. You got time for a quick coffee?'

'Aye sure. See you in the canteen in a minute.' She sounded more upbeat than the day before.

Chambers hung up, picked up a notepad and made his way to the door. He couldn't resist a quick look at the board and was vaguely surprised to see that no new quiz question had been posted since the one on Friday that had already been solved. His gaze drifted across to Forster who was staring at him. The old man gave him a lascivious wink.

'That your bird on the blower was it?'

Chambers ignored him.

'Off for a little date are you? Do me a favour will you. Can you give her a number for me.'

Chambers paused at the door. 'Sure what is it? A phone number for something?'

Forster began to laugh. 'Nah. Just give her one from me.' The old man let out a belly laugh.

Polk joined in the sniggering.

Forster turned to his nephew Pierce. 'You want a take a leaf out of John's book. He knows what to do with the birds.'

Pierce just shot him an angry look in return but didn't react. Chambers closed the door behind him. Only a few more days and he would be free of all this crap.

Tucker was already at a table with two coffees.

'Here,' she said gesturing to one of the coffees as he sat down.

'Thanks. How are you feeling now?'

'Still shocked by it all. A bit embarrassed you saw me like that. I've been to plenty of murder scenes. It was just such a surprise. I mean I was drinking with him Friday and he was in great spirits, really interested in the case you know? He seemed to think he was on the brink of solving it. She stopped and took a sip of her coffee. Chambers noticed her hand was shaking slightly. 'Then it turns out he's the murderer and then he kills himself. It's all just so bloody hard to take in.'

'I know. It's madness it really is. So how are the MIT about it?'

'Same as us. Complete state of shock. Buck's been part of the furniture here for God knows how long. Most of them have worked and drank with him for years. It's not the sort of thing you can just compartmentalise and file away like it's just another death. This is personal, painful you know?'

Chambers nodded. 'I need a favour Jess.' He said eventually.

'What is it?' She replied defensively.

'I need access to the crime scene.'

'Jesus. What on earth for? Can't you just let it lie now? Buck's gone.'

'There's something I just want to clear up. I need to do this. Call it closure if you will.'

'I don't know, if Barlow finds out I'll be for the high jump. Maybe it's best if I go alone. It will raise less questions. Tell me what it is you need to see? Buck's body's been taken to the morgue for the post mortem.'

'OK, maybe you're right. I don't want to get you in any more trouble. I just need to try and find a notepad.'

'What notepad?'

'The one he used to write the suicide note on. I just thought it was a bit strange that he would have ripped a sheet out then torn it down to a little scrap. I'd like to see the rest of the pad. He was working on something that Friday night when he got home. I had a missed call from him around midnight.'

Chambers brought up the picture on his mobile and showed it to Tucker. 'See it's got a feint blue horizontal line and looks like a red vertical line on the left margin. I've had a look through his things here at work and nothing matches.'

'John. I'll do this for you. But this is it. Do you understand? You're leaving in less than three days. I'm not. If things go belly up I'll be the one left in the shit.'

Chambers nodded solemnly. 'I really appreciate this. Can I ask, now you've had a bit of time to think about it. How do you feel about it being Buck? I mean I still can't believe it really.'

'No it's not really sunk in properly. I mean it's just so peculiar the way he did it?'

'The murders?'

'Well yes, but I meant the suicide. He hated guns. I recall him saying that on a few occasions. He had a fear and loathing of them. Why didn't he gas himself or overdose on pills or something?'

'Yeah or attached an hose to his car's exhaust?'

'Apart from the fact he didn't own a car. I'm guessing that might have caused him a problem.'

'Chambers could hear the sarcasm in her voice. He guessed she was still angry with him for what he had unwittingly led her into at Buchanan's house a few days previously. 'Yeah, good point.'

'OK, I'll head over there now. I'll call you if I find anything.' She stood up, grabbed her coffee and left Chambers mulling over what she had just said. Chambers hadn't remembered that part. But now she mentioned it, Buchanan had told him previously about his aversion to firearms but the news he didn't have a car came as a surprise. He just assumed Buchanan drove but now he couldn't be sure. It was something else he needed to check out.

Chambers was still sitting at the table five minutes later when Polk came in. He looked around and on seeing Chambers he made his way over without getting a drink.

'John. Can I have a word?'

'Sure take a seat.'

Polk seemed nervous. 'I feel bad saying this. Talking out of turn like. Just something I thought you should know.'

'Fire away. What is it?'

'It's Piercy ... Paul I mean.'

THE CHARRED FOREST MURDERS

'What about him? Is he rowing with his uncle again?'

'No it's not that. Although they're not getting on well right now. It's more about Paul's how should I put it? Preferences?'

'Preferences?'

'Sexual you know what I mean.' He had a quick look over his shoulder to make sure no one was listening. 'He's bent.' Polk quickly corrected himself, 'he's gay I mean.'

Chambers couldn't say the news came as much of a revelation; he'd had his suspicions about Pierce from day one. 'And?' Pierce's sexual persuasion was his own business and something that didn't need to be gossiped about by his colleagues as far as Chambers was concerned.

'Don't get me wrong I haven't got nothing against them. I was a bit surprised is all. You know he was always talking up his time on the pull and all that. Anyway it's just I think that bloke that was murdered the other day in Chiswick. I think that might have been his boyfriend.'

Chambers sat bolt upright. 'You what? Why do you think that?'

'My missus had been out shopping last weekend in the big Westfield up the Bush. She saw Paul and a bloke in the mall. She said she was sure it was Paul but when he saw her he disappeared sharpish. So anyway, long story short, that victim's picture was in the paper yesterday. She swears blind it was the man she saw with Paul last week.'

'Russell. I think for now you shouldn't say anything to anyone. Not until we can get a bit more information on this, right? Not a word to anyone you understand? By the way do you know Paul's home address?'

'Yeah, in fact he moved back in with his mum a month or so back. Said his girlfriend had kicked him out. That's a laugh innit?'

'Did you ever meet her? His ex I mean?'

'No, come to think of it. I've only heard about his women never met any of them. No wonder, right?'

'OK. Can you email me his address?'

'Sure. I'll do it now.' Polk got up and made his way out of the canteen.

Chambers shook his head. Whatever it was that was going on, things were getting weirder by the day.

***

Chapter 29.

Mourning lead

Thursday, 21st June 2012 – 10:12am

The previous day had been somewhat of an anticlimax. Tucker hadn't got back in touch about the notepad; only sending a text to him saying she had been pulled in for questioning about Buchanan's suicide regarding the reasons she had been out at the scene. She would get back to the house in Isleworth as soon as she could, maybe later that day or even the day after – when time permitted. Chambers had spent the rest of the afternoon idly watching the office dynamic. Since he had heard about Sandra Hayes' resignation it was now clear to him why she had spent so much time out of the office. He realised just how bad the constant sniping, sexist banter and backstabbing from Polk, Pierce and Forster had really been. He had simply filtered or tuned it out from his first day, caught up in his own thoughts and reflections. He knew he hadn't been at his best since he joined and he wasn't one for making excuses. How he had failed to grasp the full extent of just how negative an environment was present was clearly a reflection on his poor management. And now a source of embarrassment to him. He had badly let Hayes down. He should have stepped in earlier to stamp out the sexist attitude that pervaded the office but part of him had just wanted to ignore it and wallow in his own issues.

The guilt just added to his belief that he had done the right thing in deciding to leave. It was clearly time, he had taken his eye of the ball. It was just fortunate that he had managed to close a cold case and inadvertently solve several modern open cases as well, but it gave him little satisfaction that it was his friend who was ultimately the serial killer. It was just another example of how bad his judgement calls had become lately. Here was another one to add to the list. Now he couldn't wait to get away. The search for Lucy would be different. There would be no distractions and he would be totally focussed and he wouldn't rest until he had gained some closure, whether it was good news or bad.

At this stage Buchanan's suicide would be seen as just that. It was only Tucker and himself that knew about his links to the Stripper killings and as far as Barlow, and the MIT units at Brentford and other West London police stations, there was nothing linking any of the modern killings. It was probably best that way, Chambers decided. He'd only spoken to Tucker briefly at the scene of the suicide and on the phone, when he had told her then there was no point explaining their theory. The murders would stop and Buchanan suicide could be quietly filed away. It was probably in the Met's best interests anyway he figured. It wouldn't be the ideal piece of PR to admit that London's worst serial killer of all time and a case unsolved for half a century had been committed by one of their own. No it would be best if he kept his mouth shut, he just hoped Tucker would do the same. How Buchanan had been able to manipulate the three young men to take the blame was another story and one for now that he didn't care to dig into. Buchanan would have had his ways, maybe as an exchange for not arresting them or however he'd been able to manipulate people in the past. With only a couple of days left on the force it would fall to someone else to uncover, but by then he'd be long gone.

Forster, Chambers had noticed during his leisurely study of the group of three, was looking thinner than he had a few weeks before. Although he was still a big man he had definitely lost some weight since Chambers had joined the team, his face looked almost gaunt, or appeared that way despite him still looking overweight. It was the hollow eyes, Chambers decided, that were making him look thinner or unhealthier. In fact he was beginning to look desperately ill. Maybe things were coming to an end for him. The cancer that he had been battling looked like it had taken the upper hand and the war would soon be over. Chambers wanted to ask after his health but was unsure of how Forster would react to the invasion of his privacy. Badly, Chambers guessed.

The three others were deep in debate over something; Chambers could hear the occasional swear word or mocking laugh. It was as if they couldn't communicate unless they were taking the piss out of someone. It was sad, he reflected, that it was the only way they could relate to each other. But the normal warmth that Pierce had previously shown his uncle seemed to have diminished to the point of constant hostility. There was volatility between the pair. Chambers just hoped the friction didn't spill over until the following week when he had left. It was odd though, if Forster's illness was getting worse, he imagined Pierce would have been more protective, less vitriolic, not the other way round. Something had definitely changed in their relationship. The thing was that Chambers hadn't cared for them in the beginning and now with a couple of days left he didn't really care about them at all.

When Chambers arrived at work on Thursday morning it was with some relief that he noted it was one of the two guaranteed Chad-free days of the week. Pierce and Polk were in, but not the others. There was an email from Dr Bhanji waiting in his inbox. The time stamp revealed it had been sent just before midnight the previous day.

'Dear John,

Thank you for your recent enquiry about the alleged suicide note found at the DS Terrence Buchanan's residence on 18th June 2012. I have taken undertaken an extensive analysis of the *ink and also of the handwriting samples. I have attached for your reference but in short I agree with your initial speculation. I ran some tests on the ink and although all of the writing appears in blue ink – it is made up from two distinct types of ink (signature is type 2, rest is type 1 as marked in the attached PDF) although both from types of disposable pens that you could purchase in any stationary store. Also my initial investigation into the graphology suggested from the slight divergence in the slanting of the letters between the body copy to the signature reveals that the initial penmanship was created by a left handed person and the signature was written by a right handed, trying to imitate how the rest of the copy was created.*

I believe it is particularly pertinent that this information be related back to the investigating team.

Please don't hesitate to contact me.

Regards,

Parvati'

It took a moment for him to take in what just what the email meant. But if Dr Bhanji was sending, or already had sent, this information to the MIT then it would be practicable to presume that Hutchinson would be changing his view of the death of Buchanan from suicide to murder. If this was the case Chambers wanted to find that notepad before the scene of the crime got locked down. He reached over and picked up the handset and dialled Tucker, all the time thinking that one of the men who hadn't been picked up yet, maybe the murderer at Kew, or one of the others, maybe the last one in Chiswick had decided to come back and deal with Buchanan. Whatever it was Chambers wanted that notepad and quickly.

'DS Tucker.'

'Hi Jess, how was the interview yesterday?' Chambers tried to keep it light.

'Just a formality really. They just wanted to know why we were there and what Buchanan's state of mind had been.'

Chambers thought she sounded fairly relaxed. If Dr Bhanji had sent the report to someone in MIT then it clearly hadn't been made public, or he hoped, she hadn't sent it at all and was expecting me to do so. 'What did you say?'

'John,' now she sounded a bit irritated, 'I told them we had gone to pick him up on our way to go and visit a witness in a cold case who might be able to help you out on something for one of your cold cases. I only offered to drop you off as it was on my way to see a suspect of my own.'

Chambers nodded, he felt a surge of relief. 'Jess any chance you, or both of us, can get out there and have a look for that notepad? I really think if we can find something that he wrote on the day it might give us an insight into what he was thinking on his last day.' He was still being frugal with the truth, but he couldn't tell her what he had just read. Not yet anyway.

'Sure, if it will get you off my back. But I need you stay in the car. And John?'

'Yes?'

'I'm only doing this because you are gone tomorrow. I doubt you can get me into more crap before you are off. I bloody well hope so anyway.'

'OK and thanks Jess. I really appreciate everything you've done.' Chambers hung up.

**

Nearly thirty minutes later Tucker pulled the Mondeo up a hundred metres short of Buchanan's house. There was one officer working at the house and after passing the blue and white police tape that still surrounded the house, Chambers could see her enter into conversation with the officer before she moved towards the door and out of his line of sight.

Chambers sat drumming his fingers on the dashboard for what seemed like an eternity before Tucker appeared almost twenty minutes later. As she approached the front of the car, he noticed she was empty handed, but she flashed him a smile and came round to let herself into the driver's seat.

It was only when she had sat down and slammed the door closed that she slipped a notepad from inside her jacket pocket and passed it to him. Chambers eyes lit up.

'This was all I could find. It was the only one that fitted the description you gave me. It was in his bedside cabinet. The last place I looked and I've not had a chance to flick through it. The other detective there was starting to wonder what I was doing in there.'

'Thanks Jess. Let's hope this is it.'

'That's it John. I can't be doing you any more favours. Do you hear?'

'I know. Look I think it's best if I make my own way back to the station. That way it won't draw any unnecessary attention to you if we arrive back together. I'll just take a hike down to the main road and grab a 237 back.' Chambers was already opening the door and climbing out. 'Thanks again Jess. I mean it. I'm massively in your debt.'

'OK, well you bloody well better not let me down when I come to claim what's owed.' She gave him a wink.

He closed the door and she sped off along the street.

Chambers pulled a sheet of paper out of his pocket. It was the address for Paul Pierce that Polk had emailed to him the day before. Chambers had copied the address into Google maps and printed it off. The address was at the end of a dogleg cul-de-sac, King's Avenue in Hounslow East, it was about a 15-minute walk from his current location. As he set off he began flicking through the notepad. About half of its pages had notes of some sort written on, the rest was empty.

THE CHARRED FOREST MURDERS

Most of the notes were shopping lists or comprised endless rows or figures that Chambers guessed were his home accounts unless they were codes for something else, but they seemed fairly inane. The pages were filled out with these mundane insights into Buchanan's life. He began thumbing quickly to the last page entry and when he saw it he stopped dead in his tracks.

On the page were some words but an area had been torn roughly out. To the right and below the missing section read:

I'm sorry Harry is a burden to you.
Give my love to the kid.

Jock
PS. To save you and the police looking for me I'll be in the garage.

Chambers fumbled for his phone and flicked through his images until he found the one of the torn suicide note.

"I can't stick it any longer.
It may be my fault but not all of it.

Farewell, Terrence

He held up the image up to the torn notepad and saw that the two pieces fit together perfectly. The whole original message, if he deleted the additional forged name, would have read:

I can't stick it any longer.
It may be my fault but not all of it. I'm sorry Harry is a burden to you.
Give my love to the kid.
Farewell,
Jock
PS. To save you and the police looking for me I'll be in the garage.

How had he been so stupid? He had seen this before. This was the original suicide note that Buchanan had showed him for du Rose's prime suspect back in the original investigation in the sixties. This was Mungo Ireland's suicide note. It was the PS – that last line, that was the one that du Rose had argued proved beyond belief that Mungo Ireland was the killer. Now it was clear that someone had either found this note, or more probably had Buchanan write it out. Then it was just a matter of tearing the sheet to only include the parts of the first three lines and add in Buchanan's name to the right of the word 'farewell'.

Dr Bhanji's ink and graphology analysis proved the name 'Terrence' had been added later in a different hand using a different pen. This pointed to the fact his friend had been murdered and not killed himself. But it didn't prove Buchanan wasn't Jack the Stripper or was involved in the recent murders. But added to the fact Buchanan had called him to say he thought he had solved it only added to Chambers feeling that the real killer was still out there.

***

Chapter 30.

Cerise rope

Thursday, 21st June 2012 – 11:59am

Chambers stood outside the address in Hounslow East and rang the doorbell. He was still somewhat in shock about the discovery of the notepad and the adulterated suicide note. The page entries before the suicide note were no longer simple lists for household products, but notes about several policemen that Buchanan had begun to think may have been the killer back in the sixties. Detectives who had been either questioned in relation to the murders or who had later had criminal convictions against them for attempted murder, rape or other serious crimes. None of the names struck a chord with Chambers but when he got back to the station he would begin looking through Buchanan's files to see what he could unearth.

A woman answered, Chambers guessed she was in her mid- to late-sixties. She had short grey curly hair and a heavily lined faced.

'Hello, can I help you?' She said in a friendly if slightly guarded tone.

Chambers flashed his police ID. 'Hi, I'm DI John Chambers, I work with your son Paul at Brentford. Is he in?' Chambers said knowing full well he was at the station.

'Hello, er no, he's at work. What's all this about? Is he in trouble?'

'No, no,' Chambers smiled at her. 'Actually do you mind if I come in?'

'Of course not. Would you like a drink? Tea, coffee?'

'A water would be great.' Chamber said crossing the threshold as the woman directed him in to the living room and towards a faux leather sofa by the wall facing the window as she bustled into the kitchen.

When she returned she had a worried look on her face as she passed him the glass.

'Mrs …' Chambers paused.

'Pierce. Rose Pierce.' She filled in the missing blanks.

'Mrs Pierce. I'd just like a moment of your time. I'm sure it's nothing to worry about but I just noticed Paul seemed a little bit down recently and I thought it might be an idea to have a quick chat with you and see if everything is OK. I understand he's just broken up with his,' Chambers hesitated, 'his fiancé? And moved back in with you. Is that right?'

The old lady look puzzled. Fiancé? I don't think so? And he's lived here with me for the past five years.'

'Really?' Chambers was genuinely surprised that Polk had given him such misleading information. 'I'm sorry. My mistake. A friend of his told me he was a bit down after a recent relationship break up.'

'Detective Inspector, I think you ought to know my son is gay. He's battled against a lot of prejudice during his life. I don't know what he's told his colleagues and bosses. My guess is he hasn't told anyone. He's had a difficult past. It was tough for me and his father to take the news when he came out. I got used to it, he's my son. But his father never did. He walked out years ago. It brought us closer together, Paul and I. He's a good boy. He seemed happy enough recently and he'd met someone he seemed to get on with.'

THE CHARRED FOREST MURDERS

Chambers searched his memory for the name of the man found a few days before at the riverside in Chiswick. 'Wilson?'

'Yes, Henry Wilson. But how …' She tailed off. 'How did you know that if you didn't know that he was gay?'

'I'm sorry Mrs Pierce. I think somewhere I've got my wires crossed. Please forgive me for the intrusion.' Chambers began to get up from his seat but decided to change the subject, the confused look on the old woman's face wasn't reassuring him. 'How is Chad, I mean, Charlie? You know he comes in to help us out from time to time. He lives round here doesn't he?' Chambers recalled he had said something about coming from Isleworth or Hounslow not far from where Buchanan lived.

'Yes, we all grew up round here. This was my parents' house. We're the last of the originals you could say. Not many locals left, just immigrants round here now.' She said matter of factly. 'He moved into one of them new builds, Brackendale Close. It's just at the back of here, but you got to head out back to Spring Grove Road, up Jersey Road almost till you get to the A4 and it's on the right. Silly thing is it takes about 10 minutes to walk but our back gardens almost touch each other.' Her features relaxed into one of sadness. 'He's not got long left you know? The cancer is in its final stages now. He's been through a lot and I think it's taken its toll on him mentally and physically. You would think they would have found a blasted cure by now.'

Chambers nodded.

'I try and cheer him up, cook him some dinner, take it round. The place is a bit of a mess but he won't let me in to clean. He comes here for a bite sometimes. The rest of the time he's messing about with those computer things. What do you call it? Interweb or something. I'm too old for all that kind of stuff, but he was always the smart one. Always loved electric things.' She let out a sigh and said almost to herself. 'I never thought I'd outlive them both.'

'Both?' Chambers was unsure as to whom she was referring to. 'Your husband and Charlie?' He ventured.

'No, my husband is alive and well and living in Whitton. Worse luck.' She gave him a brief, grim smile. 'No my other brother, Alfred. He was a policeman as well you know? Paul was following in the family footsteps. Both his uncles and my father, god rest his soul.'

'Oh I'm sorry to hear that. It must make it all the harder to see what's happening to Charlie. Was it recent? The passing of Alfred I mean?' Chambers regretted his lack of tact in asking.

'Oh no. The poor man killed himself a long, long time ago. Back in the sixties. Such a sad affair it was. Killed himself over a woman. She broke his heart you see. I wish I had known just how much it affected him, he just kept it bottled up. Not like today. More blinking likely to go on TV or go to one of them quack doctors. But do you know what? The guilt, it never leaves you. I'm always thinking was there something I could have said or done to change things? Prevent it you know?'

'I'm sorry, I should leave you in peace, I didn't mean to come blundering in here stirring up all these emotions. Please forgive me.'

'It's OK Detective Inspector you weren't to know.'

'Maybe it's worth you and I keeping a close watch on Paul. I don't mean to pry it's just he seemed a little down is all.'

'Thank you I'll do that. Are you sure you won't have a cuppa? I've got some nice rich tea biscuits.'

Chambers felt an enormous sense of sadness for this personable old woman. Her husband run off, one brother dying of cancer, the other committed suicide, a son who had a chip on his shoulder, angry at the world with or without good reason. It made him think that if we knew the cards we were to be dealt in life would we still choose to carry on if they could be as cruel as the ones Mrs Pierce had received? 'No, I'd better be getting back.' He said moving towards the door.

'One last thing,' he stopped suddenly to face her. 'Where did your brother work? What was his station?'

'Oh, he was up Notting Hill. Going back a bit now. He must have been up there from the late fifties up until his death – 13th April 1965. That day's etched on my memory.'

Chambers tried not to show any reaction when she said the date. It was about three months after the last murder and a month after John du Rose's primary suspect, Mungo Ireland, had killed himself effectively bringing an end to the investigation.

'And his name was Alfred Forster.' Chambers said out loud but more to himself trying to think back to whether he had seen the name in any of the files or on Buchanan's notepad but he couldn't make the connection. He would check the notepad again more thoroughly when he got outside.

'No, no. He was Alfred Pierce.'

Chambers looked confused. 'I don't follow. I thought Pierce was your married name and Forster would be your maiden name same as Chad.'

'No we're all Pierce's. When I was married I became a Rattigan but after we split I went back to my maiden name.'

'But Chad … Charlie, I mean. If he's your brother how come he's a Forster?'

'Oh that,' she smiled. 'Charlie was adopted see? His parents were killed in the Blitz. My mum and dad knew his folks so they took him in. It was before I was born. It was 1944, he was a newborn baby. Alf was four years older and I came along a couple of years after Charlie was adopted. When he was 15 he found out. My parents hadn't wanted him to know, brought him up as their own. But he found a letter. I was about 13 and I remember he didn't take it too well. He changed his name from Pierce to Forster, that was his original family name. But he didn't do it immediately. He did that a few years later after he joined the police.'

'When was that, do you remember?' Chambers was intrigued by the story. He tried to imagine what impact that the news would have on a teenager, finding out that his parents had been killed by a bomb during the war.

'Before Alf, you know,' she looked wistful at the sound of his name, 'probably about '62 or '63, somewhere about there I should say.'

Chambers almost felt sorry for Chad Forster. He'd been through the mill a few times in his life, no wonder he had become the bitter old man that he was.

'Well thanks for taking the time to explain all this to me, and I'll keep an eye on Paul for you.'

She got up stiffly from her chair, 'my pleasure Detective Inspector. Anything you can do for Paul would be greatly appreciated. Let me show you to the door.' She shuffled past him.

As Chambers exited he turned and said, 'probably best we keep the visit to ourselves I don't want Paul to think we're talking out of turn about him.'

The old woman nodded and gave him a wave as he set off down the garden path and back towards the main road. He was only a few minutes from Forster's house but he decided against paying the old man a visit even though he was curious as to see the state of the house in which he dwelled.

***

Chambers was walking back down Spring Grove Road towards the 237 bus stop located outside the West Thames

College on the London Road when his phone rang. It was Tucker.

'John, where are you?'

'Heading back to the station now. Should be 10 minutes why?'

'Hutchinson has just got the post mortem results back.'

'So? I mean we both saw what happened to Buck.'

'Yes but do you recall what hand Buck used?'

'Left.' Chambers stopped walking and thought back to the grisly murder scene, visualising the slumped body of his colleague and the position of the weapon. 'The gun was definitely in his left hand.'

'Yes but the entry point under his chin was towards the right of his jaw but exited towards the left hand side of his crown. I'm not saying it's impossible to do, but it's unnatural.'

Unnatural, thought Chambers, as if blowing your brains out was a completely natural event. But he couldn't help transferring the phone to his left hand and holding it under his chin on the right hand side like a pistol and aiming up and slightly left. It was definitely an awkward position to then angle it back and have the exit point in the middle of the temple.

'So what are you saying?' After the information Chambers had received about the forged suicide note, he knew it was looking more and more likely that Buchanan had been murdered, but it didn't necessarily mean he wasn't the original Jack the Stripper or have ties to the latest murders. Chambers was still confident that he was involved but maybe he had been murdered by an accomplice.

'I'm saying Buck didn't kill himself. It's a murder and you know more about this than you're letting on. I think you'd better come back to the station and give me that notepad. I'm sure that's got something to do with all this.' She sounded extremely unimpressed.

Chambers knew it was time to come clean to Tucker at least, that way they might be able to solve the puzzle of Buchanan's death at least before he left the following day.

***

THE CHARRED FOREST MURDERS

Chapter 31.

Short amen

Li had counted a week had passed since Shen had recaptured her on the deck of the sampan when she had been so close to her freedom she could almost taste it. Shen and a colleague from the other vessel had bound and gagged her before dragging her aboard the bigger ship. She had tried not to show the pain from what she was now sure was her broken wrist.

Tied up and hidden among some packing cases in the hold of the new boat, Li could see from a high porthole the slow passing of the sun, which she couldn't see from her position but could only tell from the amount of light that entered the damp and claustrophobic ship's hold. From time to time a young boy would come down and leave a bowl of plain rice and a metal cup of water. He would take her gag off but wouldn't undo her painful bindings. The discomfort from her injuries compounded by the poor diet was beginning to take its toll on her health.

After a week with no other human contact except for the silent cabin boy, Li had reached her lowest point. She had no idea where she was getting taken to or what possible motive Shen had to be transporting her or keeping her alive for that matter. She lived in constant fear that the next time the heavy door opened it would be to introduce her tormentor or worse, her executioner.

When a week had passed, Li heard the familiar sound of seagulls that made her think they were now close to land. It was impossible for her to establish how far or where they had travelled. Eventually another of the ship's crew came in, blindfolded and gagged her before dragging her up onto the deck. She knew it was night from the lack of sun before she was taken up. The cool fresh winds were some consolation. She was dumped roughly on the deck and left in almost complete sensory deprivation for what seemed like an eternity. She could hear voices, but the language was unfamiliar to her.

Eventually she was picked up and transferred to something that seemed to be lower down than where she was at. She had given up all thoughts of resisting because she had no energy left. Whatever she had been moved to soon became clear as a motor started and the speedboat took off at great speed to yet another unknown destination. During the journey she was placed into something else that from the smell and texture she guessed was some kind of large tarpaulin bag.

The 15-minute boat ride concluded when the engine was cut and the vessel collided with something and came to a sudden stop. She was manhandled up on to what she guessed was a dock. She could only assume that if anyone happened past they would just see a large tarpaulin bag. She wanted to shout or squirm but in all honesty there was no guarantee that there would be anyone around to see her attempts to raise the alarm. For now she would hold on and conserve her energy for a better-educated attempt to escape or draw attention to her plight.

After another seemingly infinite delay, she was whisked away to a nearby building. The bag was opened and she was dragged to her feet. Her strength had deserted her and she was unable to stand unaided. A man who she didn't recognise pushed her into another room where two other women were kneeling. This room had dirty walls and a concrete floor that was strewn with what looked like red flyers. There was no direct light source where she currently was, but enough illumination emanated from the adjacent room to throw a pall of light into the grimy room.

She was pushed to her knees and told in rough Cantonese to keep quiet. There was the noise of somebody fiddling with something behind her. Then a bright flash blinded her. It had to be a camera's flash. She'd had her eyes covered and the sudden bright light came as a shock and it took her some time for eyes to adjust back to her dimly lit surroundings. Scattered about the floor were the red brochures and pamphlets but she couldn't make out what they read. The opportunity had arisen for Li to get some clues as to where she was. If she could get a look at the ephemera on the floor, she might learn of an address and she could get a better view of the women next to her she might be able to guess their ethnicity, something that could shed some light on her new place of incarceration. Slowly she leaned forward and turned to get a better look at the women to her left. They were kneeling in the same position as her, and her first thought was they were Asian but where they were from she wasn't sure. They didn't lift their eyes from staring down at the floor in front of them. She leaned further forward to get a better look to see if she could ascertain their ethnicity, as she did so, she felt a heavy blow to the back of her head that both stunned her and knocked her painfully face forward to the floor. She tumbled to her side as the first boot slammed into her back. For a moment she thought about giving up accepting her fate and letting them beat her to death, what was the point of carrying on? Instead she pulled her knees up to her chest and curled into a ball determined that she would fight on until her last breath.

***

Chapter 32.

Whiners only

Friday, 22nd June 2012 – 10:09am

Friday was Chambers last day at the Met, an organisation he had worked at for more than two decades, and it had begun in disappointing fashion. There wasn't even a full team to greet him on his arrival. Polk had emailed in sick, while Hayes and Adams were over at Ealing making slow progress in their ongoing investigation. It was only Paul Pierce and his uncle Chad Forster in the office, both gave him monosyllabic grunts of acknowledgement when he arrived. Chambers wasn't really in the mood for conversation with either of them and sat down to go through his emails that mainly consisted of farewell messages from ex-colleagues at the different teams he'd been in across London throughout his Met career. There were a couple of emails from HR outlining the procedures he needed to complete before he left later in the day, but nothing from Barlow either in terms of a farewell or the organisation of a leaving drink. He shouldn't really be surprised.

The previous afternoon he had met with Tucker and handed over the notepad but he had made sure he had taken photos of the last ten pages while he'd been riding the bus back to Brentford. And it was these he began looking at again when he finished with clearing out his inbox. Her attitude towards him was much cooler despite him agreeing with her that Buck's death was not a suicide. It didn't help that Buchanan was still the prime suspect for the Stripper murders.

THE CHARRED FOREST MURDERS

But on one of the pages was a short list of names of policemen that Buchanan had written down and annotated that they needed further investigation. Chambers began to get an odd sensation that Buchanan might have been on to something and was maybe not the killer after all.

DC D. Cushway

SI T. Butler (Flying Squad)

DC F. Pierce

DS R. Thomson

The third name on the list stood out. DC F. Pierce. It had meant nothing to him before the trip to Hounslow, but now Alfred Pierce, or possibly the F. stood for Fred, meant it was something that he needed to investigate a little more. Was Alfred Pierce somehow involved? Also he had to get to the bottom of the correlation between Milo Stone, Samuel Zook and Godfrey Stahel. At this stage no one had connected the three men together except for Buchanan, Tucker and himself, and now Buchanan was dead. Chambers felt an uneasy feeling wash over him.

If Buchanan really had nothing to do with either set of murders and had been killed for getting too close to the truth did that mean that his and Tucker's lives were now at risk? And why had Paul Pierce repeatedly been trying to log on to his terminal? Until now Chambers had assumed that Pierce had been unable to gain entry. But that wasn't necessarily the case. Maybe there was a link between the Pierce of Buchanan's list and something in Paul Pierce's past. Maybe Pierce had been able to login, but then what? What did that compromise? Chambers didn't have enough technical knowledge to know what that the implications of such action would be. Could Pierce access confidential information through his PC. He sat for a moment before emailing Tucker.

'Jess,

Have you come across the name, Alfred (or Fred) Pierce in your investigations into the Stripper case or in your discussions with Buchanan?

Cheers

John'

He pressed send then turned his attention back to the enormous pile of files relating to the original Stripper killings. This time he would see if any of the investigating officers bore the name Alfred Pierce. Opening the first file of Elizabeth Figg from 1959 he was aware that Forster had turned and was watching him, it was as if the old man knew what he was thinking. Chambers thought that maybe it was about time they had a little chat about the old man's dead brother.

'Chad,' he called across the office, 'I've just come across something interesting in the file.'

Chambers desk phone rang and he recognised the number that appeared on the caller ID as that of Tucker. He picked up the receiver and held one finger out towards Forster. That conversation could wait for a few minutes.

'Jess? You got my email then?' He lowered his voice aware that Pierce had also turned round to face him, alerted by him calling across the office.

'Yes. And in response to your email – yes he did mention that name. Seems he had a connection to all the women that were killed.'

Chamber quickly began flicking through the pages of the Figg file, looking for the names of the officers on the scene but none of them corresponded to that of Pierce.

'As an investigating officer? I can't see any reference in the Figg file, let me check Rees.'

'No, I wouldn't bother. He wasn't part of any of the investigating teams. He worked the beat up Notting Hill back in those days. Let's just say he was using and abusing his power in terms of whether he arrested these women or not. Back in the early sixties the laws relating to being a street prostitute were changing, but a solicitation charge was costly and if you racked up a few you'd be put inside. No earnings possible from there right?'

'So, you mean he was turning a blind eye for something in return?' This was a peculiar revelation; it was exactly the same thing Forster had accused Buchanan of doing. He'd been working up in Notting Hill as well. Were they in it together? Buchanan had said Forster had got his nickname of Chad because of all his voyeuristic traits, always peering over walls and watching the comings and goings. Were they all telling the truth or was one of them lying?

'Precisely.' Tucker said.

'But you think Buchanan had Pierce down as a suspect?' As soon as he said the two names out loud he regretted it. He looked up to see the other two men in the office were watching him intently. 'Fancy a coffee?' he said quickly.

'Er, OK. Everything alright?'

'Fine. Yes. See you in five.' Chambers hung up.

'What was all that about?' Paul Pierce asked. 'Why are you saying my name in relation to Buchanan? Are you suggesting I had something to do with his death?' His tone didn't sound the slightest bit amicable.

'Nah, nothing like that,' Chambers said casually, 'just another man named Pierce that's all.' He wanted to speak to Tucker urgently. Who was this Alfred Pierce? The man Rose Pierce had described as a victim of love, a man who had killed himself because of a broken heart, had been taking sexual favours of terrified prostitutes around Notting Hill during the late fifties and sixties. He no longer sounded like a victim but a corrupt and sleazy individual. So why would a man like that commit suicide? Guilt? Remorse? Something else? Or maybe his wasn't a suicide either. Chambers needed to get out of the room and clear his head. As he stood up so did Forster.

'Going for a coffee are you? Mind if I join you?' He began shuffling over towards him. 'Could do with a little relief from sitting in here.'

'What are you working on?' Chambers feigned interest. 'You still looking at the Booth case that Buck passed to you last month?'

'Nah I got bored with that. I've been doing some investigating into all them queer murders recently.' He was standing right next to Chambers now, who had stopped a few feet short of the door.

'Queer?' Chambers was confused. 'You mean odd? Why? What's have you found that's strange about them?'

'Nah, not odd. Queer, you know, as in faggot. Queer as in perverted little gays. Someone's been killing a few recently and it seems the idiots in MIT haven't made the connection. Seems no one has. Strange don't you think? Seven little buggers get murdered and no one cares. I wonder why that is? Maybe cos no one cares about the murder of queers? Don't you think? That last one what was his name? Wilson was it?'

'I, I'm not following. We're a cold case unit. It's not our remit to look at any new cases. You know that.' Chambers stuttered aware that Forster was looking over his shoulder towards Pierce. The old man was breathing heavily through his nose.

'Yes that dirty little bandit was blubbering like a little girl at the end,' he hesitated and flicked a look back at Chambers, 'so the report says anyway.' His face cracked into a broad ugly smile.

'How are you getting access to those files?' Chambers was confused now. 'You don't have an ID for HOLMES 2? I mean you don't even have computer access here.'

Almost before Chambers had finished speaking, Paul Pierce had leapt across the table and grabbed the old man by the throat, the pair of them tumbling to the floor, table screeched as chairs hit the floor. Chambers just managed to stop a monitor from crashing to the floor.

'It was you,' screamed Pierce as he tried to throttle Forster, 'you killed him.' The pair were rolling about the floor. Pierce's surprise attack and initial momentum had passed, and larger size and force of Forster appeared to be getting the upper hand. Chambers hesitated, having recovered from the initial shock and regained his balance after nearly being knocked off his feet. Part of him was content to watch the two knock seven bells out of each other. When it appeared Forster was getting the upper hand, Chambers waded in and dragged them roughly apart, pushing Pierce up against the wall.

The younger man was bleeding from the lip, his face red and tears running down his cheeks. He was shaking and snivelling. 'You killed him. You murdered him! Why? You're a sick old bastard. You're beyond help.'

Forster just laughed. 'I did nothing of the kind.' He was breathing heavily, wheezing. 'But you disgust me. You're just a dirty batty boy. You brought nothing but shame on our family.'

'Fuck you. You're not even part of my family.' Pierce retorted angrily confirming the information his mother had given Chambers the day before. 'And I know what you did to my real uncle.'

The smile disappeared from Forster's face. 'You don't know what you're talking about queer. You want to shut the fuck up before I come over and give you another beating.'

'Enough!' Shouted Chambers. 'Enough of this crap. Paul go to the toilet and get yourself cleaned up. And you,' he said turning to Forster, 'get the fuck out of this station. You're nothing more than a hurtful, miserable, bitter old man who just wants to make everyone else as unhappy as you. But it won't work and deep down you know it. Now piss off back to your Hounslow hovel.' Chambers pointed to the door. Pierce quickly made his way out and Forster after a long stare down with Chambers eventually followed. Taking a moment to clear up the mess, straighten the tables and upended chairs that the two brawling men had created, Chambers made his way out and towards the canteen.

Initially he stopped at the door, drawn by the smell of bacon cooking behind the counter, but when he took a cursory look around the canteen he saw Tucker who looked up at him and began tapping at her watch.

Chambers reluctantly approached her avoiding the near overwhelming draw of the sizzling rashers. The woman working behind the counter was busy slicing up a loaf with a large bread knife. He raised his hands in apology. 'Sorry Jess, just had to pull apart Paul and his uncle. What a pair of arseholes.' He was still buzzing due to the adrenalin coursing through his veins.

Tucker raised her eyebrows and looked past him towards the counter. Chambers turned and was surprised to see Pierce was at the counter, evidently he considered a cup of tea more important than going to splash some water on his face and get rid of the blood smeared on his face. Chambers turned back to Tucker.

'What was it all about? He looks quite marked. Is he OK?'

Chambers lowered his voice. 'I've got the feeling Paul was in a relationship with our last victim. He seems to think Chad had something to do with his death.'

'Really, that's seems a bit far-fetched doesn't it? Chad's in his seventies and on death's door with cancer.'

'Yes but he's tougher than he looks, he just got the upper hand in his little rumble with Paul just now.'

'Hey, you were asking about a name. Fred or Alfred Pierce. I had nothing on that in the records of being one of the officers on the scene or a suspect. However I did get another match for a Pierce. A PC by the name of Lee Pierce. Seems to have been on the scene at all the murders from the third one from Tailford in Hammersmith to the eighth one, O'Hara in Acton.'

Lee Pierce? Chambers thought about it, something sounded oddly familiar. He turned and called over to Pierce. 'Paul, have you got a minute?'

Pierce came over reluctantly a mug of tea cradled in his shaking hands.

'What?' He said defensively.

'Have a seat. Are you OK?' Asked Tucker.

'I'm fine. Just that stupid vindictive old bastard.'

'What was that all about? What was that you said about your uncle's suicide being his fault?' asked Chambers.

'Years ago. He was round at ours for Christmas. Did his usual. Brought nothing. Ate everything, complained about the food. Ungrateful old shit that he is. Anyway he got into mum's single malt, and it's the only spirit that seems to make him mellow out as well as getting him to drop his guard. So my mum had gone to bed and it was late and he starts on about my uncle. How everyone thought it was a suicide. But it wasn't. Seems my uncle had been doing things he shouldn't have up in Notting Hill.' Pierce stopped, taking a sip from the shaking cup.

'Doing things? Like what?' Tucker pressed.

'He was banging prostitutes. Getting it for free so as he didn't arrest them. I think a few of them were into it up there.'

'When was this?'

'Late fifties I guess. All that trouble up there with the riots, seems it changed him. That's what my mum always said. Anyway seems he got real shaken up when the prostitutes who did him these favours, well they all started turning up dead, didn't they? He was sure he was going to get investigated, so he decided he was going to hand himself in. Next thing he turns up dead. Seems like he took the easy way out.'

'But I thought you said Chad told you it wasn't a suicide?' Chambers asked.

'Well my mum always said it was a broken heart. That's all I knew. Then Chad tells me that it wasn't suicide over a woman, it was something more sinister. Said he knew his brother was murdered. Then the old bugger passed out. He never mentioned it again. I don't know if it was a suicide or Chad or someone else killed him. I could never allow myself to believe it was Chad. My mum used to say Chad had uncle Alf on a pedestal when they grew up. Couldn't do anything wrong. Then in the late fifties, it must have been, they had a falling out. This was not long after Chad followed him into the force. And a few years later Alf killed himself.'

Chambers was baffled. 'But then what was all that about earlier? Why did you suddenly attack him?'

'Did you see how he was looking at me? Goading me he was, talking about gay killings. I know that last bloke who was murdered.' Then Pierce added defensively. 'Just mates that's all right?' He said too defensively.

'Sure.' Chambers encouraged. 'Henry Wilson?'

Pierce took a sharp intake of breath at the mention of the name. 'Yes that's him.' He nodded slowly it was obviously painful for him to talk about. 'But my uncle was looking at me like he knew. Like he knew that he was a friend of mine. I never told him about Henry, so how did he know? He knows cos he killed him.'

Tucker nodded slowly. 'Paul, I know you're upset about your friend's death but really do you think Chad is involved? I mean, let's be fair, he's on his last legs.'

'I dunno.' Pierce shook his head. He looked like he was going to cry.

'Paul, your uncle Alfred. Was he known as Alf, Alfred or Fred?'

'Hmmm, all three at different times. Alf at home, Fred at work. Why?'

'No reason. What about Chad?'

'At work he was Chad cos he was forever snooping in other people's business I know that. But my mum still calls him Lee.'

'Lee?' Chambers sat bolt upright. 'Not Chas or Charlie?'

'No he's always been Lee at home. Why? What's going on? What's all this about?'

'Nothing. One last question,' Chambers was thinking about the log in issues. 'How come you've tried to log on to my PC? Is yours having problems.'

Pierce looked blank. 'No idea what you're banging on about.'

'Anyone else know your password?' Chambers had a sinking feeling.

'Chad why? He said he needed access and you hadn't provided him with a PC.'

Chambers jumped up from the table. 'Shit. If he's had access to my emails he knows everything we've been looking into. No wonder he was always in the loop.'

'John?' Tucker said, looking confused.

'He's a bloody computer expert, that's what Mrs Pierce told me.' Chambers said realising too late what he had said.

'You've been round to my house? Why?' Pierce looked surprised then worried. 'What did my mum tell you?'

'Nothing. Just that Chad was big into computers.'

'Yes the old man's on Craigslist all the time, god knows what he's up to. You sure my mum didn't say anything else?'

Chambers knew what Pierce was alluding to but he ignored it. What he was coming to realise was that the young PC known to colleagues as Lee Pierce was also the man he knew as Chad Forster. The man he now believed was Jack the Stripper. And now he was too old to commit murder himself he had been recruiting guns for hire, probably through Craigslist or some online forum, to kill young gay men who had been Paul Pierce's lovers or ex-partners. Why had the murders started again? The dates coincided perfectly with Forster's diagnosis of terminal cancer. That's why he couldn't recreate the murders in chronological order. There simply wasn't the time. He didn't have five years.

Buchanan had been murdered with a shot to the head that was made to look like a suicide. The doctored suicide note acting as the perfect cover up. Forster had paid a visit to Buchanan's house after he knew the latest victim Henry Wilson had been confirmed murdered. There was no sign of forced entry as Buchanan would have welcomed in an old colleague. Forster must have been concerned that from what he had read on Chambers' emails and other documents that Buchanan was starting to join the dots and it wouldn't be long before he linked the name of Lee Pierce to Charlie 'Chad' Forster – HR would have coughed up the records eventually. Easier to do away with Buchanan and make it look like he was the bad guy by spreading carefully constructed lies about Buchanan to Chambers; to create doubt in his mind.

Chambers was sure Forster had been monitoring his emails. The old man had reacted immediately to the mail he had just sent to Tucker only a few minutes before. He had been monitoring their whole investigation. No wonder he had suddenly come back to the Brentford police station the year before. He had returned just at the same time the murders had started and had put himself in the perfect position to monitor the investigation into his crimes. Chambers was also confident if he went into the search history of Firefox or one of the other browsers he didn't use, he would find a log in on Craigslist or something similar with all the requests for 'business'. What did they call it in the USA? Housepainters required – it was an old Mafia code for hiring a hitman.

It was possible to hire cheap immigrants to commit murder in mirror images of his murder scenes all those years ago when he'd been murdering prostitutes who had slept with his brother. Soiling the image of his hero making him human, less than human. That, and finding out he was adopted, and not even related to his idol maybe had driven him over the edge. Who knew what pushed people into doing these things? Mental problems. Sickness. But Chambers was sure Forster was the man they were looking for. Buchanan was on to something when he suggested it was a policeman. Someone who knew the subdivisions, who could dump the bodies to cause maximum confusion between the investigating teams. He had been killed for getting too close.

'Earth calling John.' Tucker called. 'Come in John.'

'It's him.' Chambers said quietly returning his gaze to his two seated colleagues.

'Who?'

'Chad, Lee, Charlie. Whatever you want to call him. He's the Stripper and he's the man behind these other murders.'

Before he had time to explain. Paul Pierce was out of his seat. He charged across to the counter, grabbed the long breadknife the cook had been using to slice the baguettes and ran from the room.

By the time Tucker and Chambers reacted Pierce was already out of the canteen door. When they got to the corridor, there was no sign of Pierce.

'Head out to the road. He's probably gone out after Chad.' Chambers said to Tucker. 'I'll check around the station.'

As Tucker began descending the stairs they heard a gurgling scream coming from Chambers' office. They darted back to the office and as they entered the room they saw Forster on the floor by the side of Chambers' desk. Kneeling on top and thrusting the blade frantically into the prone body of Chad Forster was Paul Pierce, who was crying and cursing Forster for murdering his uncle and his partner. By the time they could restrain Pierce and get the knife out of his blood soaked hands, Chad Forster lay dead in a pool of his own blood. Jess Tucker was screaming for help and Chambers was vaguely aware that other police officers had rushed into the room. Frozen to the spot, all he could do was stand and stare at the scene of carnage that had unfolded in front of him. The knowledge that it was over and the murders would stop offered him little consolation amid the mayhem.

***

THE CHARRED FOREST MURDERS

Epilogue

Merchantman? Harsh job

Monday 25th June 2012 – 10:17am

Chambers was on his way to Heathrow airport. He was no longer a serving member of the Metropolitan Police. His last day hadn't quite been shuffling out with a whimper that he had expected. It had gone with more than a bang. Chad Forster murdered at Chambers' desk. Murdered by his nephew in a fit of rage. Chambers wished he had kept his mouth shut. It was him that had alerted Pierce to Forster's role in all of the deaths and inadvertently caused the old man's death. Chambers didn't feel any culpability. Forster was responsible for the deaths of eight women in the fifties and sixties and another seven young men over the past 12 months. At least all of the senseless killing would end with Forster's own. Pierce would be charged with murder but was more likely to be charged with manslaughter due to diminished responsibility or whatever his lawyers could conjure up. They'd have plenty of material to work with.

Forster, Chambers was sure, was the man who had murdered those eight young women all those years before. The vitriol possibly subsiding with the death of his elder brother, whether by his hand or by suicide Chambers would only be guessing. The anger reignited when Forster discovered he was dying of cancer compounded by his discovery that his only nephew was homosexual. Forster's killing urge had returned and he had targeted his nephew's ex-boyfriends or lovers as his new choice of victims. It had been easy enough for a man of Forster's talents to log into Chambers computer with Pierce's login details. Cloning his emails and other source material, Forster had been able to monitor everything going on with their investigation. The 'From Rotting Hell' letter was another of his sick jokes. Chambers had wondered exactly how the killer knew to send the letter to the Brentford cold case unit. Now the answer was painfully clear, because the perpetrator was sitting a few feet away.

Chambers thought about how the shock Forster must have felt when he realised Buchanan had made the leap to discover the link between then and now, and that it was a former policeman who was responsible. It was clear that Forster was aware of how close Buchanan was coming to solving the case and had decided to take matters into his own hands to make sure not only did he clear the meddlesome Buchanan out of the way he would conveniently make sure he would also carry the can for the murders. He only needed a little more time to complete his second set of murders. The eighth murder to coincide with that of Mary Fleming on the 11th of July was just a matter of weeks away. Had Forster got away with it until then, would he have stopped at eight? Who really knew? Maybe his desire to kill would have been satiated or the desire may have diminished. Maybe he would have carried on killing until he eventually succumbed to his cancer. For now it was mere conjecture on Chambers' part. In reality no one would ever know.

Pierce had only become aware when his current partner had been murdered. Forster, physically incapable of doing it himself, had employed others to do his dirty work. Hiring cheap assassins through his extensive network formed via social media and the numerous chat rooms he subscribed to, putting his technical knowledge to criminal use. Instructing his hired killers to replicate the murders while leaving his hands clean, but still giving him the gratification and satisfaction of watching others suffer.

***

THE CHARRED FOREST MURDERS

There would be a time when Chambers would need to return to give evidence but for now his time as a policeman was over. Now he could put the horrors behind him. In a few hours he would be airborne. Next stop Bangkok, Thailand and hopefully one step closer to finding out the fate of Lucy and that of her captor Tomar Shen. This, he feared, would be the toughest investigation of his career and he dared not think that the outcome could be anything other than positive.

***

Acknowledgements

I'd like to thank my father for his support in writing this novel. I also appreciated the help of the local history staff from Chiswick Library who were the only local people I conversed with who had some knowledge of these bizarre events. Also I'd like to thank those who pointed me in the right direction at the National Archives at Kew. Despite not being able to gain access to the Jack the Stripper files for legal reasons, the resources and material available for public research are a goldmine of fascinating information of Britain's rich and varied history. Last but by no means least a huge thank you to Allan and Sybil (Ma) Wallis for their generous assistance in helping me to complete this book.

As usual, any mistakes in this book are mine and mine alone.

***

Bibliography

DuRose, John - *Murder Was My Business*, Mayflower Books, 1971

McConnell, Brian - *Found Naked And Dead*, New English Library, 1974

Milkins, Neil - *Who was Jack the Stripper?*, Rose Heyworth Press 2011

Seabrook, David - *Jack Of Jumps*, Granta Books, 2006

For an overview of the Jack the Stripper case –

http://en.wikipedia.org/wiki/Jack_the_Stripper

***

About the author

Andrew Woodward was born in London to Scottish parents. He travelled extensively before settling down to reside in Sydney, Australia for just over a decade. However, his desire to seek new challenges led him to a short sojourn in the deserts of the Middle East before finding his true calling as an author in Hong Kong. And it was in this vibrant city that features as the location for his debut novel, The Water Dragon, featuring the intrepid Detective Inspector John Chambers. Andrew released the sequel, The Fire Walker, which is set in Scotland, in mid-2012. The third installment of the DI Chambers series - The Silverbird's Sign, is set both in Hong Kong and sub-Saharan Africa (released early 2013) and is a continuation of the author's split narrative approach. The fourth novel in the Elements series, The Charred Forest Murders was released in August 2013. Andrew is currently researching material the fifth and final novel of his Elements pentalogy that is scheduled for release in mid-2014.

His writing style in the first two novels encompassed the traditional thriller and detective mode of writing, while his third novel saw him switch to the classic whodunnit plot line. The combination of murder-mystery with a rich and evocative travel writing style help to bring the settings to the fore, making the locations an integral part of the narrative that add a depth and reality rarely found in the genre.

***

Printed in Great Britain
by Amazon.co.uk, Ltd.,
Marston Gate.